ROAD TRIP

The Good Words
Book For Success

Written by:

Rick Alan Randall

Copyright © 2025 Rick Randall
All rights reserved
First Edition

Library of Congress Control Number: 2025907319

ISBN 978-1-963851-77-9 (Paperback)
ISBN 978-1-963851-75-5 (Hardback)
ISBN 978-1-963851-76-2 (Ebook)

All rights reserved. No part of this publication may be reproduced,
distributed, or transmitted in any form or by any means, including
photocopying, recording, or other electronic or mechanical methods,
without the prior written permission of the publisher, except in the case
brief quotations embodied in critical reviews and other noncommercial
uses permitted by copyright law.

The views expressed in this book are solely those of the author and
do not necessarily reflect the views of the publisher, and the publisher
hereby disclaims any responsibility for them.
First originally published by Olympus Story House 2025

Olympus Story House

Road Trip – Likely to Succeed A-Z

A very good friend of mine once suggested that he
could sum up life with just one word.
"What would that be?" I asked. He said, "Vocabulary."
I laughed and said, "Vocabulary seems like it is more than one word."
Then he laughed and said, "Exactly, life is about the words that you know."

Likely to Succeed A-Z is the result of over 40 years of life, living and thinking about it.

My friend was right.

Vocabulary is one of the most important words that you should know and understand.

Vocabulary defined, is the stock of words used by or known to a particular person or group.

On average, the words that we use on a daily basis, our daily vocabulary, consists of about 1,500 words. Road Trip – The Good Words Book for Success, Likely to Succeed A-Z, is based on the idea that if we only have 1,500 words in our bag of words, we should fill our bag with as many Good Words as we can. The more Good Words that you know and use will significantly enhance the quality of your life.

Here is how it works: Think about anything. What words show up? How do the words that show up in your thinking make you feel or what do they make you want to do? The words that we know, and use, are our tools to describe or define our thoughts and what is going on in our lives and the world around us. The words that we know, and use, write our thoughts, determine our emotions and direct our behavior. Important.

Thoughts – Thoughts happen all the time, but we can only think one thought at a time. The cool thing is that the thought that we think about is up to us. If a thought shows up that does not feel good or isn't consistent with the experience that we would like to have, we can rewind, rewrite and replay a better thought. The key word is rewrite.

Use Better Words, use Positive Words, use Good Words and write a Better Thought. Your thoughts are the seeds from which your future grows. Pay attention to what you are thinking. Focus on your thoughts. Your thoughts are up to you. You decide which of your thoughts get to stay in the house. Get good at good thoughts. It seems pretty simple, because it is. I believe your mind and body will do what it is trained to do. This is mental training, not to be confused with brainwashing, however, sometimes it is a good idea to take a mental shower.

Emotions – how we feel about our lives and what is going on around us. What words do we use to describe or define how we feel about life, and feel about what we do? If we made better choices with the words that we use, would we feel better and behave differently? Yes, it is Possible. This is the concept.

Perhaps an example: Say "stressed out" or "Pumped Up". What feels better? Both could apply to the same situation or circumstance. Which is the better choice? When our bag of words is full of Good Words, our thoughts and our emotions will be better, our behavior will be better, we will feel better, and we will In Joy a better life experience.

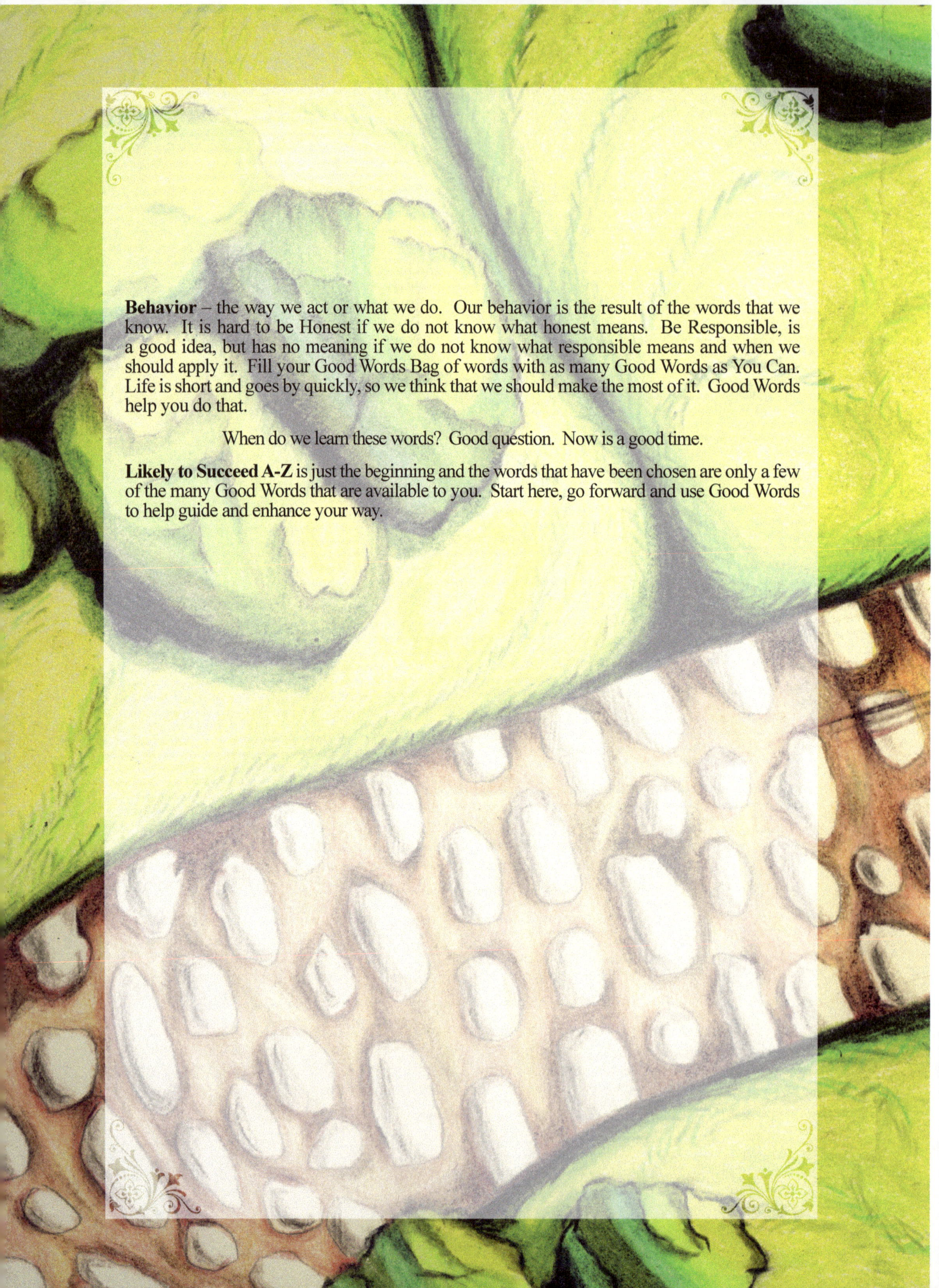

Behavior – the way we act or what we do. Our behavior is the result of the words that we know. It is hard to be Honest if we do not know what honest means. Be Responsible, is a good idea, but has no meaning if we do not know what responsible means and when we should apply it. Fill your Good Words Bag of words with as many Good Words as You Can. Life is short and goes by quickly, so we think that we should make the most of it. Good Words help you do that.

When do we learn these words? Good question. Now is a good time.

Likely to Succeed A-Z is just the beginning and the words that have been chosen are only a few of the many Good Words that are available to you. Start here, go forward and use Good Words to help guide and enhance your way.

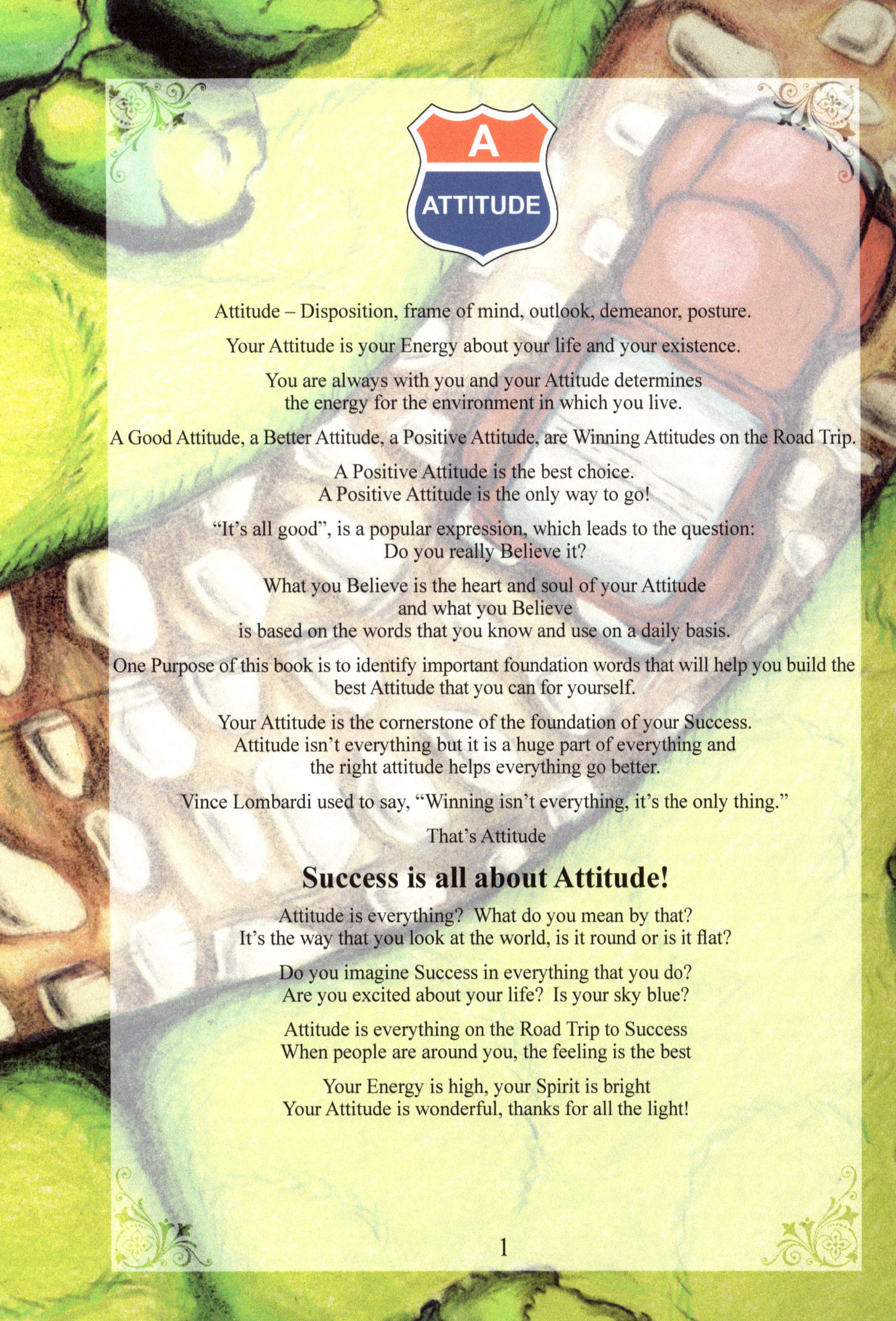

Attitude – Disposition, frame of mind, outlook, demeanor, posture.

Your Attitude is your Energy about your life and your existence.

You are always with you and your Attitude determines
the energy for the environment in which you live.

A Good Attitude, a Better Attitude, a Positive Attitude, are Winning Attitudes on the Road Trip.

A Positive Attitude is the best choice.
A Positive Attitude is the only way to go!

"It's all good", is a popular expression, which leads to the question:
Do you really Believe it?

What you Believe is the heart and soul of your Attitude
and what you Believe
is based on the words that you know and use on a daily basis.

One Purpose of this book is to identify important foundation words that will help you build the
best Attitude that you can for yourself.

Your Attitude is the cornerstone of the foundation of your Success.
Attitude isn't everything but it is a huge part of everything and
the right attitude helps everything go better.

Vince Lombardi used to say, "Winning isn't everything, it's the only thing."

That's Attitude

Success is all about Attitude!

Attitude is everything? What do you mean by that?
It's the way that you look at the world, is it round or is it flat?

Do you imagine Success in everything that you do?
Are you excited about your life? Is your sky blue?

Attitude is everything on the Road Trip to Success
When people are around you, the feeling is the best

Your Energy is high, your Spirit is bright
Your Attitude is wonderful, thanks for all the light!

Ambition – Drive, zeal, desire, aspiration, goal, aim, intent, purpose.

Ambition is the fuel for the engine.

It is the juice that gets you going.

Ambition encourages the Motivation to have and to be and to do.

It is Energy.

It is Excitement.

Ambition is Enthusiasm about you and your life.

It is the drive needed to attain, achieve and accomplish
your hopes and dreams and the goals you have for your life.

Ambition comes from the inside out.

Your Ambition is up to you.

How much Ambition is in your bucket?

What do you want?

Why do you want it?

What do you have to do to realize it?

Will you do it?

This is where Ambition comes in.

Success is full of Ambition

Ambition they say is all up to you
It is the Energy to go, and get up and do

Wake up in the morning and put your Ambition hat on
You will Love how it feels, like you have already won

What are you thinking? How high will you go?
With a bucket full of Ambition there are no limits you know

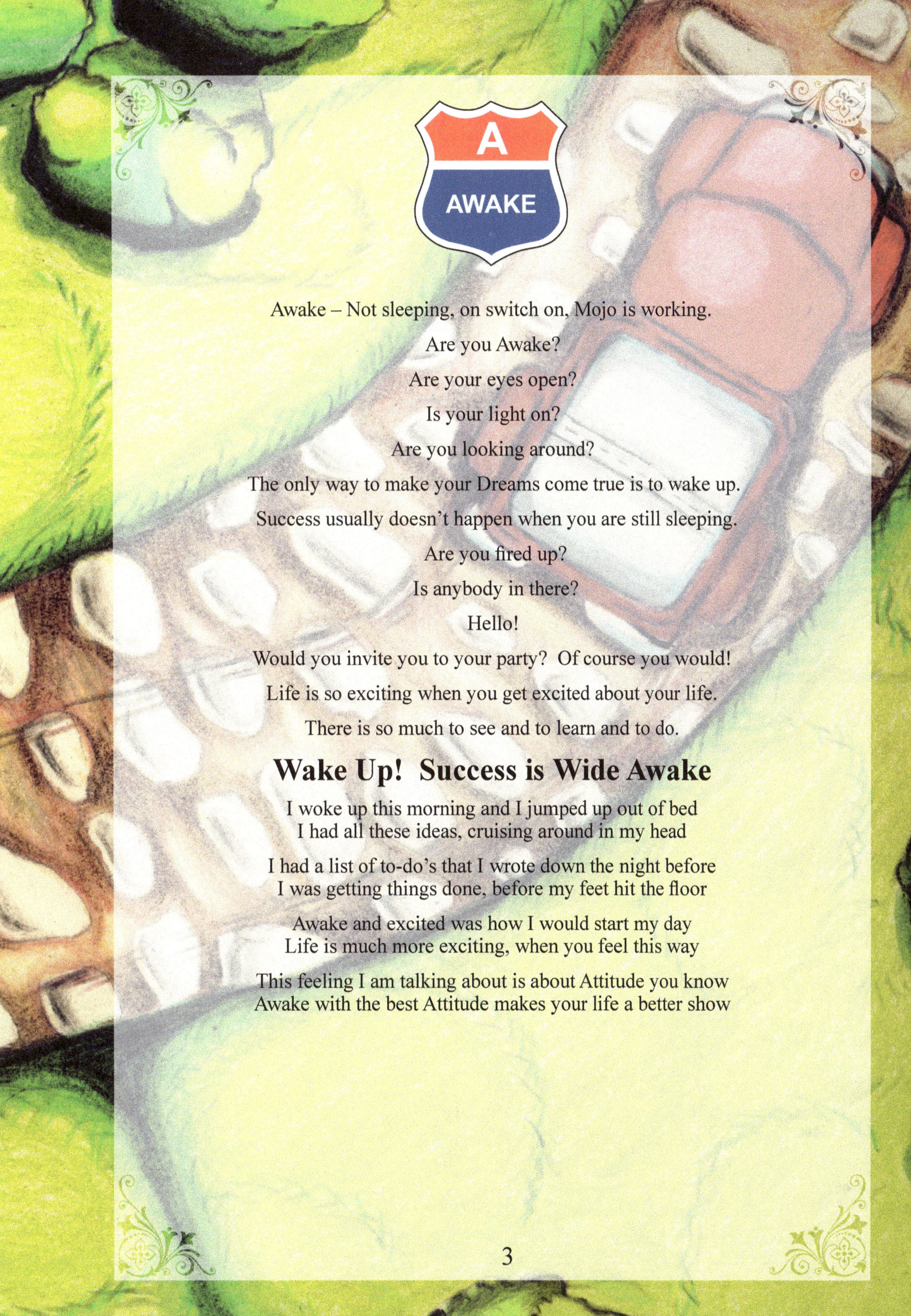

Awake – Not sleeping, on switch on, Mojo is working.

Are you Awake?

Are your eyes open?

Is your light on?

Are you looking around?

The only way to make your Dreams come true is to wake up.

Success usually doesn't happen when you are still sleeping.

Are you fired up?

Is anybody in there?

Hello!

Would you invite you to your party? Of course you would!

Life is so exciting when you get excited about your life.

There is so much to see and to learn and to do.

Wake Up! Success is Wide Awake

I woke up this morning and I jumped up out of bed
I had all these ideas, cruising around in my head

I had a list of to-do's that I wrote down the night before
I was getting things done, before my feet hit the floor

Awake and excited was how I would start my day
Life is much more exciting, when you feel this way

This feeling I am talking about is about Attitude you know
Awake with the best Attitude makes your life a better show

Acceptable – What is allowable, tolerable, worthy, satisfactory, suitable, good to you?

What is Acceptable to you?

What is Acceptable for you?

What is Acceptable to you regarding your behavior? Behavior – what you do.

Do you have a code of conduct that you live by?

What is Acceptable to you regarding others that you live with?

Work with?

Or the people that you Accept into your inner circle?

This is about the words in this book and establishing your code of behavior.

Your code of behavior is better because of the Good Words that you choose to live by.

Your Success is Acceptable!

Good enough is not good enough
Acceptable gets you out of the rough

Acceptable is about living in the top drawer
Your code of behavior raises your score

We sometimes fall and we stumble, but we get back up
Acceptable behavior, grab yourself a cup

Keep your eye on the goal and raise the standard a bit
Care about what is happening, choose an Acceptable that fits

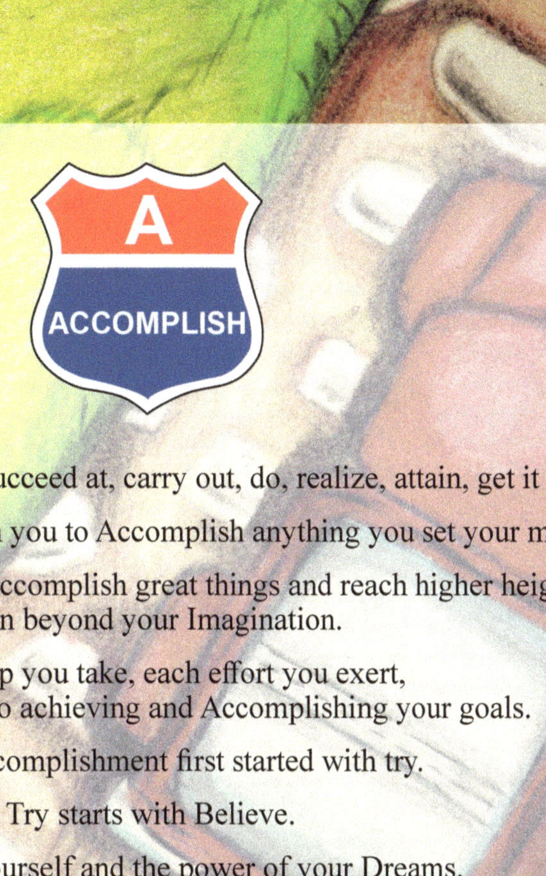

Accomplish – Achieve, succeed at, carry out, do, realize, attain, get it done.

You have the ability within you to Accomplish anything you set your mind to.

You have the potential to Accomplish great things and reach higher heights…..
even beyond your Imagination.

Each step you take, each effort you exert,
brings you closer to achieving and Accomplishing your goals.

Every Accomplishment first started with try.

Try starts with Believe.

Believe in yourself and the power of your Dreams.
As you go closer to it, it comes closer to you.

It's about taking that first step, no matter how big or how small
in the direction of your Dreams.

With determination and perseverance, you will overcome obstacles
and Accomplish what may seem impossible at first.

Set your sights high, Believe in yourself, go forward with Confidence and
In Joy the incredible feeling of Accomplish!

Accomplish Success!

I started with a Goal that seemed too big to do
It was something that I wanted but I'm not sure if I could see it through

Then I got started, I just kept moving right along
I was gaining momentum, I was feeling pretty strong

Accomplish the Goal was the mission today
As soon as I got started, the goal started coming my way

Amazing how it works, great how it feels
Accomplish Success, Manifestation makes it real

The first part about Be is Be You.
Be the Best you that you can Be.

Road Trip is about getting good at playing the game of life.

Likely to succeed A-Z is about your choice to Be?

A few suggestions perhaps:

Be Ambitious, Be Awesome, Be Bold, Be Caring, Become.

Be Compassionate, Be Concerned, Be Confident, Be Consistent, Be Courageous.

Be Energetic, Be Enthusiastic, Be Fun, Be Generous.

Be Genuine, Be Good, Be Happy, Be Honest.

Be Independent, Be Kind, Be Life, Be Love, Be Nice, Be Noble.

Be Passionate, Be Patient, Be Persistent, Be Positive, Be Real, Be Reliable.

Be Responsible, Be Sincere, Be Wise, Be the difference.

You are the most qualified person to Be You.

You are someone special.

You make a Positive difference for the planet and everyone else around you…
because You are You.

Be You.

Just Be You and You will Be Successful

When you look in the mirror who or what do you see?
You are a beautiful You, Be the Be You that you want to Be

Love the Be You that reflects back in the mirror
When you Accept the Be You, the reflection gets much clearer

So smile back at the mirror and let yourself Be
Be the amazing You that you are, say Yes and you will see

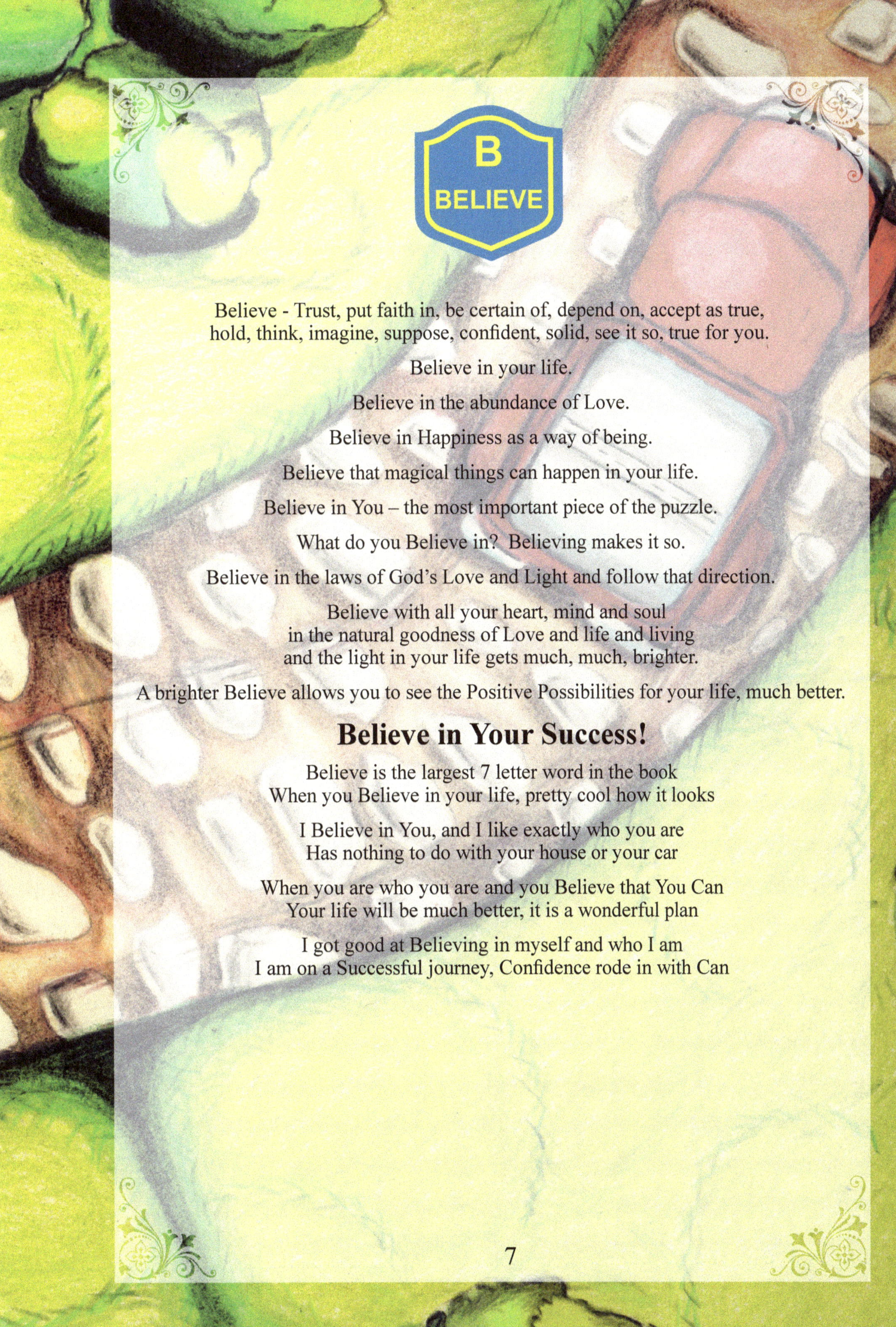

Believe - Trust, put faith in, be certain of, depend on, accept as true,
hold, think, imagine, suppose, confident, solid, see it so, true for you.

Believe in your life.

Believe in the abundance of Love.

Believe in Happiness as a way of being.

Believe that magical things can happen in your life.

Believe in You – the most important piece of the puzzle.

What do you Believe in? Believing makes it so.

Believe in the laws of God's Love and Light and follow that direction.

Believe with all your heart, mind and soul
in the natural goodness of Love and life and living
and the light in your life gets much, much, brighter.

A brighter Believe allows you to see the Positive Possibilities for your life, much better.

Believe in Your Success!

Believe is the largest 7 letter word in the book
When you Believe in your life, pretty cool how it looks

I Believe in You, and I like exactly who you are
Has nothing to do with your house or your car

When you are who you are and you Believe that You Can
Your life will be much better, it is a wonderful plan

I got good at Believing in myself and who I am
I am on a Successful journey, Confidence rode in with Can

Balance – Harmony, middle ground, stability, steadiness, composure.
Coolness, presence, steady, stable, level.

Success thrives on Balance.

Could you imagine walking on a tightrope and being out of Balance?
You won't necessarily fall if you get out of Balance,
as long as you don't stay out of Balance.

There are highs and lows, ups and downs, curves and straight aways.
Balance keeps you on the road.

Embrace the ebb and flow and find harmony between work and play, ambition and relaxation.

The heart works really hard for 30% of the time and rests for 70% to stay in Balance.
Interesting.

What is the ratio for your Success?

In the symphony of your life, let Balance be the conductor, shall I play or maybe no.

Keep your Success in Balance

Too much, too little, just the right amount is good
Balance and Success need to be well understood

If I go too fast, the wheels might blow
but I will never get there if I go too slow

Balance and Success are wrapped in the same cloth
When you are out of Balance, Success will be lost

Stay in Balance is the moral of the story here
In Joy Balance on the Road Trip, keeps your buggy in gear

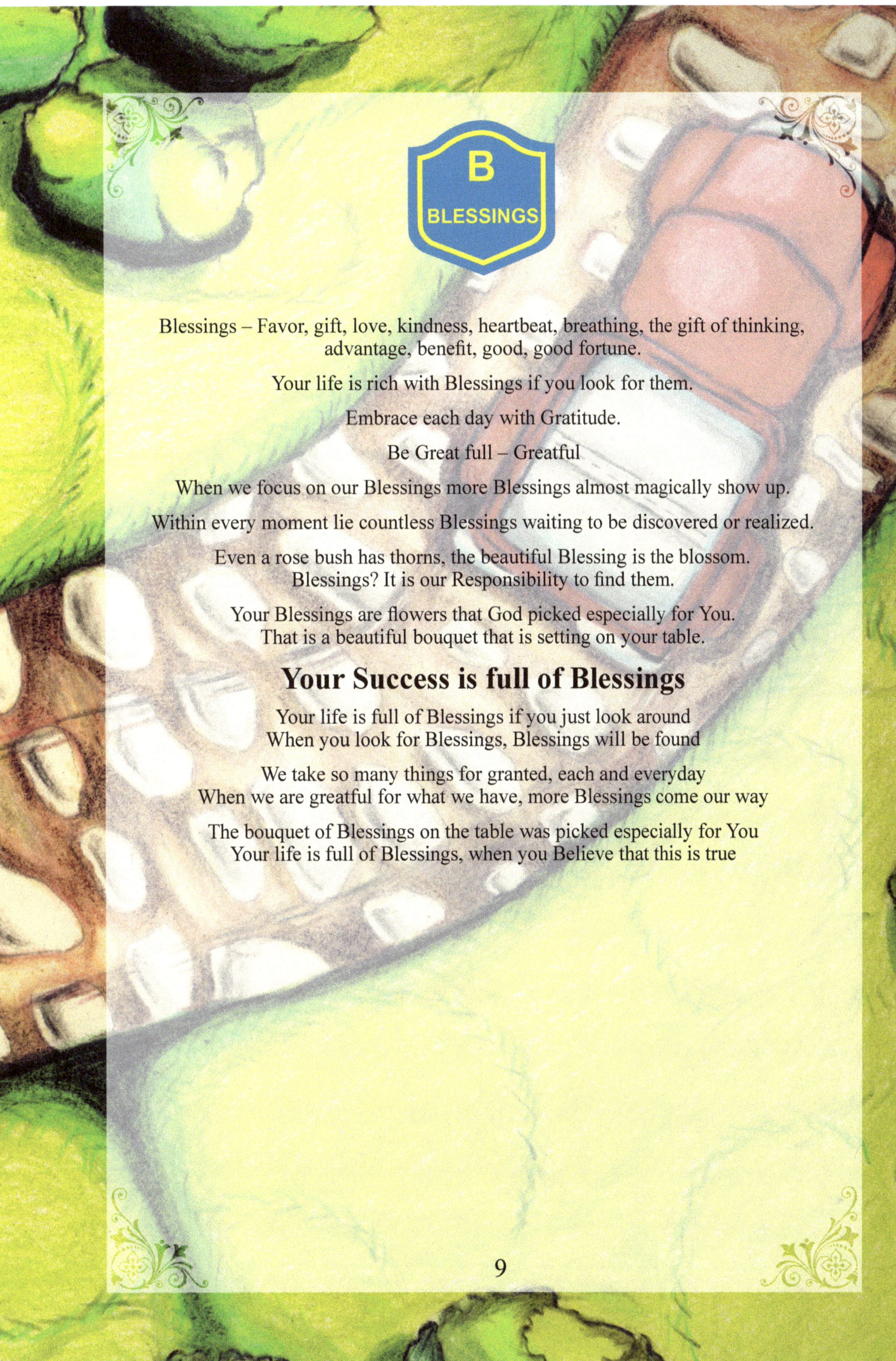

Blessings – Favor, gift, love, kindness, heartbeat, breathing, the gift of thinking, advantage, benefit, good, good fortune.

Your life is rich with Blessings if you look for them.

Embrace each day with Gratitude.

Be Great full – Greatful

When we focus on our Blessings more Blessings almost magically show up.

Within every moment lie countless Blessings waiting to be discovered or realized.

Even a rose bush has thorns, the beautiful Blessing is the blossom. Blessings? It is our Responsibility to find them.

Your Blessings are flowers that God picked especially for You. That is a beautiful bouquet that is setting on your table.

Your Success is full of Blessings

Your life is full of Blessings if you just look around
When you look for Blessings, Blessings will be found

We take so many things for granted, each and everyday
When we are greatful for what we have, more Blessings come our way

The bouquet of Blessings on the table was picked especially for You
Your life is full of Blessings, when you Believe that this is true

Build – Create, make, produce, develop, magnify, originate, manifest.

Build the building for your Success.

Every step you take is another brick, building the building of your Success one brick at a time.
Your potential building can have as many bricks as you choose.

With each effort, you are progressively building
the foundation and the structure for your Success.

Use Good Words to Build your building.
Goals, Courage, Determination, Perseverance and Believe are good bricks.

Keep building and keep growing.
In Joy the process of building.

The building of your Success is Built by You.

Build your Success

Get a hammer and a ladder, perhaps a saw or two
Build a classic structure, Build your Success is what you do

Believe in what you are building, Success starts with this thought in mind
The building of Success that you are building is Built one brick at a time

Build your Success with confidence in the direction that you want to go
You are building a Successful building; Believe it and you know

Begin – Set out, commence, initiate, embark on, take the first step, start.

A good bit of time is spent just thinking about getting started.
Once you Begin, you are off and running.

Half of the completion of any goal or objective is just getting started.
Fifty percent finished by just getting started? Pretty much.

It is surprising how true this is.

It is never as big as it seems, and it is only as big as you make it.

Look in the D words and find Determination.
Check the E words and find Enthusiasm.
Then go to the P words and find Passion and getting started is automatic.

Begin, get started.
Now is a good time to Begin.

Just get it started and Begin Your Road Trip to Success

My list was full and there was lots for me to do
I was pretty darn excited, I just had to think it through

The first thing is to just get started and Believe and just Begin
The list of things gets checked off, each check is another win

The Road Trip to Success is one of the best rides of your life
Begin and get it started, Success is about the ride

Confidence – Self-confidence, trust, Faith in oneself, Believe in, probable, certainty, Can.

This is another one of the most important pieces of your Success story.

Believe in yourself.
Believe in your plan.
Confidence leads to Can.

There are no limits with Can.

Yes you Can.
Of course you Can.
Know that you Can!

You Can do it.
Be Positive.
I think you Can.

Confidence is Knowing that you are a Winner
and you will Succeed when you Believe you Can.

Say Yes because it is true.

Go forward with Confidence in the direction of your goals and your objectives
and Confidence and Can will guarantee your Success.

Have Confidence in your Success

Confidence is a wonderful feeling, it comes from deep inside
When you Believe in you and you are Confident, the Road Trip is a better ride

It is that talk that you have in the morning, a board meeting with you and you
You are Confident that you Can, do whatever you want to do

Build your Success with Confidence and you will surely Succeed
Confidence leads to Can, your Success is guaranteed

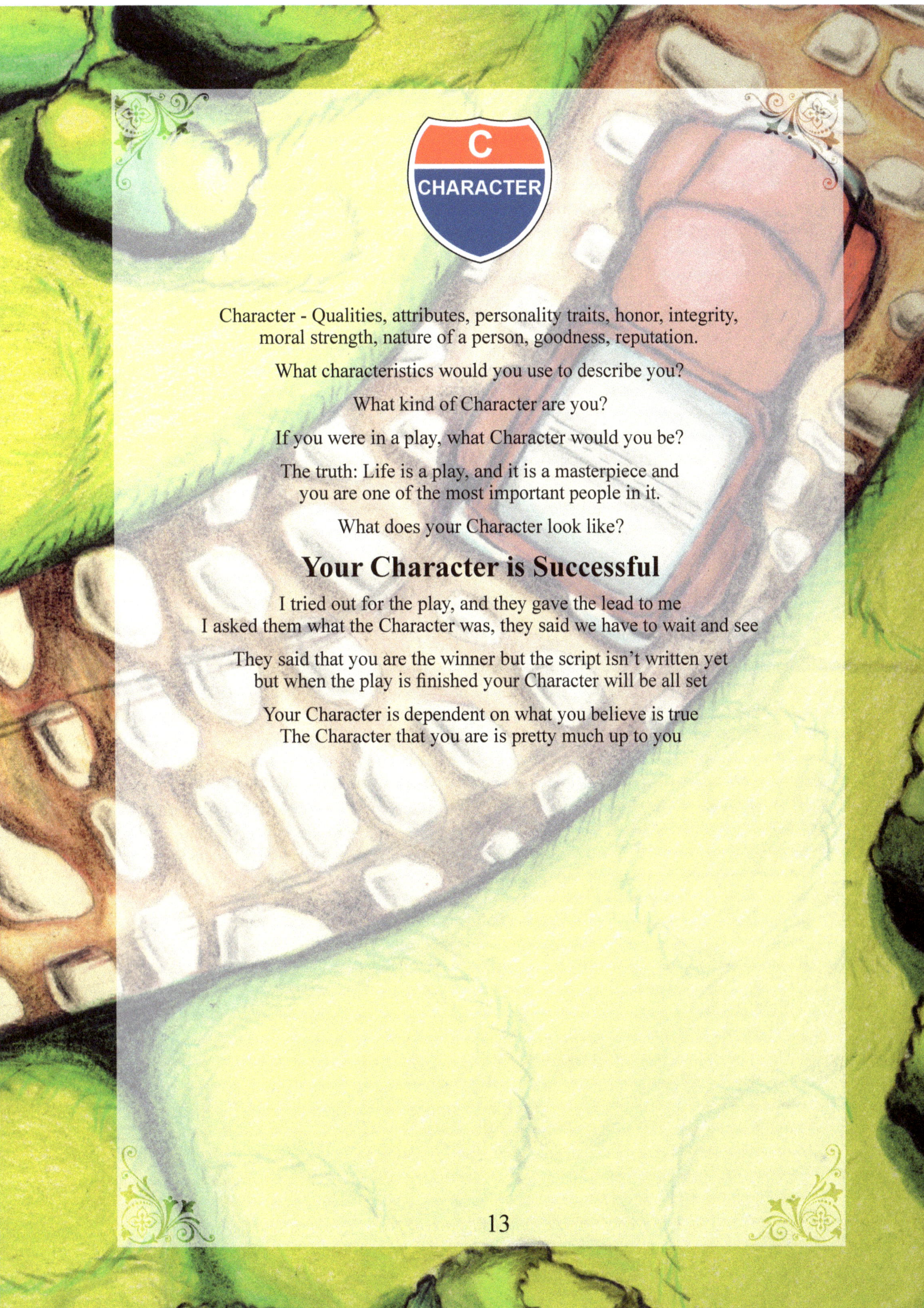

Character - Qualities, attributes, personality traits, honor, integrity, moral strength, nature of a person, goodness, reputation.

What characteristics would you use to describe you?

What kind of Character are you?

If you were in a play, what Character would you be?

The truth: Life is a play, and it is a masterpiece and you are one of the most important people in it.

What does your Character look like?

Your Character is Successful

I tried out for the play, and they gave the lead to me
I asked them what the Character was, they said we have to wait and see

They said that you are the winner but the script isn't written yet
but when the play is finished your Character will be all set

Your Character is dependent on what you believe is true
The Character that you are is pretty much up to you

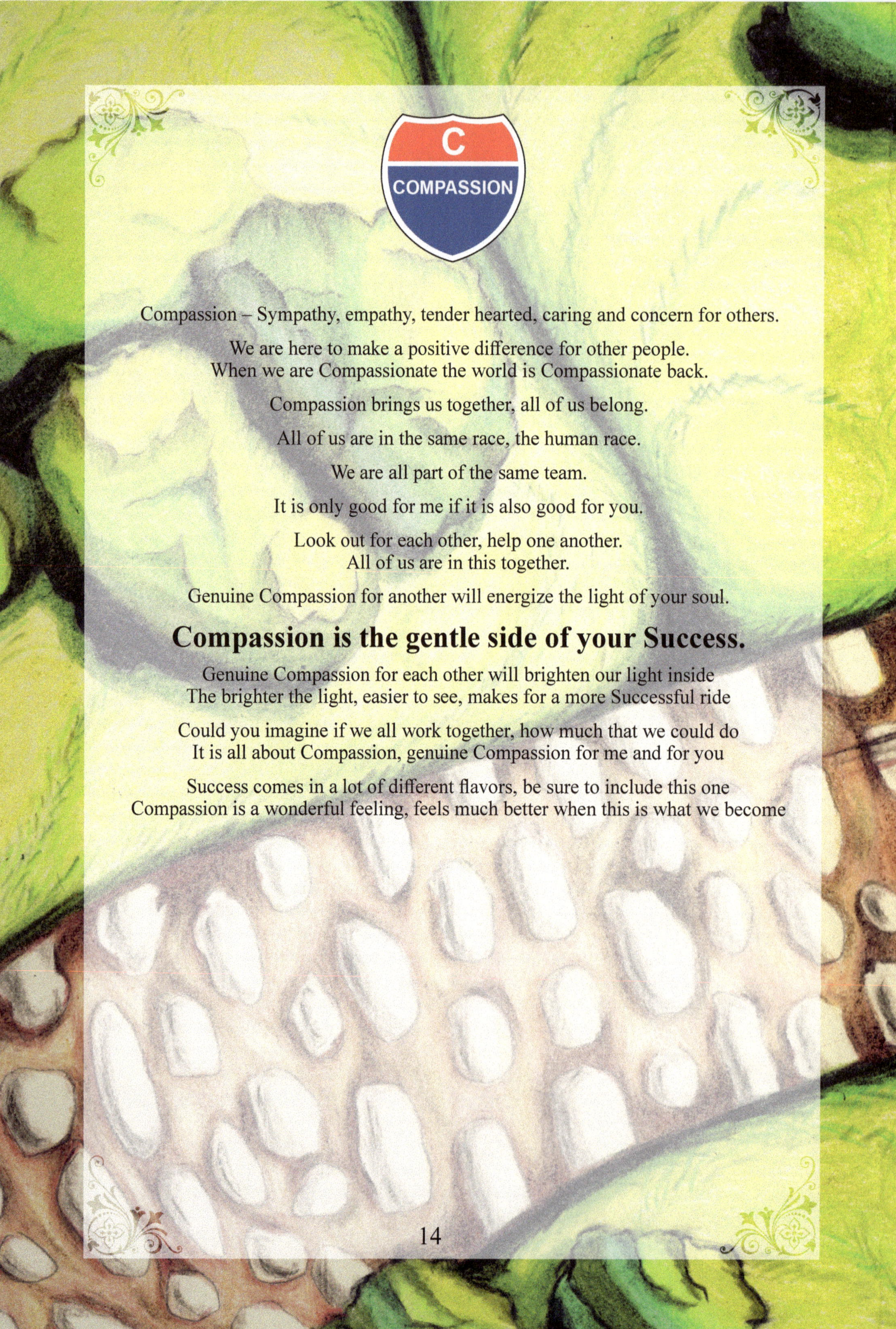

Compassion – Sympathy, empathy, tender hearted, caring and concern for others.

We are here to make a positive difference for other people.
When we are Compassionate the world is Compassionate back.

Compassion brings us together, all of us belong.

All of us are in the same race, the human race.

We are all part of the same team.

It is only good for me if it is also good for you.

Look out for each other, help one another.
All of us are in this together.

Genuine Compassion for another will energize the light of your soul.

Compassion is the gentle side of your Success.

Genuine Compassion for each other will brighten our light inside
The brighter the light, easier to see, makes for a more Successful ride

Could you imagine if we all work together, how much that we could do
It is all about Compassion, genuine Compassion for me and for you

Success comes in a lot of different flavors, be sure to include this one
Compassion is a wonderful feeling, feels much better when this is what we become

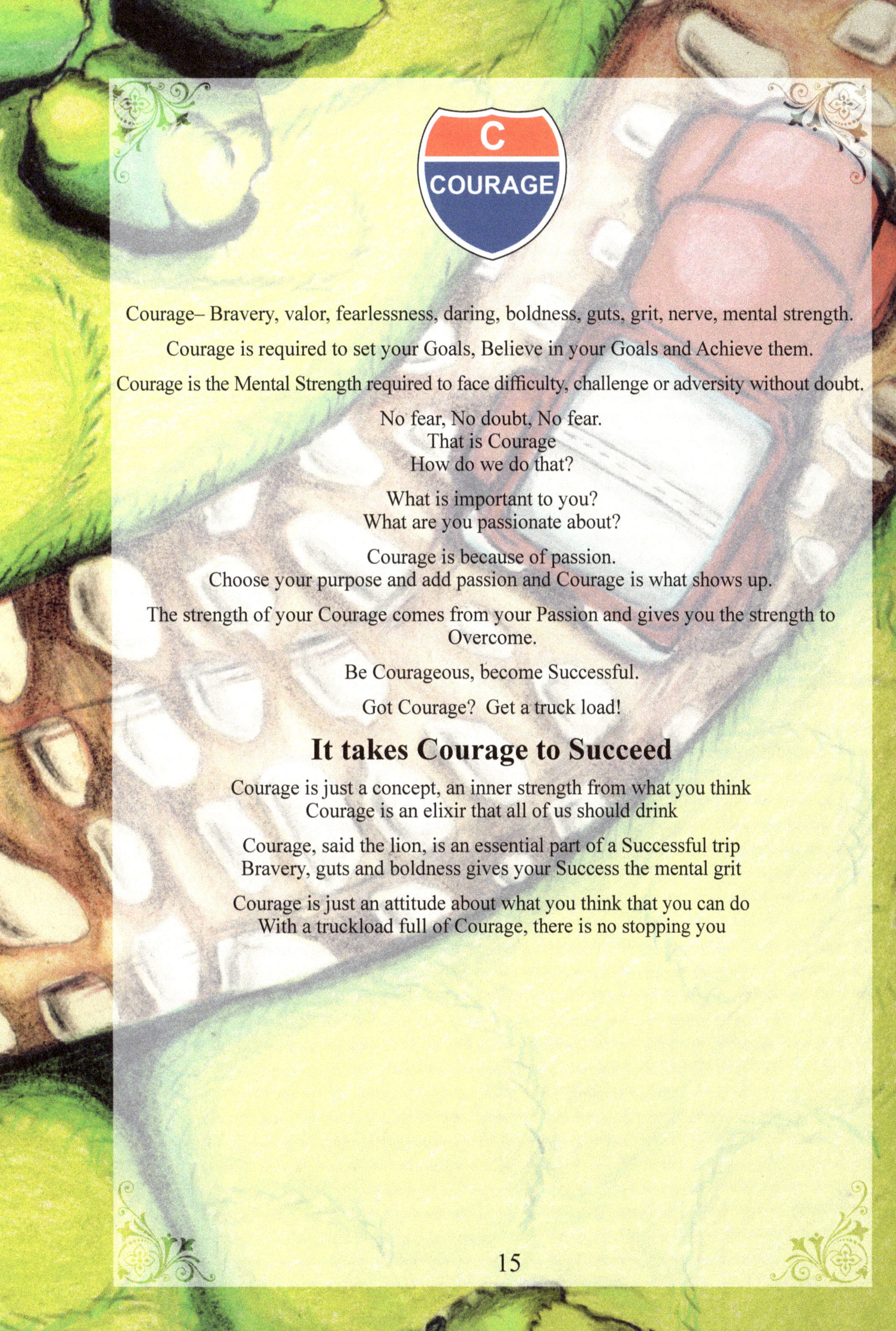

Courage– Bravery, valor, fearlessness, daring, boldness, guts, grit, nerve, mental strength.

Courage is required to set your Goals, Believe in your Goals and Achieve them.

Courage is the Mental Strength required to face difficulty, challenge or adversity without doubt.

No fear, No doubt, No fear.
That is Courage
How do we do that?

What is important to you?
What are you passionate about?

Courage is because of passion.
Choose your purpose and add passion and Courage is what shows up.

The strength of your Courage comes from your Passion and gives you the strength to Overcome.

Be Courageous, become Successful.

Got Courage? Get a truck load!

It takes Courage to Succeed

Courage is just a concept, an inner strength from what you think
Courage is an elixir that all of us should drink

Courage, said the lion, is an essential part of a Successful trip
Bravery, guts and boldness gives your Success the mental grit

Courage is just an attitude about what you think that you can do
With a truckload full of Courage, there is no stopping you

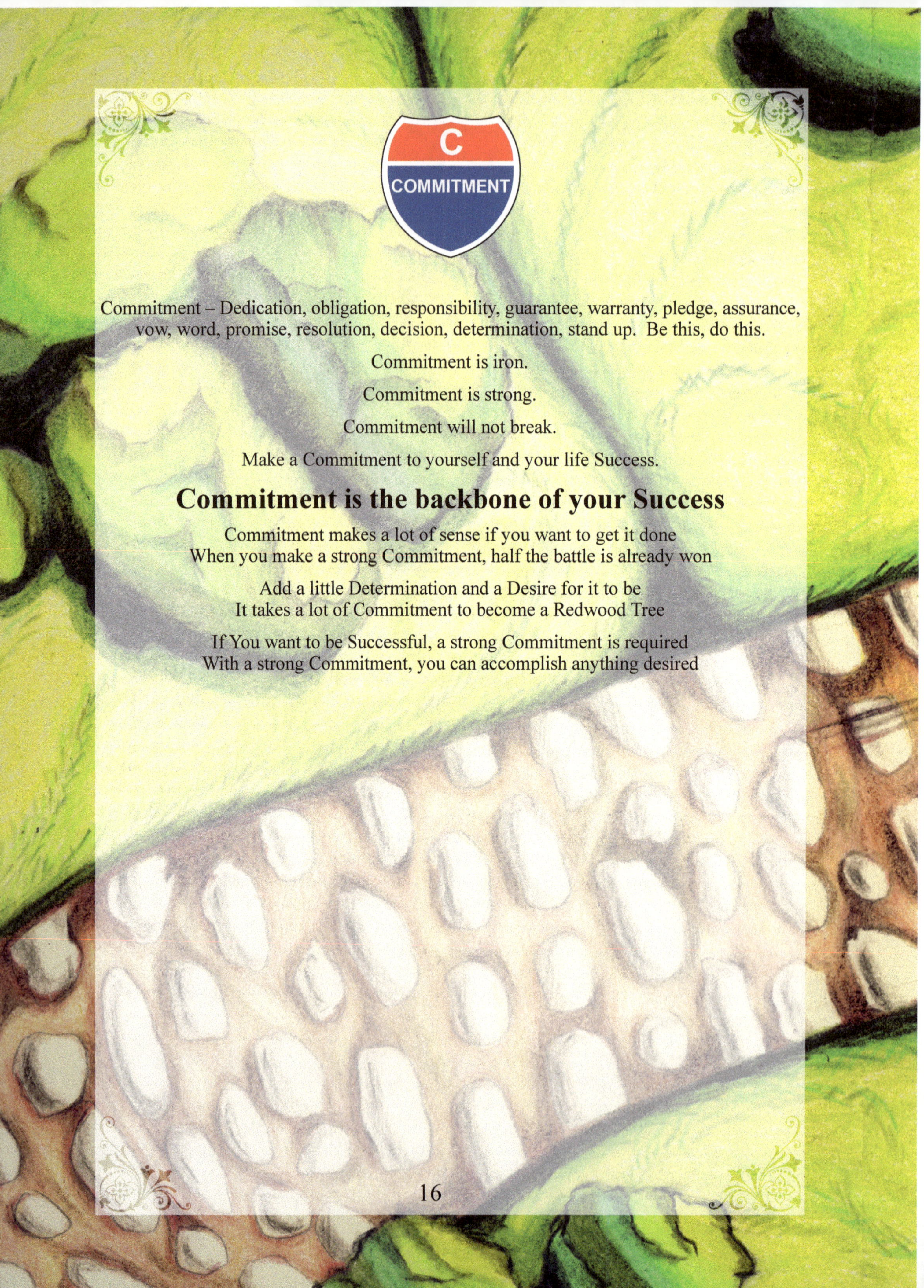

Commitment – Dedication, obligation, responsibility, guarantee, warranty, pledge, assurance, vow, word, promise, resolution, decision, determination, stand up. Be this, do this.

Commitment is iron.

Commitment is strong.

Commitment will not break.

Make a Commitment to yourself and your life Success.

Commitment is the backbone of your Success

Commitment makes a lot of sense if you want to get it done
When you make a strong Commitment, half the battle is already won

Add a little Determination and a Desire for it to be
It takes a lot of Commitment to become a Redwood Tree

If You want to be Successful, a strong Commitment is required
With a strong Commitment, you can accomplish anything desired

Conquer – Prevail, defeat, succeed, survive, victory, overcome, win.

The most important thing to Conquer on the journey is self-doubt.

Whatever the challenge, Believe in You.

Have Faith in the power of Believe and Can and Conquer shows up.

Trust in your abilities and resolve to Conquer any challenge that dares to stand in your way.

Focus on the mountain to climb, it only takes a mustard seed of Faith to move it.

Believe in yourself and Conquer is inevitable.

You Can Conquer Success!

Conquer is domination, overwhelm the opposing foe
Whatever the challenge, Conquer gives you the giddy up and go

Could you imagine if you were an explorer and Conquer was not around?
What about the ocean, other lands would not have been found

Conquer your fear of anything in the way of your Success
Believe in the strength of your desire and Conquer does the rest

Care – Empathy, compassion, think about, interested, concern, it matters.

Care about it.

Care about your life, Care about others, Care about your Relationships.

Care about where you live and what it looks like.

Care about your family.

Care about who you are and where you are going.

Care about what you look like. Care about how you smell.
I washed my face and combed my hair and what about the teeth?

It is true that soap and a hot shower are good for Mental Health
Check out The Adventures of Rick and Jack.com and learn all about it.

Care about your Health, Exercise, and Care about what you eat.

Care about what you do.

Care about how you do it.

When you Care about who you are and what you do and who you are with,
your life is full of Possibles and Probables. Add Care and in Joy a better life experience.

Life is so much more meaningful when you Care about it.

Care about your Success!

If you add Care to your Road Trip, more meaning will show up
Care about Succeeding and Success will erupt

When You Care about what is happening, the trip is way more fun
Care is essential to get the Road Trip done

Care and Compassion sometimes walk together hand and hand
Care about who you are and what you are doing, Success is where you will land

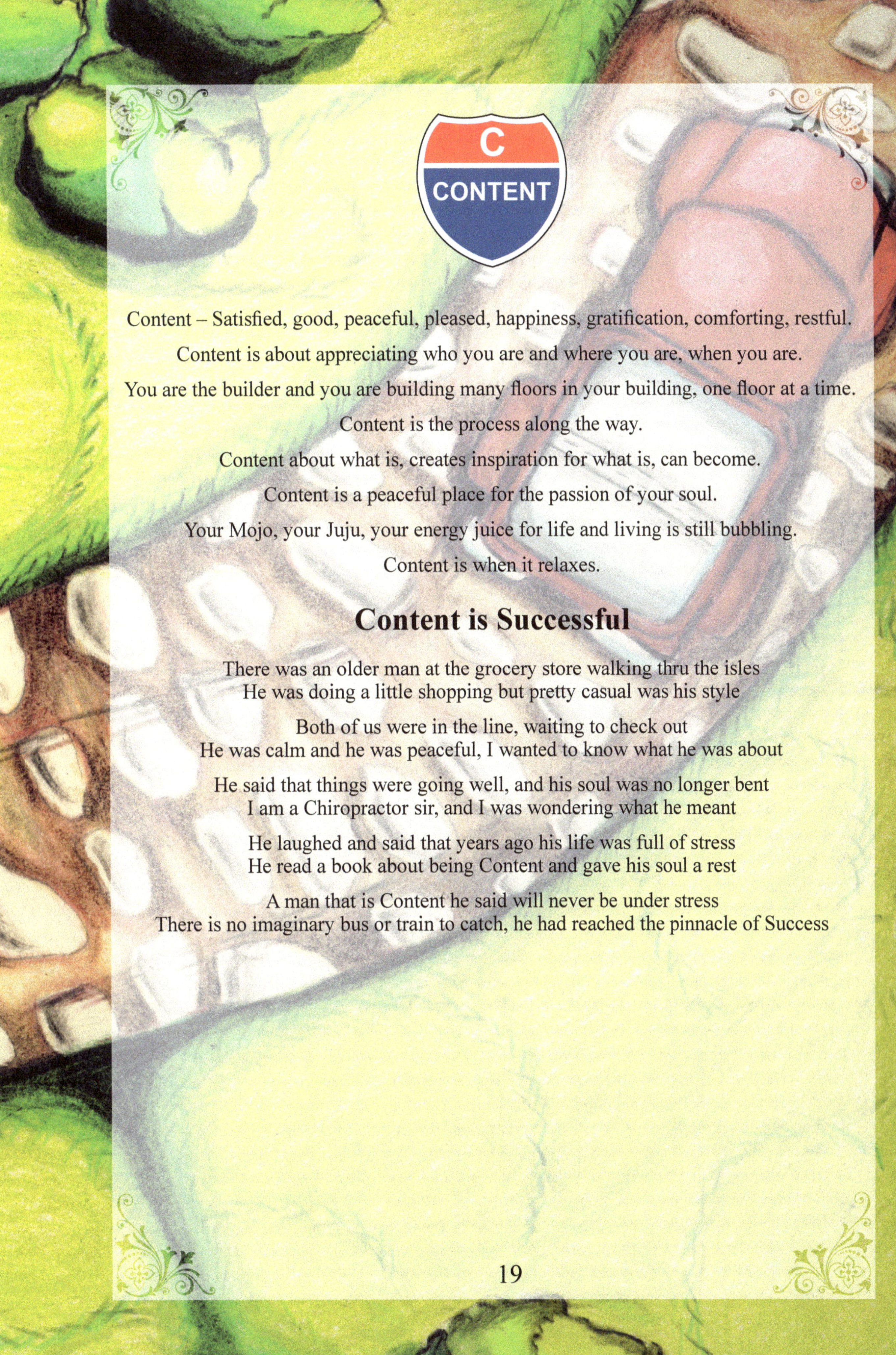

Content – Satisfied, good, peaceful, pleased, happiness, gratification, comforting, restful.

Content is about appreciating who you are and where you are, when you are.

You are the builder and you are building many floors in your building, one floor at a time.

Content is the process along the way.

Content about what is, creates inspiration for what is, can become.

Content is a peaceful place for the passion of your soul.

Your Mojo, your Juju, your energy juice for life and living is still bubbling.

Content is when it relaxes.

Content is Successful

There was an older man at the grocery store walking thru the isles
He was doing a little shopping but pretty casual was his style

Both of us were in the line, waiting to check out
He was calm and he was peaceful, I wanted to know what he was about

He said that things were going well, and his soul was no longer bent
I am a Chiropractor sir, and I was wondering what he meant

He laughed and said that years ago his life was full of stress
He read a book about being Content and gave his soul a rest

A man that is Content he said will never be under stress
There is no imaginary bus or train to catch, he had reached the pinnacle of Success

Discipline – Self-control, code of conduct, instructions, rules to live by, cement for the bricks.

Success and Discipline both ride in the front seat on the Road Trip.

It's the daily commitment to your goals.

Discipline is self-imposed.

What do you want to do or accomplish?

What do you have to do to get it done?
This is where Discipline comes in.

Discipline is the unwavering dedication to doing what you have to do.
It is the courage required to push yourself beyond your reach and do it.

Usually, by just getting started, the how to will show up.
Learn how to do it in the doing of it and don't give up.
Discipline is what allows this to happen.

Discipline is the bridge between your goals and the accomplishment of them.

Discipline plays a key role when building the foundation
and the structure that your Success will live in.

Success requires Discipline

Discipline? You mean Discipline, like Discipline? Required for Success?
To Achieve my Hopes and Dreams and Goals? I would rather lay on the couch and rest

You can lay on the couch all day long, but this is what I know is true
When you add a little Discipline, it is amazing what you can do

It starts with a target that you want to hit
Discipline is required and you will conquer it

Discipline is a Character trait that stands tall among the rest
Discipline gives your Fortitude an interesting little test

Discipline is just a principle of what you say that you will do
Discipline determines your Success, makes you become a better you

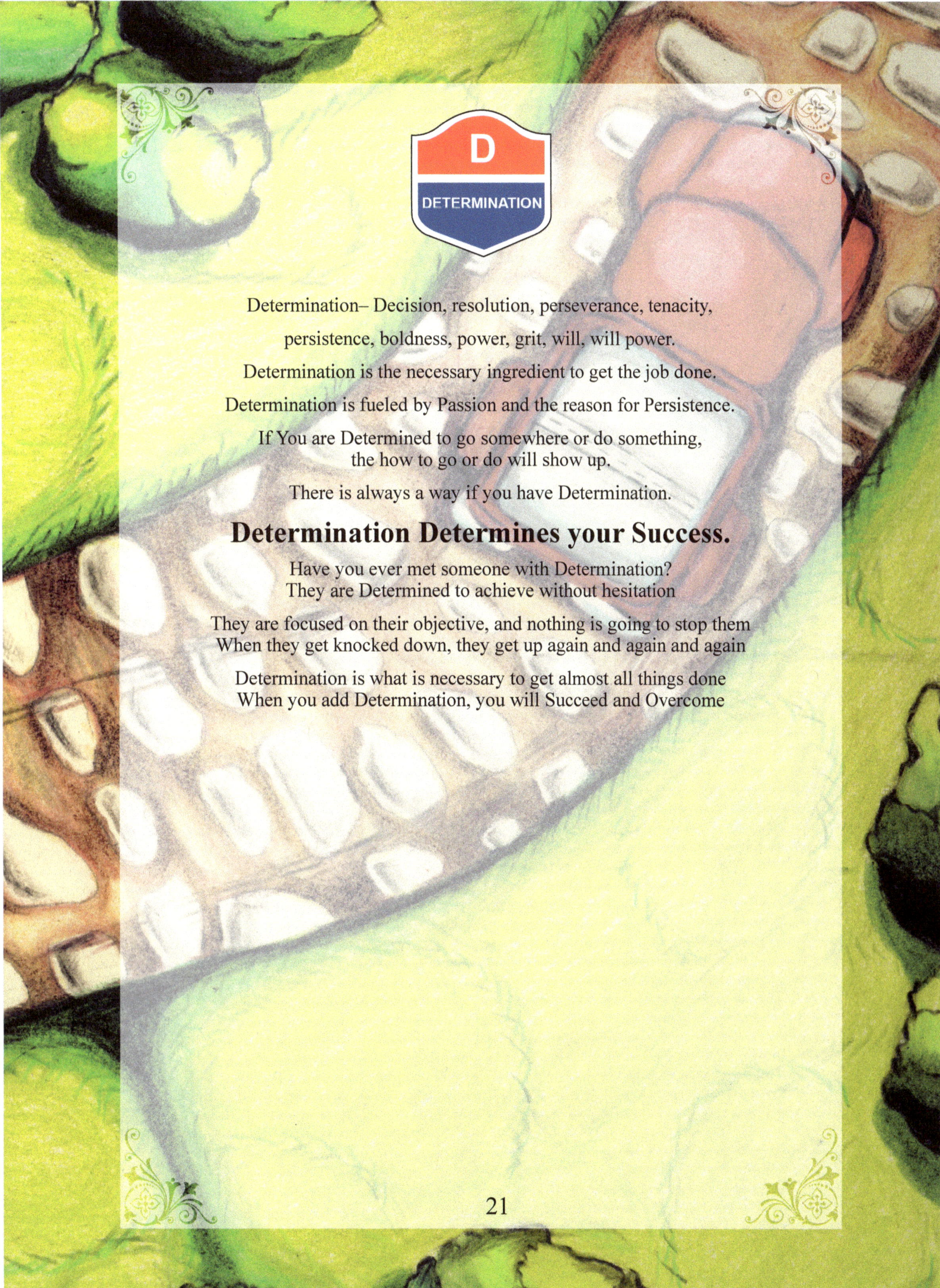

Determination– Decision, resolution, perseverance, tenacity,

persistence, boldness, power, grit, will, will power.

Determination is the necessary ingredient to get the job done.

Determination is fueled by Passion and the reason for Persistence.

If You are Determined to go somewhere or do something,
the how to go or do will show up.

There is always a way if you have Determination.

Determination Determines your Success.

Have you ever met someone with Determination?
They are Determined to achieve without hesitation

They are focused on their objective, and nothing is going to stop them
When they get knocked down, they get up again and again and again

Determination is what is necessary to get almost all things done
When you add Determination, you will Succeed and Overcome

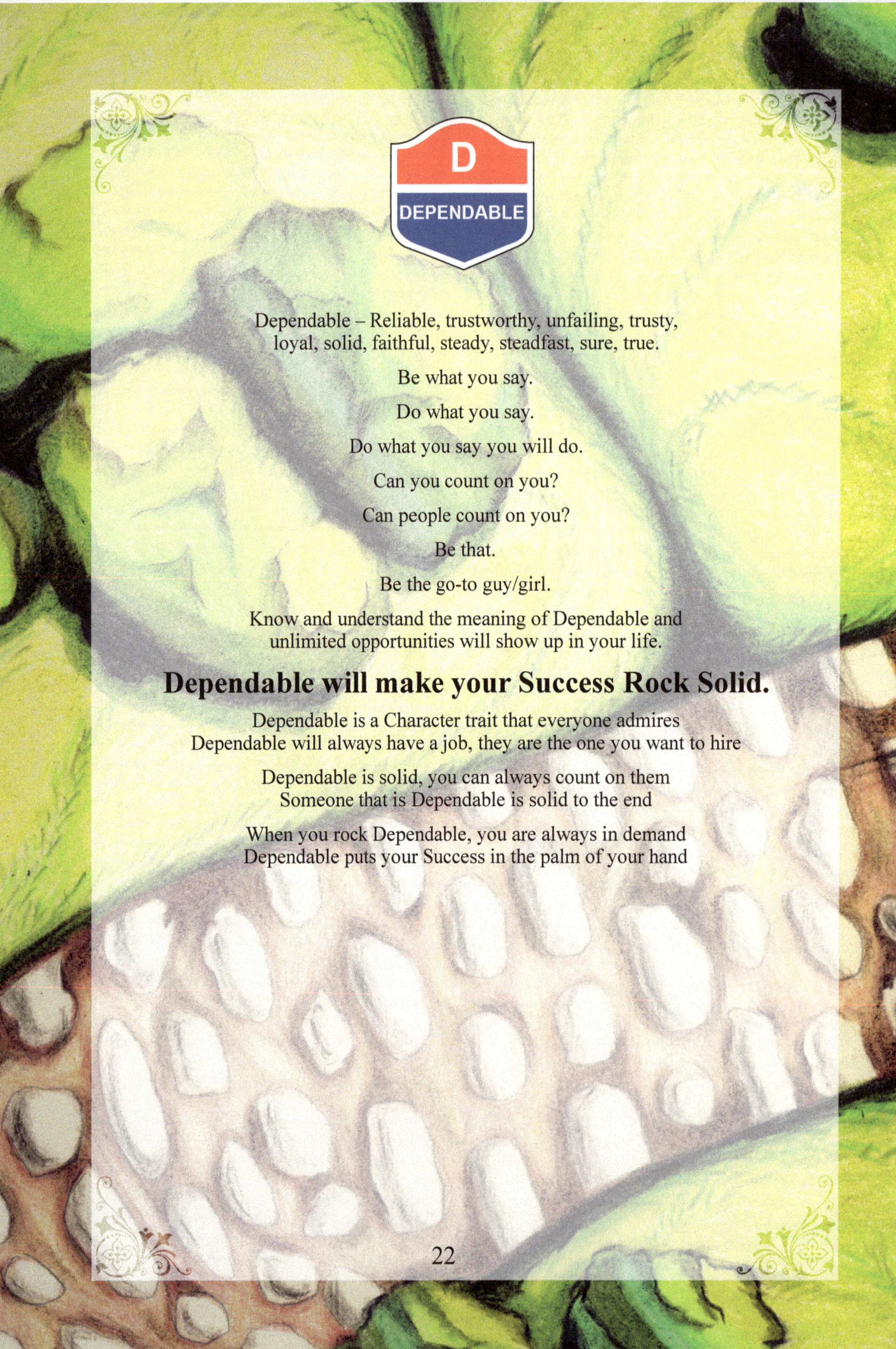

Dependable – Reliable, trustworthy, unfailing, trusty,
loyal, solid, faithful, steady, steadfast, sure, true.

Be what you say.

Do what you say.

Do what you say you will do.

Can you count on you?

Can people count on you?

Be that.

Be the go-to guy/girl.

Know and understand the meaning of Dependable and
unlimited opportunities will show up in your life.

Dependable will make your Success Rock Solid.

Dependable is a Character trait that everyone admires
Dependable will always have a job, they are the one you want to hire

Dependable is solid, you can always count on them
Someone that is Dependable is solid to the end

When you rock Dependable, you are always in demand
Dependable puts your Success in the palm of your hand

Dream – Desire, wish, goal, hope, possible, think, imagine, pretend.

This is so important and it is so much fun to take an Imagication vacation.
On a daily basis, think and Dream about your life.

"In my own little corner, in my own little chair I can be whatever I want to be."
The immortal words of Cinderella.
or
Get a big chair, take it to the beach, high on the mountain top, deep in the forest,
incredible sunrise and have one of the best times Dreaming about your life.

Dreams don't usually come true when you are still sleeping.

Dreams do come true but you have to be awake for this part.
This is the awake part of dreaming.

When you engage your imagination and Dream about you and your life,
the Road Trip gets started.

Your imagination can create magic things to happen in your life.

I call it "Imagication"- when Dreams come true.

Dreams do come true but first you have to have some.

Dream more
Dream often
Dream more often

Dream big dreams…
all the time.

Dream On and Imagicate your Success.

He was a fine young lad; he was always dreaming that he would win
His teachers thought he wasn't paying attention because he was dreaming again

So one day I asked him what he was dreaming about, and this is what he told me
I am dreaming about my future, I am dreaming about what I want to be

I am going to be Successful doing whatever I choose to do
If I keep on dreaming, I know that some of my Dreams will come true

Energy = MC². Einstein said that the mass times the speed of light squared, equals Energy.

It was profound and has changed the world.

What about your Energy?

How much Energy fuels your Desire?

Your Desire = your mass. How much mass? = How much Desire?

Speed of light squared? Sounds really fast, really bright.

What about You?

How much light do you have on?

How fast is it traveling?

Your Energy = Desire lit up!

Most of the ideas in this book are a choice.

If you want your life to be more exciting,
you have to get more excited about your life.
This is Energy.

Energy is life lit up.

You are here to In Joy being here.
Your Energy is up to you.

Success is all about MC²

Energy is a concept motivated by loving what you do
Mix your energy with ambition and watch your Success as it comes true

Love is Positive Energy, really good energy for the trip
The Road Trip to Success, requires a lot of "It".

Success requires Energy, it is all about the Love inside
Fill your pick-up, up with Love Energy and have a Successful ride

Enthusiasm – Excitement, zeal, zest, exuberance, elation, interest, passion, love,
devotion, craze, childlike, energized, contagious, unstoppable.

Are You pumped up about your life?

Is your Mojo on?

Would you want to hang around with you?

Is your life torch burning HOT? It should be.

Turn on your juice.

Power up.

Flame on.

Get excited to be alive.

Everyday is a new day full of potential and loaded with opportunities.

Seize the moment.

Miss nothing.

Right Now, is the only time you truly have.

If You are full of Enthusiasm in each moment,
memories of yesterday will be full of satisfaction
and your tomorrows will be full of promise.

Enthusiasm is a very important part of your Success.

Your Attitude, your Energy, your Personality, your Mojo,
is because of the light that is on in your life.

Enthusiasm is your light.

Enthusiasm for Success

There was this girl in the band, playing louder than the rest
She was full of Enthusiasm abounding with way more zest

I sat down and I listened, I could have listened to her all day
She was so Enthusiastic, she absolutely loves to play

Put Enthusiasm in the tank on your Road Trip to Success
Enthusiasm about what you are doing? I call that Happiness

Exceed - Go above the norm, go over the top, surpass, superior, go beyond, outreach, outrun, overdo, excel. Super achiever.

Exceed is an Attitude that allows you to have and to be and to do…more.

Good enough is not good enough.

Aim higher

Do more plus one

Go the extra mile

Exceed expectations.

Blow past the target.

Exceed!

Exceptional, Outstanding, Wonderful, Greatness, Excellence……Success
Exceed!

Exceed and Succeed, it is as simple as that
When you are working that much harder there is no turning back

The target was one thing, but they blew past that Goal
They just kept on going, perhaps they did not know

I asked what they were doing, their eyes welled up with pride
They were constantly outperforming, Exceed was on their side

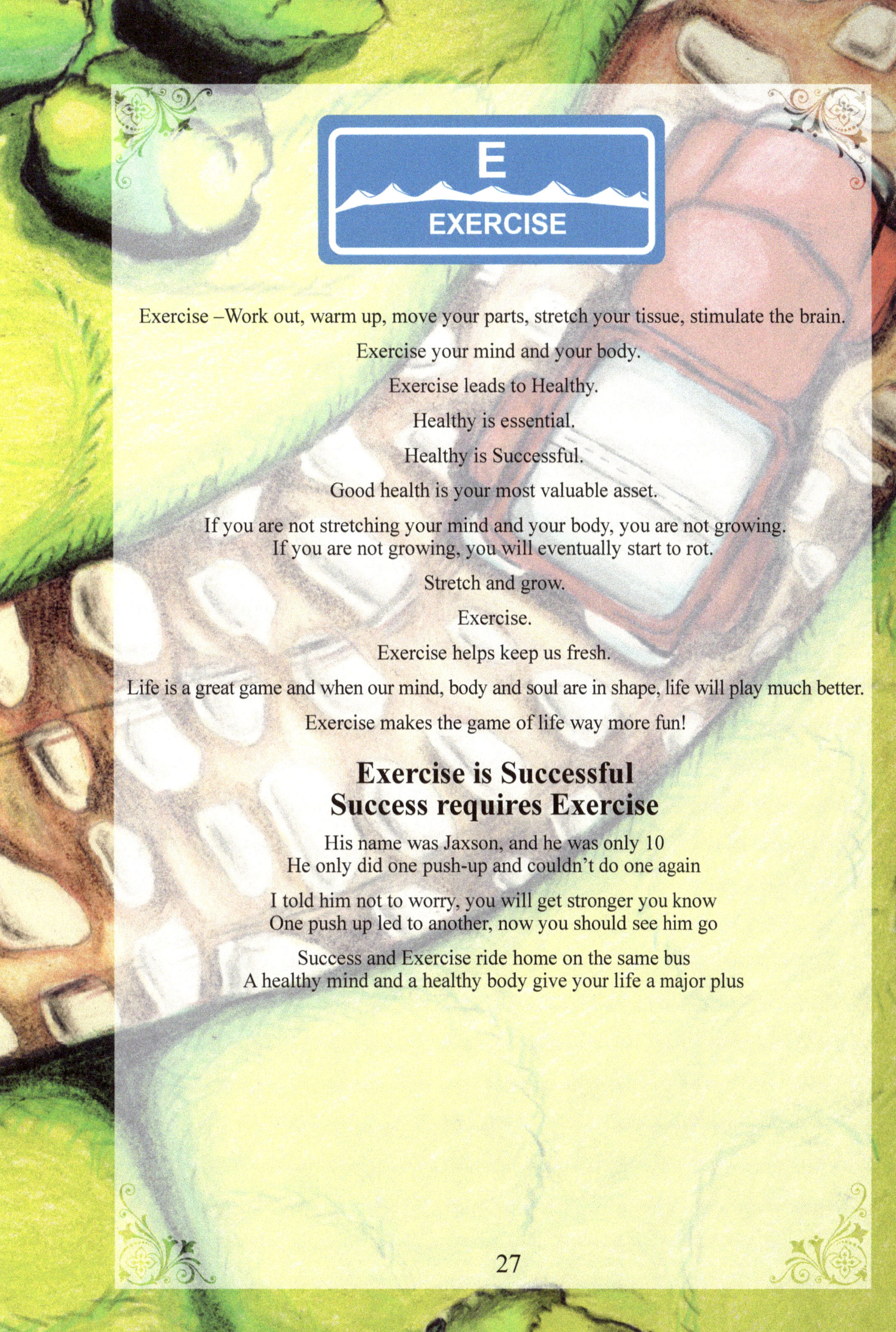

E
EXERCISE

Exercise –Work out, warm up, move your parts, stretch your tissue, stimulate the brain.

Exercise your mind and your body.

Exercise leads to Healthy.

Healthy is essential.

Healthy is Successful.

Good health is your most valuable asset.

If you are not stretching your mind and your body, you are not growing.
If you are not growing, you will eventually start to rot.

Stretch and grow.

Exercise.

Exercise helps keep us fresh.

Life is a great game and when our mind, body and soul are in shape, life will play much better.

Exercise makes the game of life way more fun!

Exercise is Successful
Success requires Exercise

His name was Jaxson, and he was only 10
He only did one push-up and couldn't do one again

I told him not to worry, you will get stronger you know
One push up led to another, now you should see him go

Success and Exercise ride home on the same bus
A healthy mind and a healthy body give your life a major plus

Faith – Belief, confidence, trust, security, reliance, assurance, certainty.

Faith is Believing in a source of incredibly Positive Energy that is available to all of us.

Faith makes all things possible in our lives.

There is huge comfort in knowing that the universe is not your responsibility,
but all of us have an important and responsible role in it.

There is an extremely wise and intelligent Energy that guards and guides us.

This Energy is called God and Love by some and Light by others,
but whatever you choose to call it; Faith is how you access it.

The greater the Faith, the greater the Energy that we have access to.

This is HUGE.

We are surrounded by an infinite supply of Positive Energy,
really good stuff, if only we Believe.

What do you Believe in? Believing makes it so.

It has been stated that it only takes a little bit of Faith and mountains will be moved.
The mountains are much smaller when the Faith is much larger.

Believe that this is true.

Have Faith in your Success

We are guarded and guided by an incredible source
Faith is your access to this amazing force

Imagine Success in everything that you do
Faith and Believe can make your Dreams come true

Have Faith in your Success and follow your plan
There is unlimited Energy that is at your command

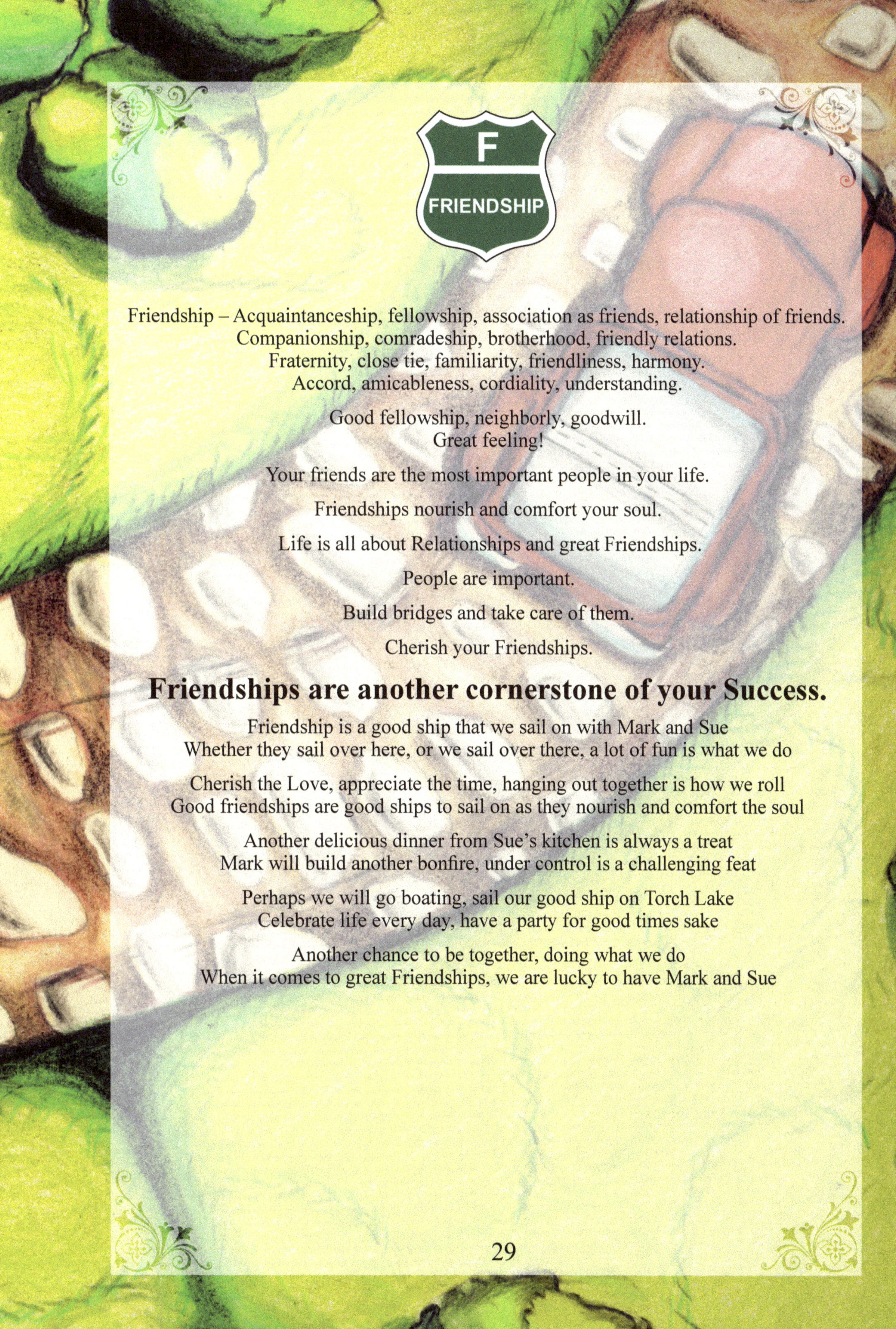

Friendship – Acquaintanceship, fellowship, association as friends, relationship of friends.
Companionship, comradeship, brotherhood, friendly relations.
Fraternity, close tie, familiarity, friendliness, harmony.
Accord, amicableness, cordiality, understanding.

Good fellowship, neighborly, goodwill.
Great feeling!

Your friends are the most important people in your life.

Friendships nourish and comfort your soul.

Life is all about Relationships and great Friendships.

People are important.

Build bridges and take care of them.

Cherish your Friendships.

Friendships are another cornerstone of your Success.

Friendship is a good ship that we sail on with Mark and Sue
Whether they sail over here, or we sail over there, a lot of fun is what we do

Cherish the Love, appreciate the time, hanging out together is how we roll
Good friendships are good ships to sail on as they nourish and comfort the soul

Another delicious dinner from Sue's kitchen is always a treat
Mark will build another bonfire, under control is a challenging feat

Perhaps we will go boating, sail our good ship on Torch Lake
Celebrate life every day, have a party for good times sake

Another chance to be together, doing what we do
When it comes to great Friendships, we are lucky to have Mark and Sue

Focus – The point or target of your concentration, present time consciousness, being present, do one thing at a time, stay tuned, stay between the lines.

Are you looking around?
Are you watching?

Pay Attention.

Pay Attention to what you are doing.

I once heard a story about a person that when they were here,
they were thinking about over there,
and when they were over there
they were thinking about over here.

Because they were not thinking about where they were, when they were,
they were never really anywhere.

Success in any effort depends on what you Focus on.

Remember the magnifying glass on a sunny day and
if you held it steady on a point it would start to burn.

Your Focus is the magnifying glass.

Concentrate your Focus on your Goals and your Objectives and
the target gets real hot, real fast.

That's a good thing.

Focus on your Success!

In everything that you do, Focus on what you are doing
Do not get distracted and keep things moving

If you Focus intently, you will get the job done
It is like being the designated hitter and hitting a homerun

Keep your eye on the task, Focus on the Goal
Success is more likely, pay attention, stay in control

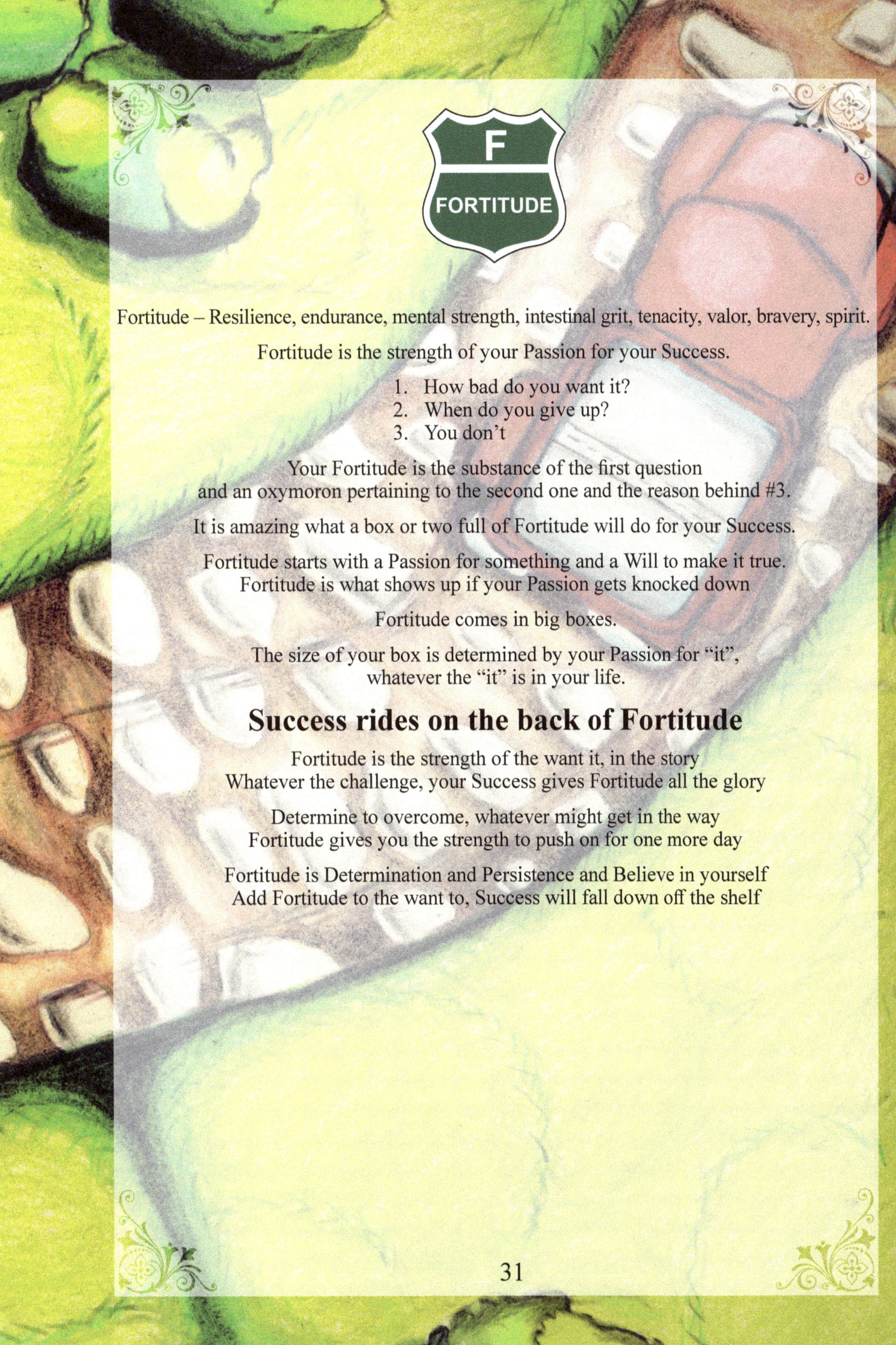

Fortitude – Resilience, endurance, mental strength, intestinal grit, tenacity, valor, bravery, spirit.

Fortitude is the strength of your Passion for your Success.

1. How bad do you want it?
2. When do you give up?
3. You don't

Your Fortitude is the substance of the first question
and an oxymoron pertaining to the second one and the reason behind #3.

It is amazing what a box or two full of Fortitude will do for your Success.

Fortitude starts with a Passion for something and a Will to make it true.
Fortitude is what shows up if your Passion gets knocked down

Fortitude comes in big boxes.

The size of your box is determined by your Passion for "it",
whatever the "it" is in your life.

Success rides on the back of Fortitude

Fortitude is the strength of the want it, in the story
Whatever the challenge, your Success gives Fortitude all the glory

Determine to overcome, whatever might get in the way
Fortitude gives you the strength to push on for one more day

Fortitude is Determination and Persistence and Believe in yourself
Add Fortitude to the want to, Success will fall down off the shelf

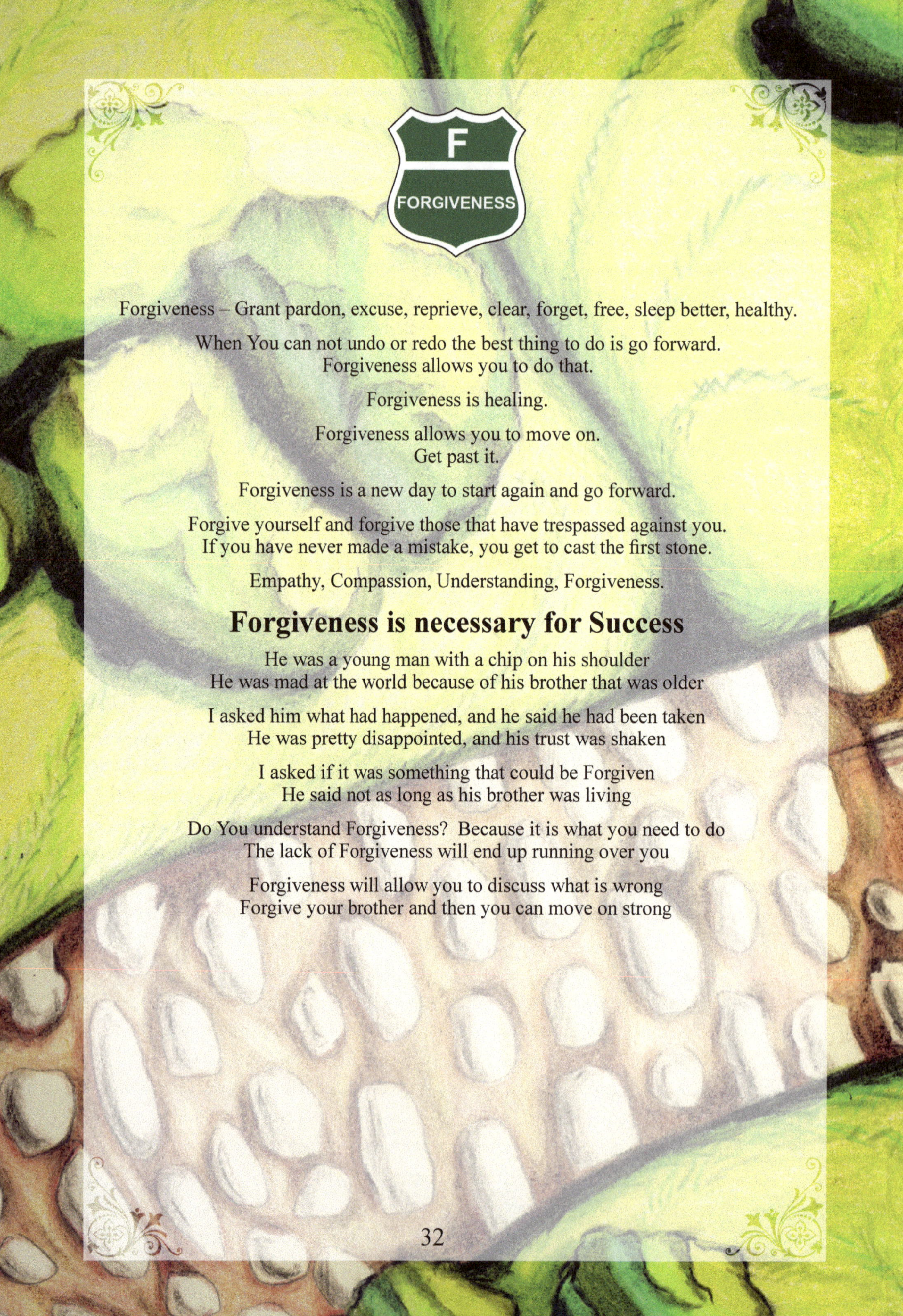

Forgiveness – Grant pardon, excuse, reprieve, clear, forget, free, sleep better, healthy.

When You can not undo or redo the best thing to do is go forward.
Forgiveness allows you to do that.

Forgiveness is healing.

Forgiveness allows you to move on.
Get past it.

Forgiveness is a new day to start again and go forward.

Forgive yourself and forgive those that have trespassed against you.
If you have never made a mistake, you get to cast the first stone.

Empathy, Compassion, Understanding, Forgiveness.

Forgiveness is necessary for Success

He was a young man with a chip on his shoulder
He was mad at the world because of his brother that was older

I asked him what had happened, and he said he had been taken
He was pretty disappointed, and his trust was shaken

I asked if it was something that could be Forgiven
He said not as long as his brother was living

Do You understand Forgiveness? Because it is what you need to do
The lack of Forgiveness will end up running over you

Forgiveness will allow you to discuss what is wrong
Forgive your brother and then you can move on strong

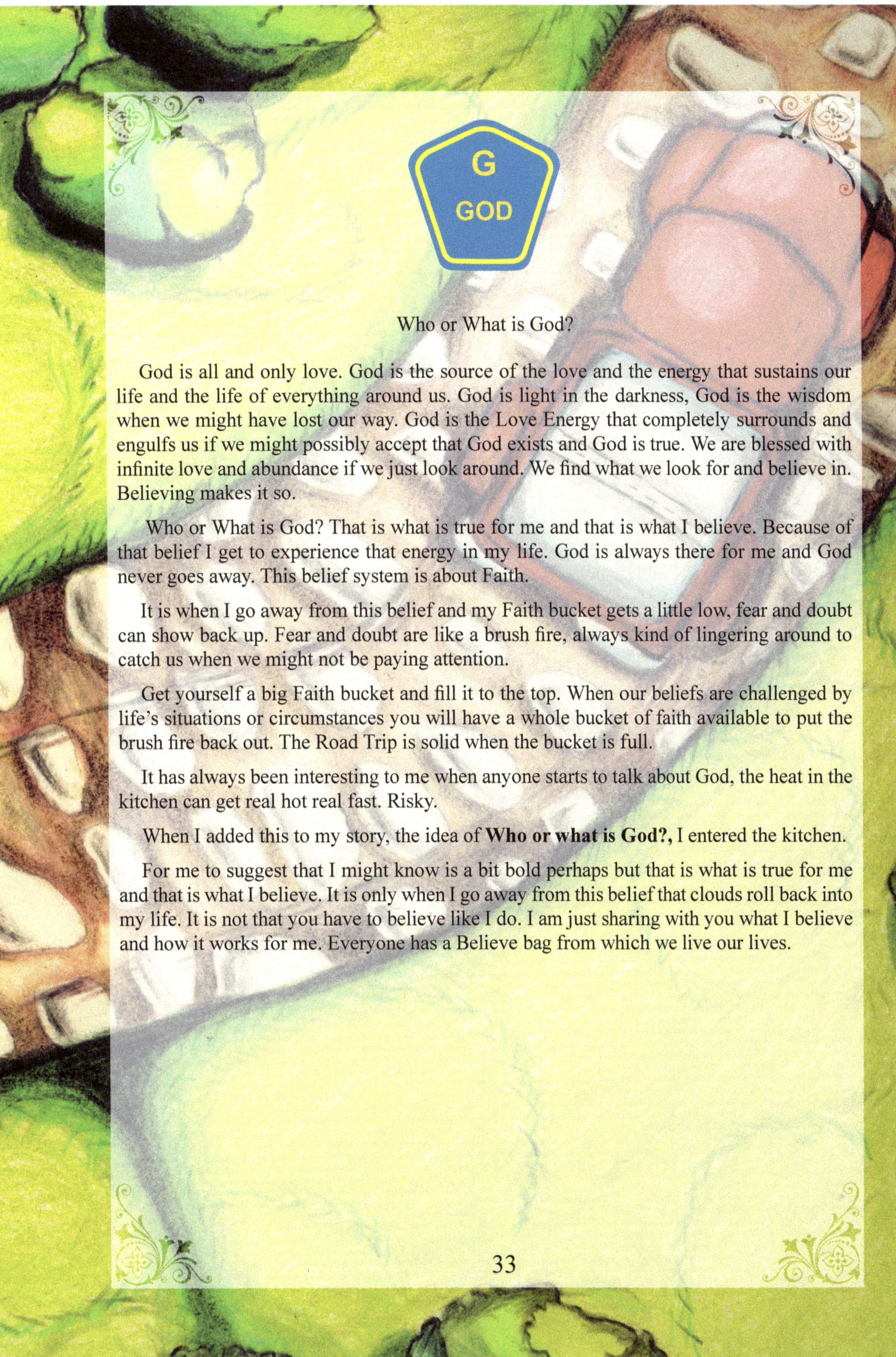

Who or What is God?

God is all and only love. God is the source of the love and the energy that sustains our life and the life of everything around us. God is light in the darkness, God is the wisdom when we might have lost our way. God is the Love Energy that completely surrounds and engulfs us if we might possibly accept that God exists and God is true. We are blessed with infinite love and abundance if we just look around. We find what we look for and believe in. Believing makes it so.

Who or What is God? That is what is true for me and that is what I believe. Because of that belief I get to experience that energy in my life. God is always there for me and God never goes away. This belief system is about Faith.

It is when I go away from this belief and my Faith bucket gets a little low, fear and doubt can show back up. Fear and doubt are like a brush fire, always kind of lingering around to catch us when we might not be paying attention.

Get yourself a big Faith bucket and fill it to the top. When our beliefs are challenged by life's situations or circumstances you will have a whole bucket of faith available to put the brush fire back out. The Road Trip is solid when the bucket is full.

It has always been interesting to me when anyone starts to talk about God, the heat in the kitchen can get real hot real fast. Risky.

When I added this to my story, the idea of **Who or what is God?,** I entered the kitchen.

For me to suggest that I might know is a bit bold perhaps but that is what is true for me and that is what I believe. It is only when I go away from this belief that clouds roll back into my life. It is not that you have to believe like I do. I am just sharing with you what I believe and how it works for me. Everyone has a Believe bag from which we live our lives.

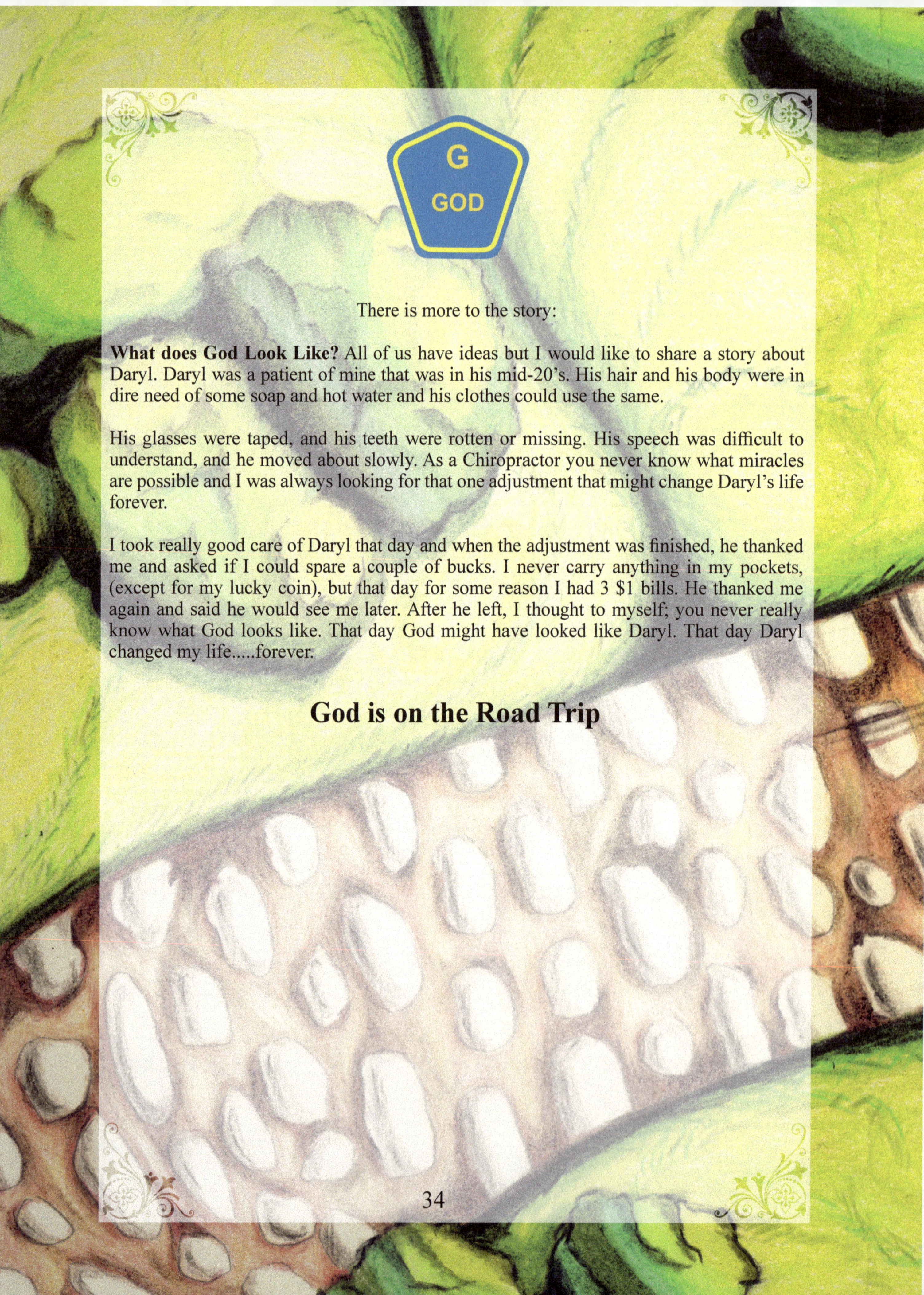

There is more to the story:

What does God Look Like? All of us have ideas but I would like to share a story about Daryl. Daryl was a patient of mine that was in his mid-20's. His hair and his body were in dire need of some soap and hot water and his clothes could use the same.

His glasses were taped, and his teeth were rotten or missing. His speech was difficult to understand, and he moved about slowly. As a Chiropractor you never know what miracles are possible and I was always looking for that one adjustment that might change Daryl's life forever.

I took really good care of Daryl that day and when the adjustment was finished, he thanked me and asked if I could spare a couple of bucks. I never carry anything in my pockets, (except for my lucky coin), but that day for some reason I had 3 $1 bills. He thanked me again and said he would see me later. After he left, I thought to myself; you never really know what God looks like. That day God might have looked like Daryl. That day Daryl changed my life.....forever.

God is on the Road Trip

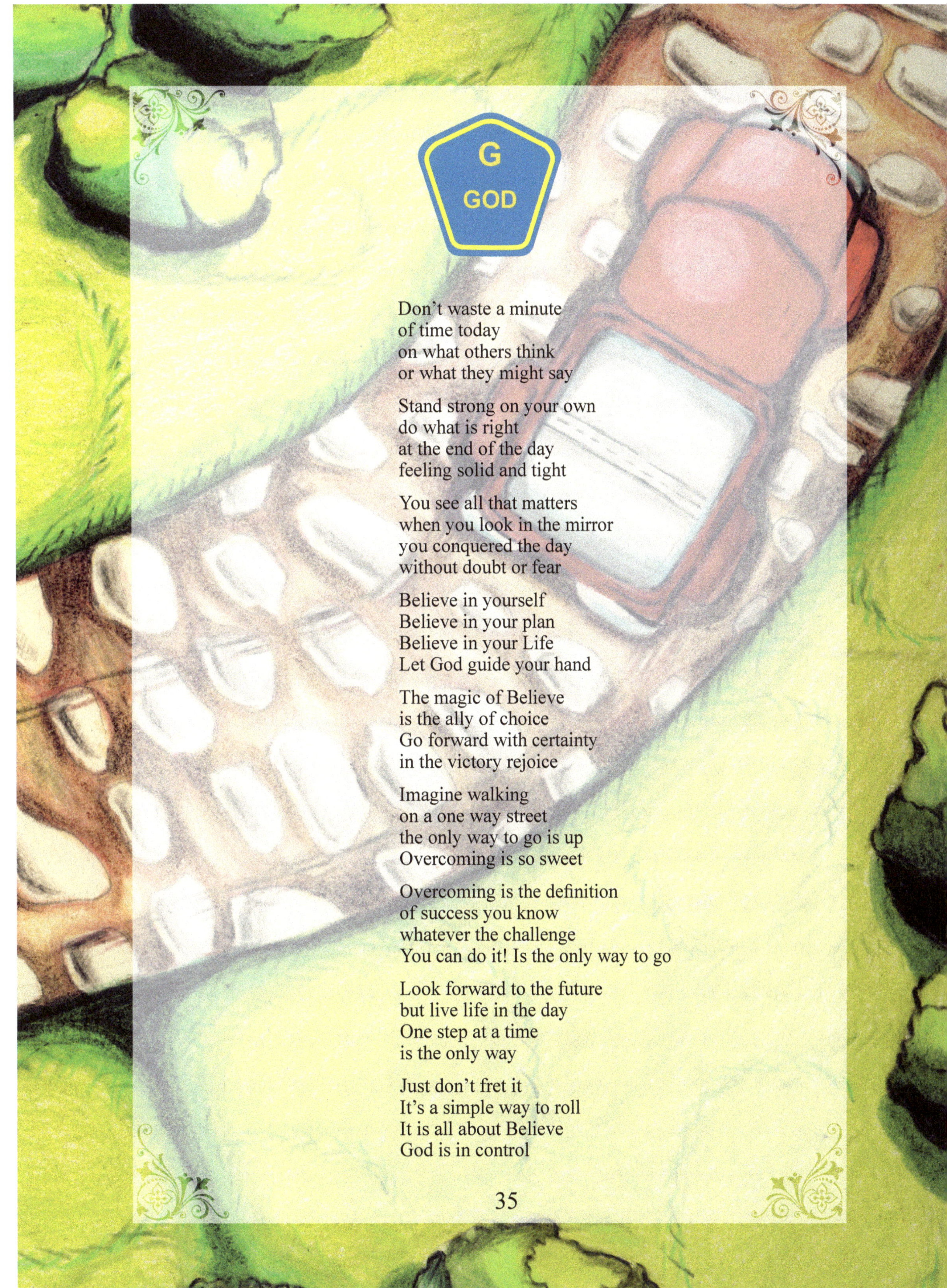

Don't waste a minute
of time today
on what others think
or what they might say

Stand strong on your own
do what is right
at the end of the day
feeling solid and tight

You see all that matters
when you look in the mirror
you conquered the day
without doubt or fear

Believe in yourself
Believe in your plan
Believe in your Life
Let God guide your hand

The magic of Believe
is the ally of choice
Go forward with certainty
in the victory rejoice

Imagine walking
on a one way street
the only way to go is up
Overcoming is so sweet

Overcoming is the definition
of success you know
whatever the challenge
You can do it! Is the only way to go

Look forward to the future
but live life in the day
One step at a time
is the only way

Just don't fret it
It's a simple way to roll
It is all about Believe
God is in control

Goals – Aim, objective, ambition, purpose, object, intent, intention, design, end, target.

The result(s) toward which effort is directed.

The idea: I did something to get something and after I did it, I got it.
The get something and got it were the Goal.

If you do not know where you are going, I promise you will never get there.
Eventually we call this lost.

Your written Goals give you a Road Map for your Road Trip to Success.

Establish a Goal and what it is that you want to do.
What is the behavior required to achieve the Goal?
Practice the behavior and get good at it.

A good game to play is called My Life.
The object of the game is your life Success and the way to play is
to sit down and write 100 Goals for you and your life.

Divide big Goals into little Goals; first downs help build a scoring momentum.

As you achieve a Goal, scratch it off the list and add a new Goal.

You can have more than 100 Goals but typically when you have
Goals to focus on Goal accomplishment will occur.

You will have fun keeping up with 100 Goals at a Time.

My Life Success is determined by the Goals that you achieve.

The best part about this game is that there are only winners.

Here is what is also true.
Winning here is synonymous with Success.
The definition of Success on your Road Trip is Overcoming.

Goals, Road Map, Road Trip, Overcome, Get There, Pretty Successful.

The recipe for Goal Achievement

1. Establish the Goal(s), write them down and read them
2. Determine what is the Behavior required to Achieve the Goal(s)
3. Practice the Behavior
4. Add Believe and Can

Goals, Success, Good Time.

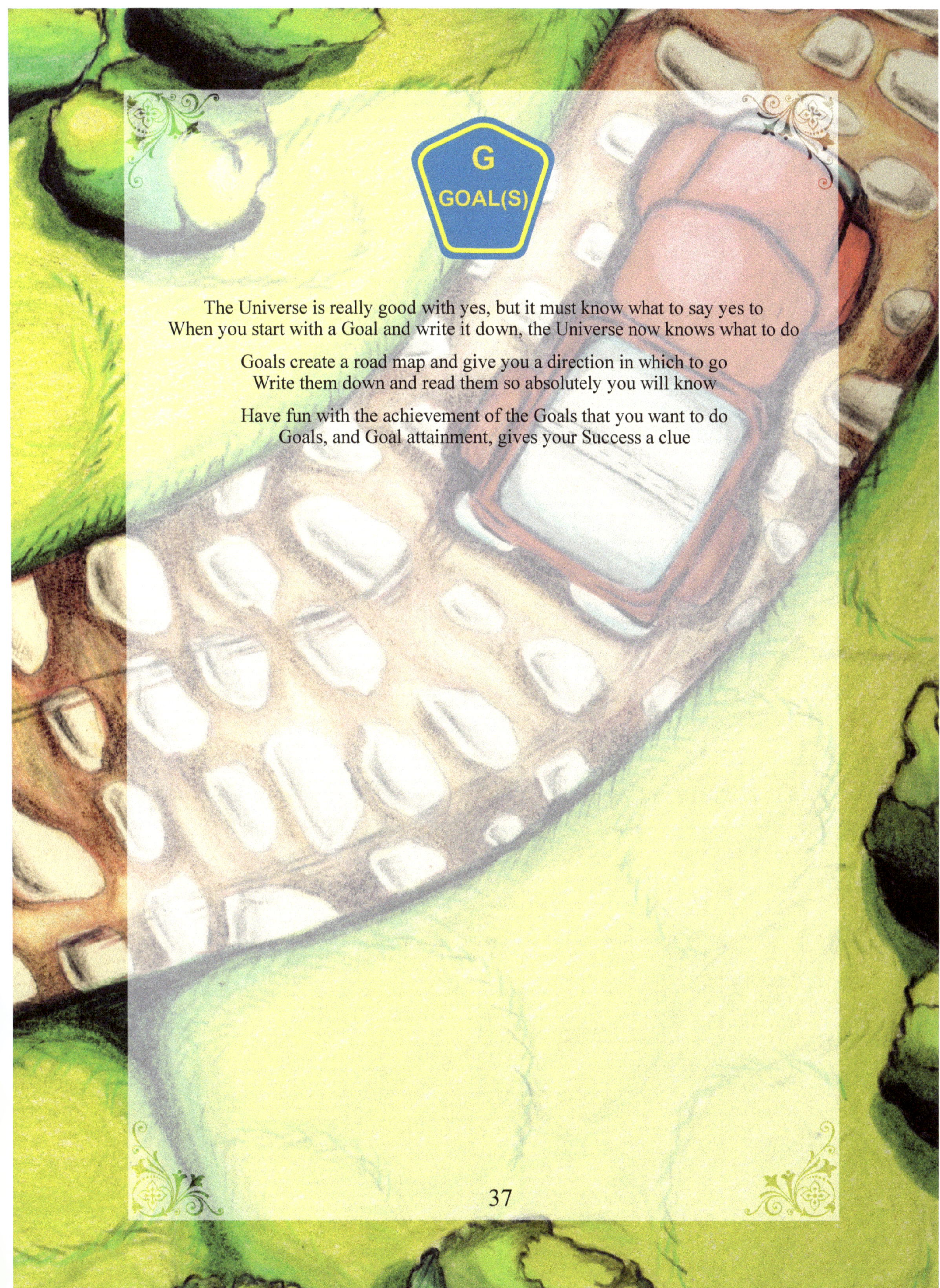

The Universe is really good with yes, but it must know what to say yes to
When you start with a Goal and write it down, the Universe now knows what to do

Goals create a road map and give you a direction in which to go
Write them down and read them so absolutely you will know

Have fun with the achievement of the Goals that you want to do
Goals, and Goal attainment, gives your Success a clue

Gratitude - Thankful, grateful, appreciation, thanks, thankfulness, thanksgiving.

Give thanks.

Thank you.

Focus on the positive elements in your life and
You will realize how much there is to be thankful for.

Count your blessings.
Start your day with Gratitude.

Appreciate what is going on around you and
what is going on around you will get even better.

Most of us have been richly blessed.
Our heart beats, our lungs breathe, and our brains are working.
Just a few things to think about.

Your blessings are the flowers
that God picked especially for you

What a beautiful bouquet that is,
setting on your table

Thank you

Gratitude is the air in your tires on your Road Trip!

Gratitude is extremely important and an essential part of the trip
Success is about appreciating your blessings, never should you forget

Just the fact that you are here, is where it should start
Be greatful for your heart and your lungs and a few other parts

Opportunity is all around you, remember that part too
Success is about Gratitude just watch what it can do

When we realize our many blessings, we are blessed even more
Gratitude is just an Attitude that opens many doors

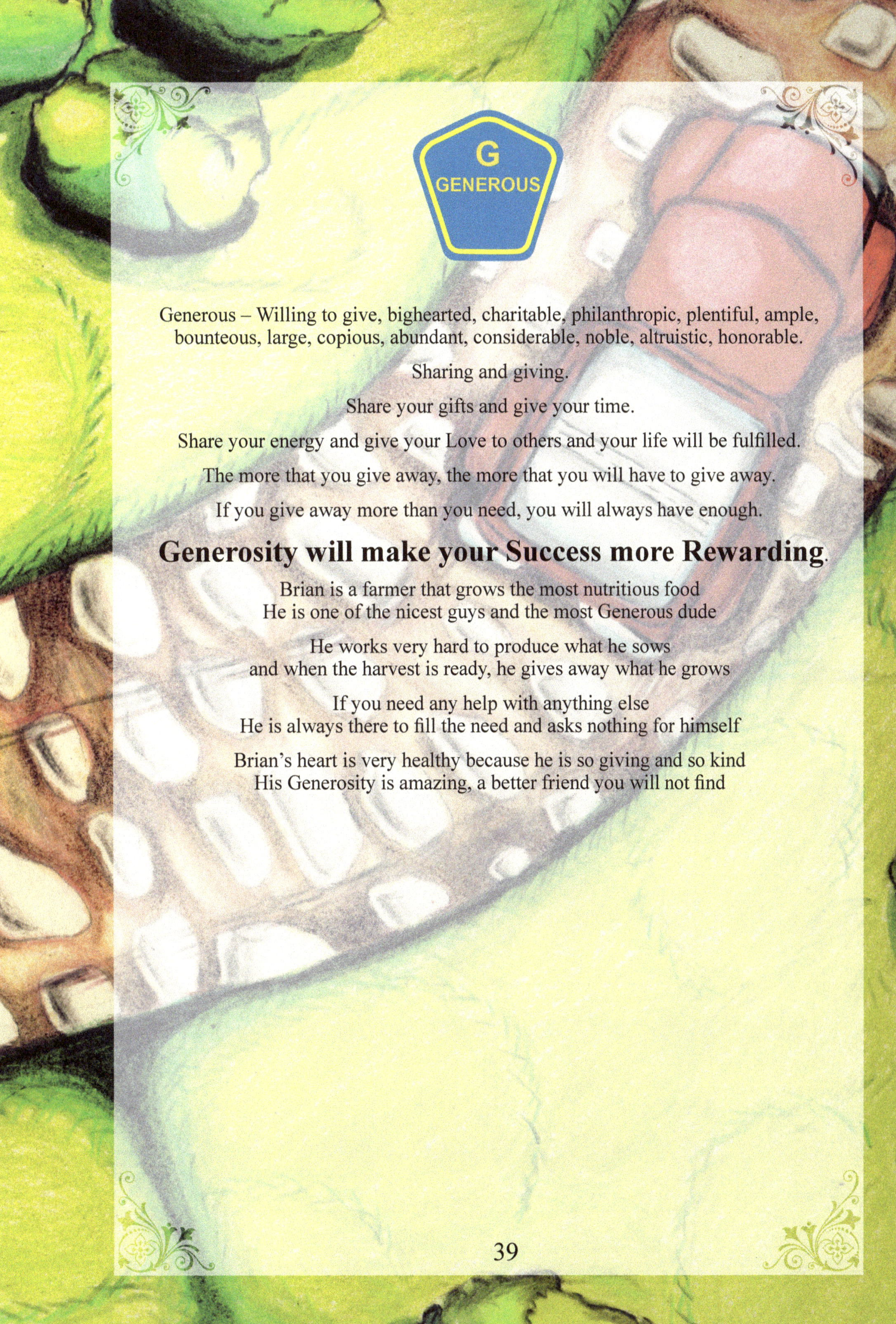

Generous – Willing to give, bighearted, charitable, philanthropic, plentiful, ample, bounteous, large, copious, abundant, considerable, noble, altruistic, honorable.

Sharing and giving.

Share your gifts and give your time.

Share your energy and give your Love to others and your life will be fulfilled.

The more that you give away, the more that you will have to give away.

If you give away more than you need, you will always have enough.

Generosity will make your Success more Rewarding.

Brian is a farmer that grows the most nutritious food
He is one of the nicest guys and the most Generous dude

He works very hard to produce what he sows
and when the harvest is ready, he gives away what he grows

If you need any help with anything else
He is always there to fill the need and asks nothing for himself

Brian's heart is very healthy because he is so giving and so kind
His Generosity is amazing, a better friend you will not find

Grow – Become larger, grow taller, spring up, shoot up, fill out,
expand, increase, swell, widen, stretch, spread, extend,
magnify, amplify, develop, mature, sprout, bud, blossom,
flower, bloom, thrive, flourish, develop, prosper,
enlarge, increase, skyrocket, Succeed.

Pretty impressive list of words.
Pick your favorite 20.

Growing starts with thinking.

Your thoughts are the seeds that Grow into your future.

Good Words create good thoughts to plant in the garden of your Success.
Gardens grow.

If you are not planting Seeds, you are not Growing.
If you are not Growing, then you are slowing and eventually you will stop.

Plant and Grow.

Grow into your Success

You mean it was once a tiny seed and now it is a mighty Oak tree
How is that possible? How could that be?

Your thoughts are the seeds from which your future Grows
Choose your thoughts from Good Words and let your life Success unfold

Think about your future, Grow into your Success
Sowing and reaping, Good Words seeds are the best

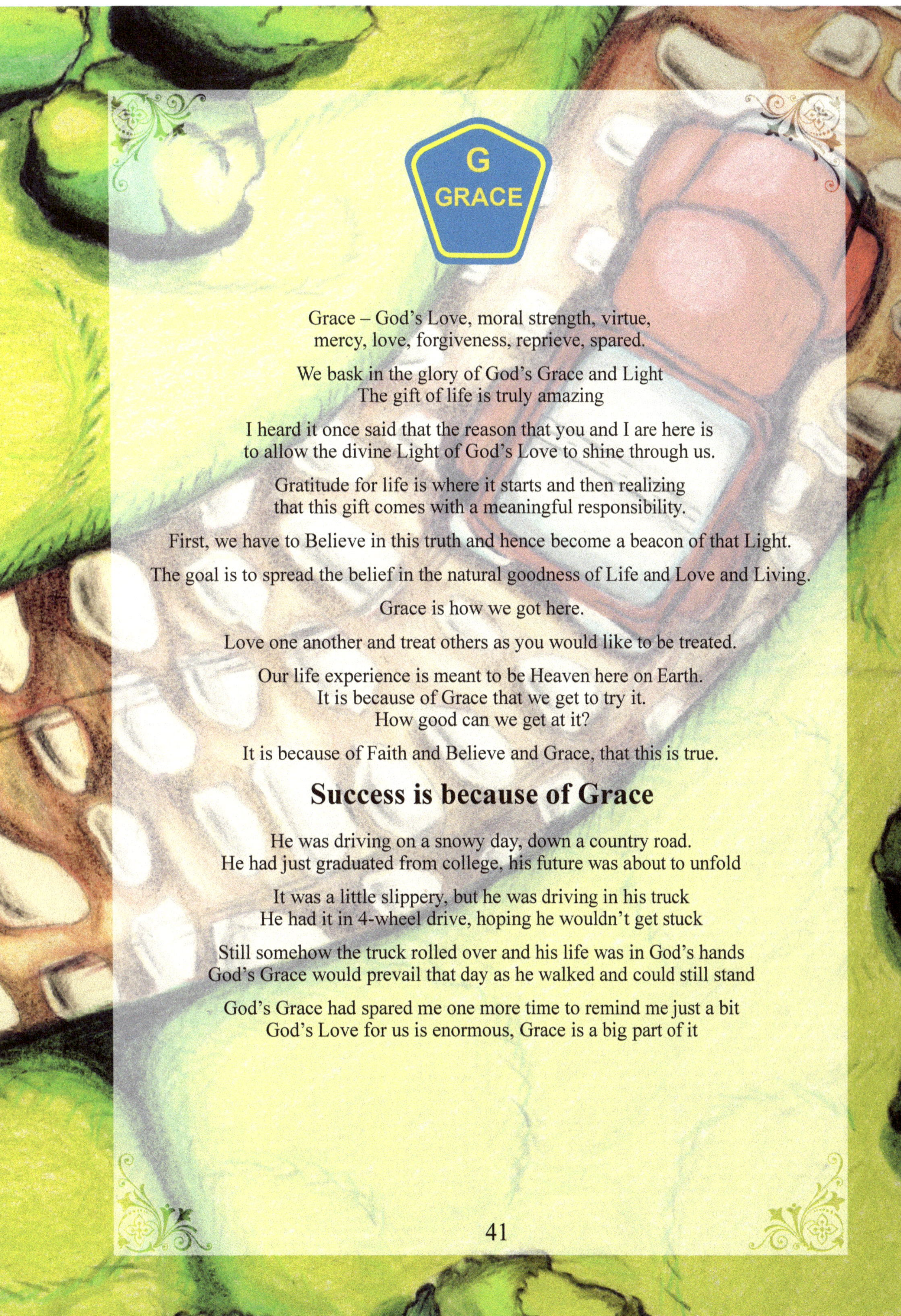

Grace – God's Love, moral strength, virtue,
mercy, love, forgiveness, reprieve, spared.

We bask in the glory of God's Grace and Light
The gift of life is truly amazing

I heard it once said that the reason that you and I are here is
to allow the divine Light of God's Love to shine through us.

Gratitude for life is where it starts and then realizing
that this gift comes with a meaningful responsibility.

First, we have to Believe in this truth and hence become a beacon of that Light.

The goal is to spread the belief in the natural goodness of Life and Love and Living.

Grace is how we got here.

Love one another and treat others as you would like to be treated.

Our life experience is meant to be Heaven here on Earth.
It is because of Grace that we get to try it.
How good can we get at it?

It is because of Faith and Believe and Grace, that this is true.

Success is because of Grace

He was driving on a snowy day, down a country road.
He had just graduated from college, his future was about to unfold

It was a little slippery, but he was driving in his truck
He had it in 4-wheel drive, hoping he wouldn't get stuck

Still somehow the truck rolled over and his life was in God's hands
God's Grace would prevail that day as he walked and could still stand

God's Grace had spared me one more time to remind me just a bit
God's Love for us is enormous, Grace is a big part of it

Be Honest – Truthful, fair, just, righteous, honorable, true,
dependable, reliable, solid, genuine, sincere.

There is no substitute for being Honest.

Honesty feels good because it is.

Honesty lasts forever, dishonesty does too.

You will never repair the bridge of dishonesty.

Tell the truth……all the time.

Tell the truth all the time because it is better.

Tell the truth all the time because it is the right thing to do.

Honesty is another cornerstone of Success

Tell the truth, is what the teacher said to me
I thought it would be better if the truth she did not see

So I came up with a story, that would sidestep responsibility
I know that I look suspicious, but it had nothing to do with me

I was sticking to my story, when she shook her head
It would have been better if you had told the truth, that is what she said

I wanted to believe your story, because I trusted you
But now because you were not Honest, the trust we had is through

I felt so bad when I realized what it was that I had done
I did not want to be the person that I had now become

That day I learned a lesson, about being Honest and Honesty
From that moment forward, Honest is how I would be

Humility – Modesty, humbleness, confidence without the cocky,
empathy, compassion, thoughtful, considerate, caring.

Humility is the realization that none of us are all that.
Humility is balance between all that and not so much.

Be Humble.

Enter: "The Swiss Cheese Philosophy of Humanity."

All of us are big pieces of Swiss cheese and all of us have holes or weak spots.
None of us are whole individually but collectively, when we come together,
we fill in the holes and support the weak spots.

We need each other.

Humility brings us together.

Together we are "whole" again.

Humility is the charming side of your Success

The older minister was dearly loved, and he had been there for a long time
There was also a new young minister, waiting patiently in line

He was a fine young man and stood pretty proud
He knew if he got a chance, he could woo the crowd

So up the aisle he went, a little more humble would have been better
The older minister gave him advice but he didn't read the letter

He stumbled and faltered and mumbled along
When it was all over, he wasn't feeling quite as strong

The young minister learned about Humility in an awkward way
The older minister took him aside, he had something to say

If you would have walked up, like you walked down,
you could have walked down like you walked up and in joyed looking around

Humility is a virtue, the young man learned about that day
He would forever be Humble and forever behave that way

Humility Part II

It took me a while to learn this, when I was growing up
I thought I was pretty special, touting the Champion's Cup

God has a sense of humor, I learned about it in a funny way
When I was thinking that I was all that, a different energy came to play

All dressed up and looking good, the envy of the crowd
but would you believe I had a booger, obvious and proud

I said hello to everyone and shook their hands too
Nice to see you, hello how are you? Kind of what I do

When I went back to my truck, all pumped up
I looked in the mirror and saw the booger that was stuck

I had to laugh at me that day when I learned about Humility
It is better to stay Humble, it's just a better place to be

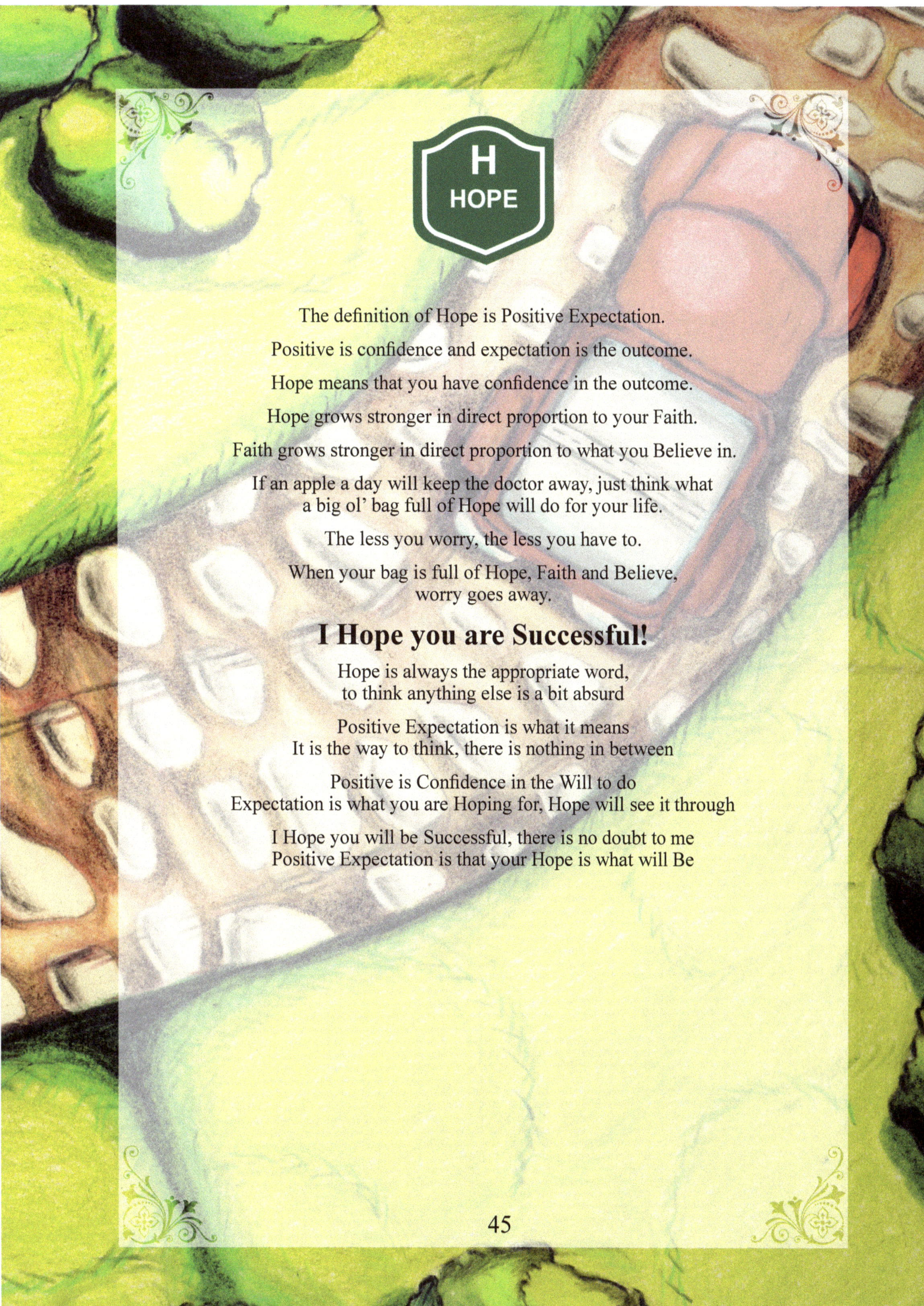

The definition of Hope is Positive Expectation.

Positive is confidence and expectation is the outcome.

Hope means that you have confidence in the outcome.

Hope grows stronger in direct proportion to your Faith.

Faith grows stronger in direct proportion to what you Believe in.

If an apple a day will keep the doctor away, just think what
a big ol' bag full of Hope will do for your life.

The less you worry, the less you have to.

When your bag is full of Hope, Faith and Believe,
worry goes away.

I Hope you are Successful!

Hope is always the appropriate word,
to think anything else is a bit absurd

Positive Expectation is what it means
It is the way to think, there is nothing in between

Positive is Confidence in the Will to do
Expectation is what you are Hoping for, Hope will see it through

I Hope you will be Successful, there is no doubt to me
Positive Expectation is that your Hope is what will Be

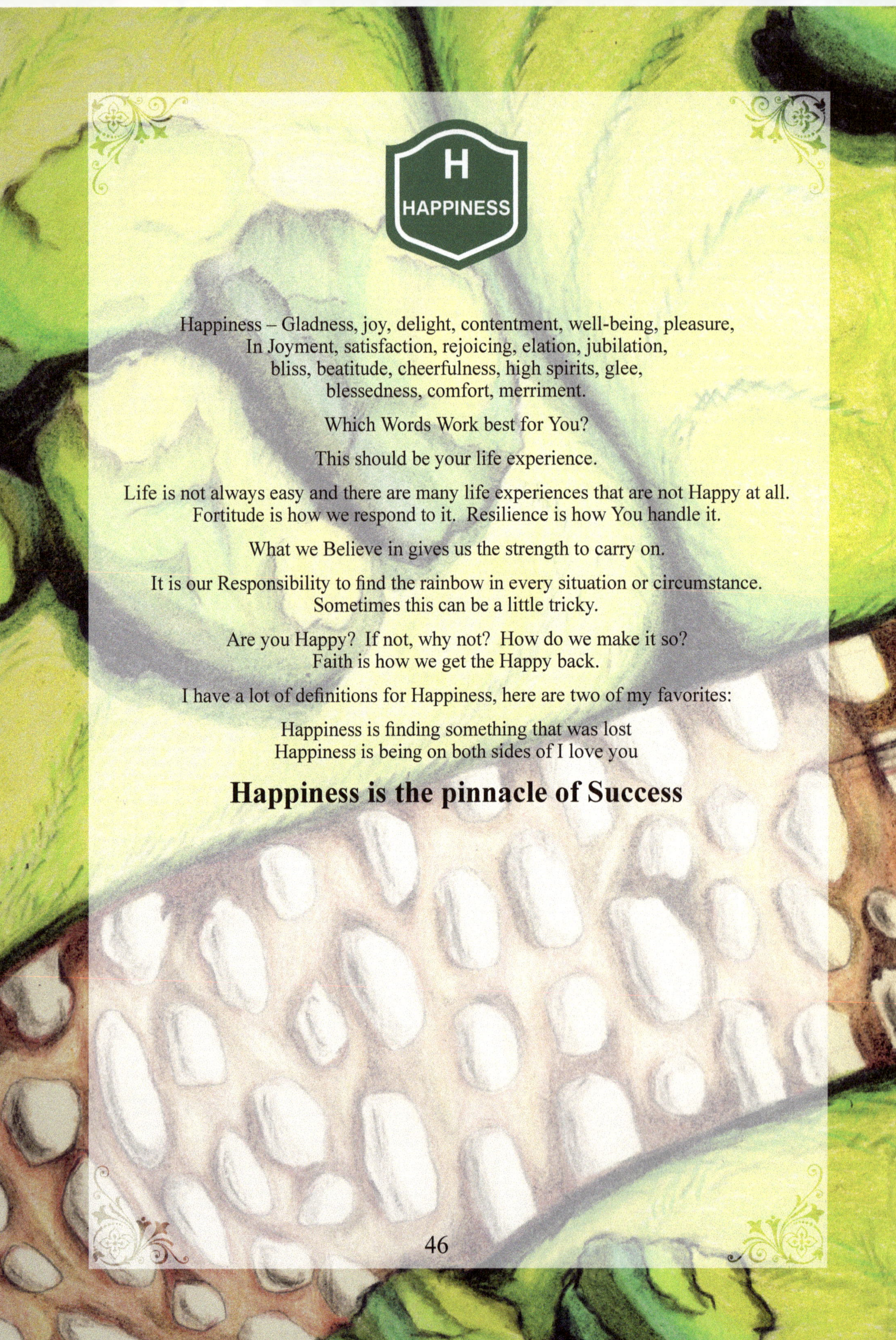

Happiness – Gladness, joy, delight, contentment, well-being, pleasure,
In Joyment, satisfaction, rejoicing, elation, jubilation,
bliss, beatitude, cheerfulness, high spirits, glee,
blessedness, comfort, merriment.

Which Words Work best for You?

This should be your life experience.

Life is not always easy and there are many life experiences that are not Happy at all.
Fortitude is how we respond to it. Resilience is how You handle it.

What we Believe in gives us the strength to carry on.

It is our Responsibility to find the rainbow in every situation or circumstance.
Sometimes this can be a little tricky.

Are you Happy? If not, why not? How do we make it so?
Faith is how we get the Happy back.

I have a lot of definitions for Happiness, here are two of my favorites:

Happiness is finding something that was lost
Happiness is being on both sides of I love you

Happiness is the pinnacle of Success

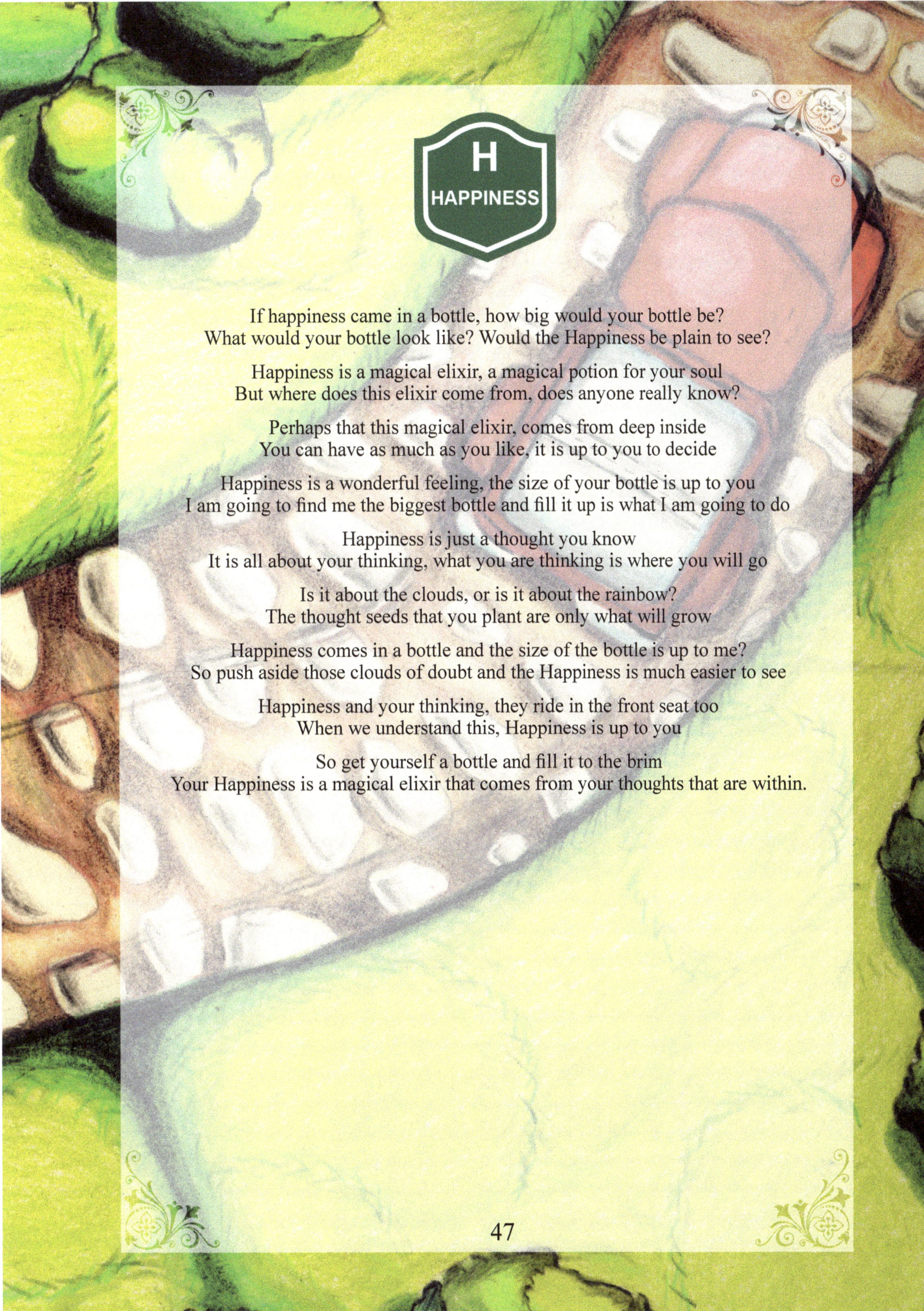

If happiness came in a bottle, how big would your bottle be?
What would your bottle look like? Would the Happiness be plain to see?

Happiness is a magical elixir, a magical potion for your soul
But where does this elixir come from, does anyone really know?

Perhaps that this magical elixir, comes from deep inside
You can have as much as you like, it is up to you to decide

Happiness is a wonderful feeling, the size of your bottle is up to you
I am going to find me the biggest bottle and fill it up is what I am going to do

Happiness is just a thought you know
It is all about your thinking, what you are thinking is where you will go

Is it about the clouds, or is it about the rainbow?
The thought seeds that you plant are only what will grow

Happiness comes in a bottle and the size of the bottle is up to me?
So push aside those clouds of doubt and the Happiness is much easier to see

Happiness and your thinking, they ride in the front seat too
When we understand this, Happiness is up to you

So get yourself a bottle and fill it to the brim
Your Happiness is a magical elixir that comes from your thoughts that are within.

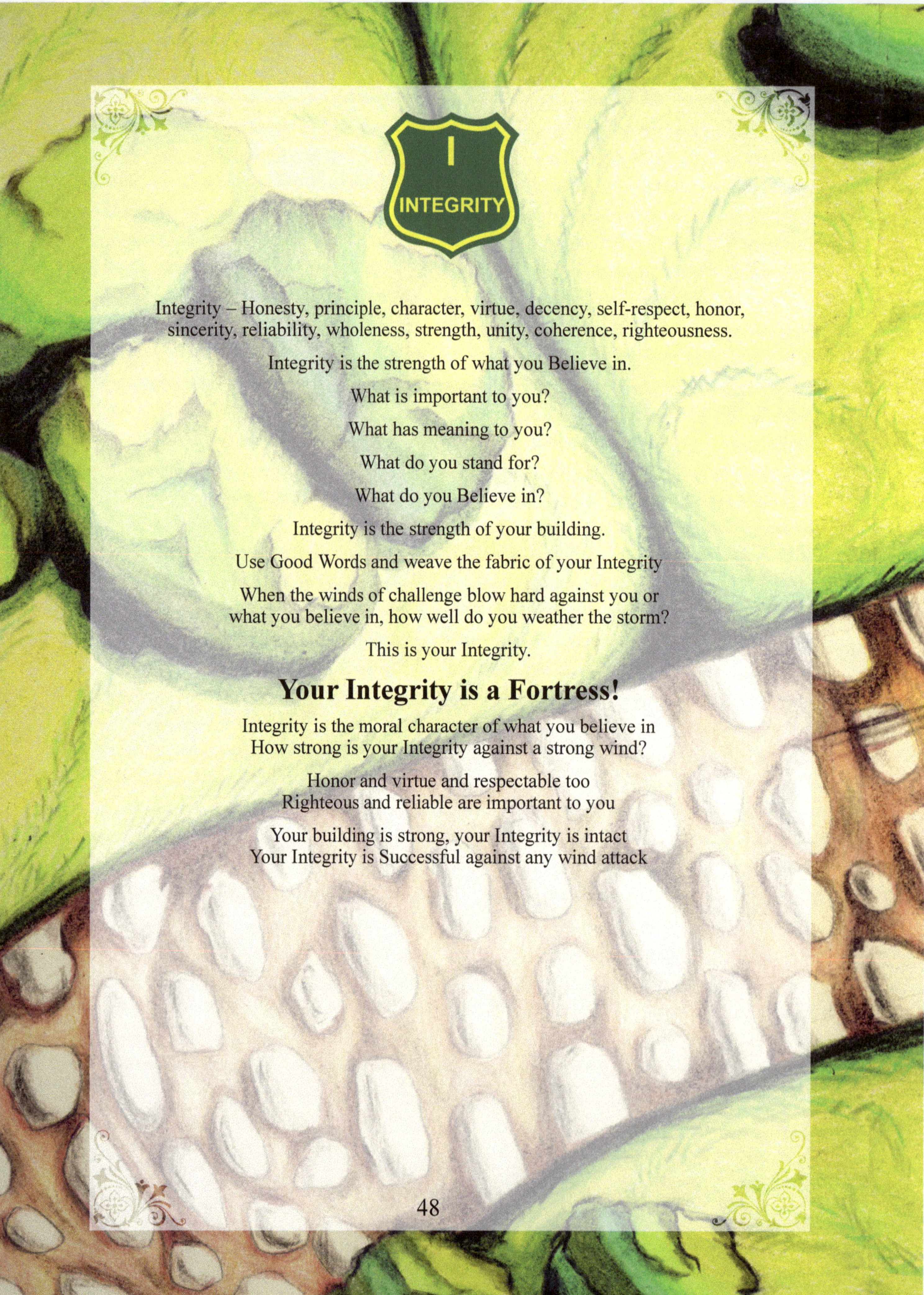

Integrity – Honesty, principle, character, virtue, decency, self-respect, honor, sincerity, reliability, wholeness, strength, unity, coherence, righteousness.

Integrity is the strength of what you Believe in.

What is important to you?

What has meaning to you?

What do you stand for?

What do you Believe in?

Integrity is the strength of your building.

Use Good Words and weave the fabric of your Integrity

When the winds of challenge blow hard against you or what you believe in, how well do you weather the storm?

This is your Integrity.

Your Integrity is a Fortress!

Integrity is the moral character of what you believe in
How strong is your Integrity against a strong wind?

Honor and virtue and respectable too
Righteous and reliable are important to you

Your building is strong, your Integrity is intact
Your Integrity is Successful against any wind attack

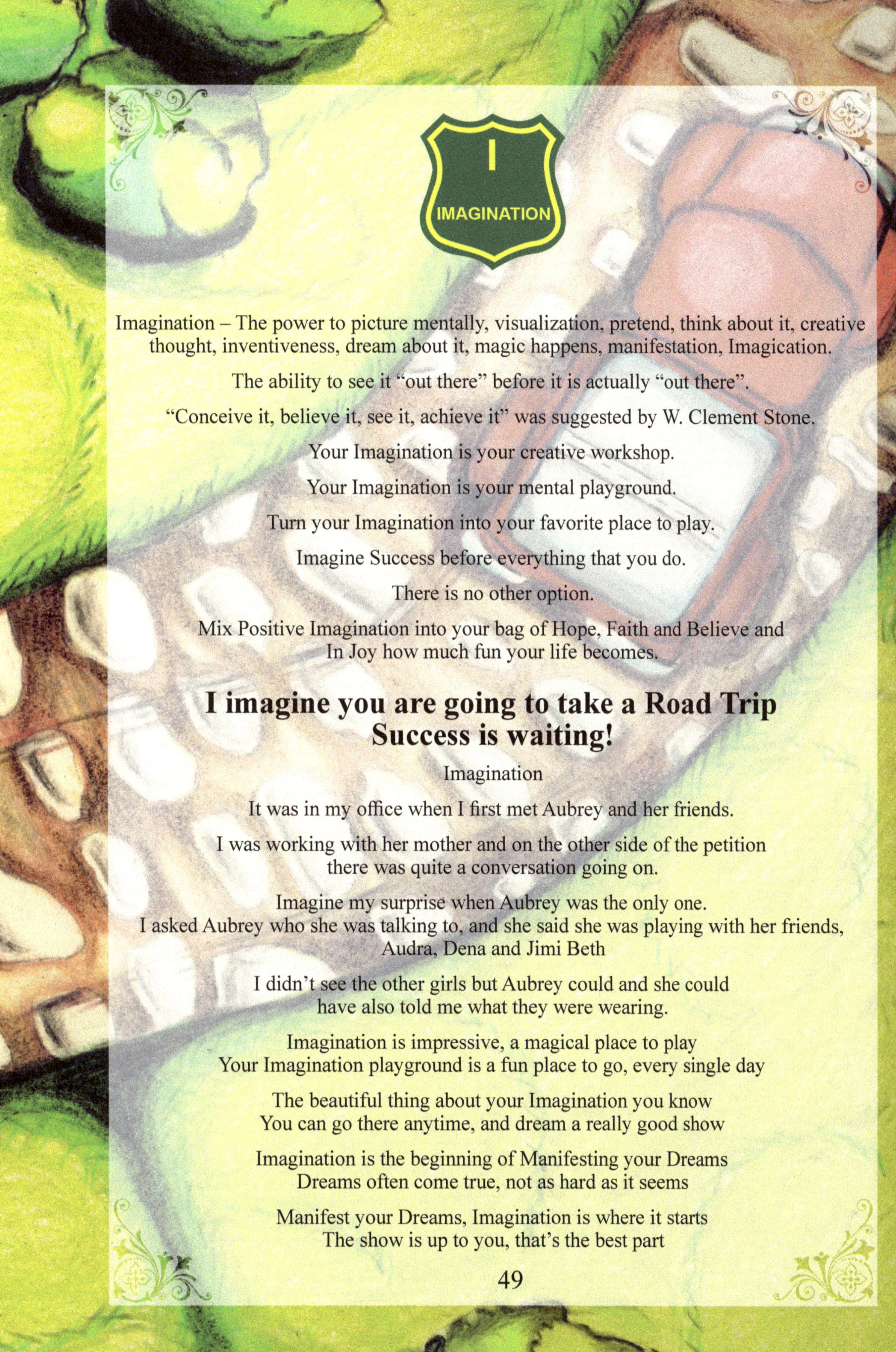

Imagination – The power to picture mentally, visualization, pretend, think about it, creative thought, inventiveness, dream about it, magic happens, manifestation, Imagication.

The ability to see it "out there" before it is actually "out there".

"Conceive it, believe it, see it, achieve it" was suggested by W. Clement Stone.

Your Imagination is your creative workshop.

Your Imagination is your mental playground.

Turn your Imagination into your favorite place to play.

Imagine Success before everything that you do.

There is no other option.

Mix Positive Imagination into your bag of Hope, Faith and Believe and
In Joy how much fun your life becomes.

I imagine you are going to take a Road Trip
Success is waiting!

Imagination

It was in my office when I first met Aubrey and her friends.

I was working with her mother and on the other side of the petition
there was quite a conversation going on.

Imagine my surprise when Aubrey was the only one.
I asked Aubrey who she was talking to, and she said she was playing with her friends,
Audra, Dena and Jimi Beth

I didn't see the other girls but Aubrey could and she could
have also told me what they were wearing.

Imagination is impressive, a magical place to play
Your Imagination playground is a fun place to go, every single day

The beautiful thing about your Imagination you know
You can go there anytime, and dream a really good show

Imagination is the beginning of Manifesting your Dreams
Dreams often come true, not as hard as it seems

Manifest your Dreams, Imagination is where it starts
The show is up to you, that's the best part

Infinite – enormous, great, tremendous, unlimited, endless,
knowing no limit, inexhaustible, forever. On and on and on.

Realize that this is your potential.

I absolutely know that this is true.

You have Infinite potential to have and be and do,
whatever you want to have and be and do.

You never know how this might look.

Road Trip is about giving you ideas for your life based on
the Good Words that you incorporate into your life.

Infinite? Goes forever.
One Road Trip at a time.

Infinite means your room has no ceiling.
Become a limitless thinker.

You do not yet know the difference that you will make by being here.

Thank you for realizing that you have Infinite Potential.

Your Success will be an Infinite Road Trip
What a Concept!

Infinite potential seems like a lot
Unlimited potential, you should find out what you got

It starts with Believe in your life and believing in yourself
You have Infinite potential; it is up to you and no one else

Realize this is true and imagine it so
You have Infinite potential, have fun where you go

Initiative - The energy and enthusiasm to originate, leadership, team leader, begin, get started, charge ahead, lead the way, lights, camera, action.

Initiative is the gusto to make something happen.

Take the Initiative and move forward with your life and your goals and your objectives.

Get it started.

Start something.

Begin.

It is on!

If you want something to happen,
do you have the Initiative to "get the ball rolling?"

Take the Initiative and step into action and let the adventure begin.

The recipe for Success includes Motivation, Ambition and Determination but you have to stir the pot.

That is where Initiative comes in.

Get it going and Initiate your Road Trip to Success!

Initiate, begin, just get started right now
In the doing of things, you will figure out how

I was a small little kid when I was eight
I wanted a treehouse, but my dad told me to wait

Dad laughed when he saw me get the ladder instead
He was proud of my Initiative, that's what he said

Initiative he said, will never let you down
So we built a really cool treehouse, 10 feet off the ground

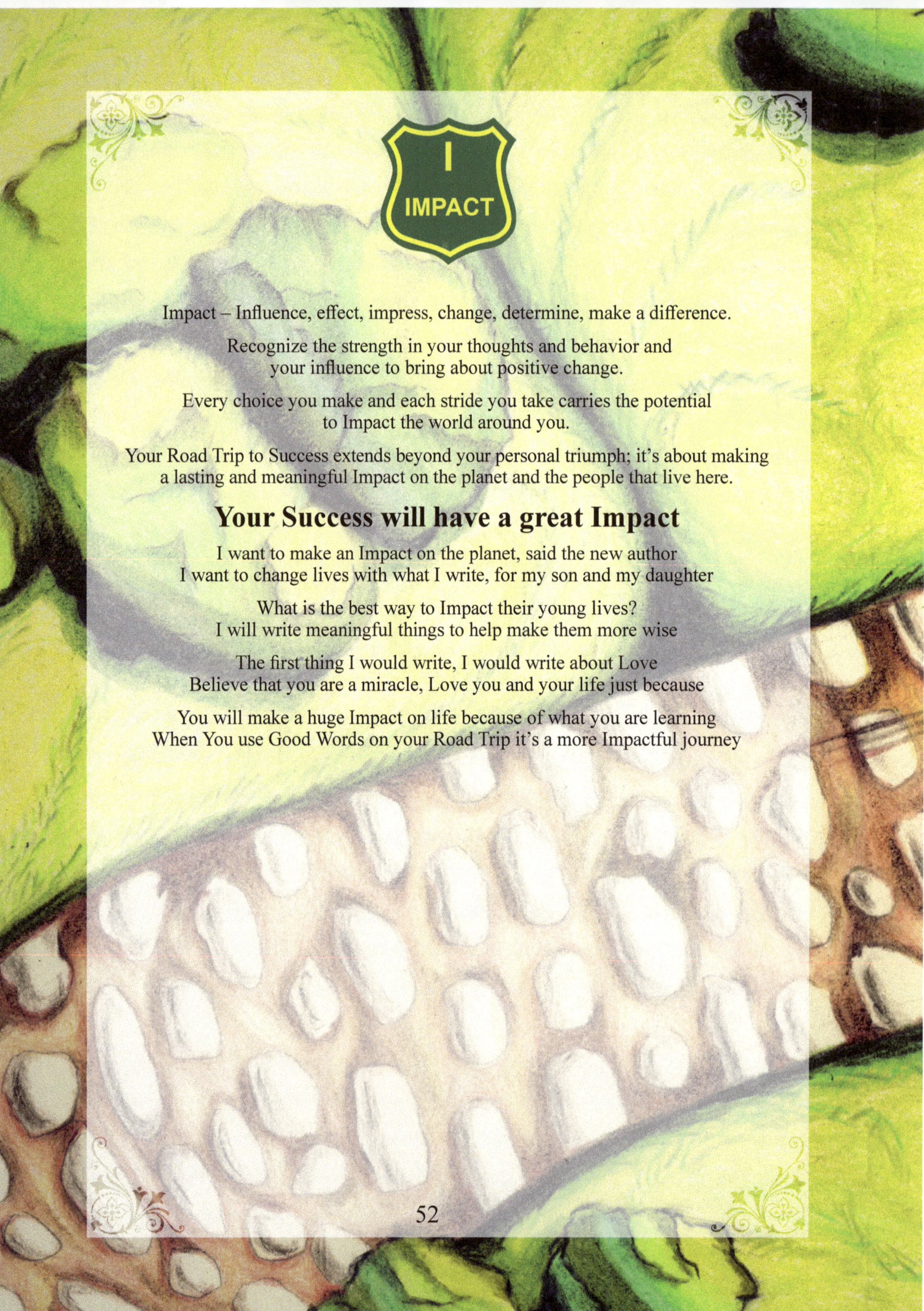

Impact – Influence, effect, impress, change, determine, make a difference.

Recognize the strength in your thoughts and behavior and
your influence to bring about positive change.

Every choice you make and each stride you take carries the potential
to Impact the world around you.

Your Road Trip to Success extends beyond your personal triumph; it's about making
a lasting and meaningful Impact on the planet and the people that live here.

Your Success will have a great Impact

I want to make an Impact on the planet, said the new author
I want to change lives with what I write, for my son and my daughter

What is the best way to Impact their young lives?
I will write meaningful things to help make them more wise

The first thing I would write, I would write about Love
Believe that you are a miracle, Love you and your life just because

You will make a huge Impact on life because of what you are learning
When You use Good Words on your Road Trip it's a more Impactful journey

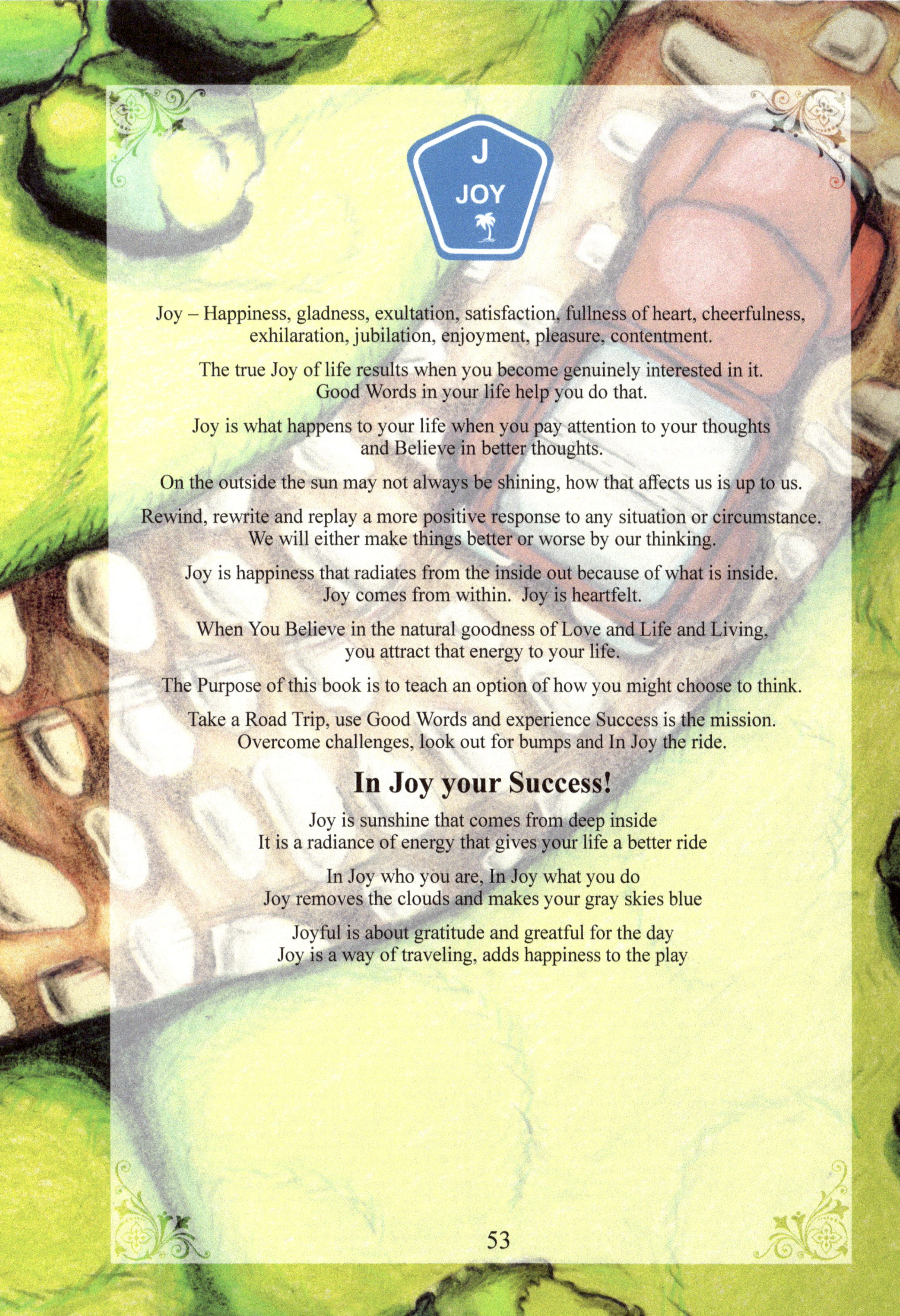

Joy – Happiness, gladness, exultation, satisfaction, fullness of heart, cheerfulness, exhilaration, jubilation, enjoyment, pleasure, contentment.

The true Joy of life results when you become genuinely interested in it.
Good Words in your life help you do that.

Joy is what happens to your life when you pay attention to your thoughts
and Believe in better thoughts.

On the outside the sun may not always be shining, how that affects us is up to us.

Rewind, rewrite and replay a more positive response to any situation or circumstance.
We will either make things better or worse by our thinking.

Joy is happiness that radiates from the inside out because of what is inside.
Joy comes from within. Joy is heartfelt.

When You Believe in the natural goodness of Love and Life and Living,
you attract that energy to your life.

The Purpose of this book is to teach an option of how you might choose to think.

Take a Road Trip, use Good Words and experience Success is the mission.
Overcome challenges, look out for bumps and In Joy the ride.

In Joy your Success!

Joy is sunshine that comes from deep inside
It is a radiance of energy that gives your life a better ride

In Joy who you are, In Joy what you do
Joy removes the clouds and makes your gray skies blue

Joyful is about gratitude and greatful for the day
Joy is a way of traveling, adds happiness to the play

Just – Fair, equitable, trustworthy, honest, moral, upright, good, ethical,
honorable, righteous, solid, strong, worthy, appropriate.

Just might seem like an antique or a relic in society today. But it isn't.
That is why our Good Words bag has words like, Honest, Integrity and True.

If we are all living by Good Words and Acceptable behavior,
Win – Win still Wins.

It is only good for me if it is also good for you.
Just be Just.

It is better when you sleep like a baby.
Just thoughts and Just actions help You do that.

Just is a perfect policy for Success

The pendulum of life swings both ways you know
the seeds that you are planting determine what you grow

The garden of life is a miraculous thing
the seeds that you plant is what the harvest will bring

Just plant Just seeds and cover the ground
Just is a good seed to plant all year round

Just seeds grow Just plants and eliminates the strife
A simple little lesson in gardening, that is also a lesson for life.

Plant Just seeds of Love and Kindness and Friendship
you are more likely to In Joy the ride on the Road Trip

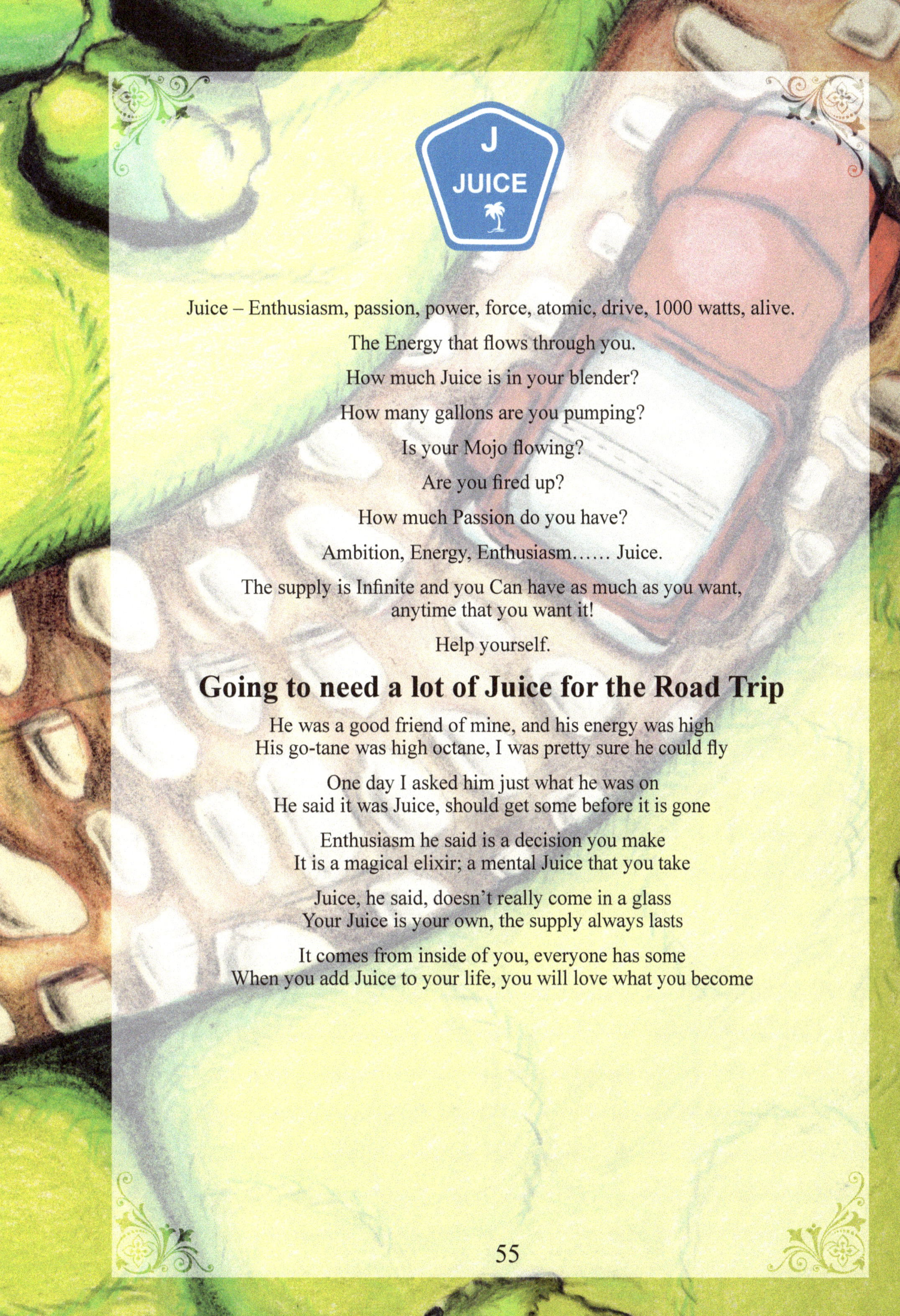

Juice – Enthusiasm, passion, power, force, atomic, drive, 1000 watts, alive.

The Energy that flows through you.

How much Juice is in your blender?

How many gallons are you pumping?

Is your Mojo flowing?

Are you fired up?

How much Passion do you have?

Ambition, Energy, Enthusiasm…… Juice.

The supply is Infinite and you Can have as much as you want,
anytime that you want it!

Help yourself.

Going to need a lot of Juice for the Road Trip

He was a good friend of mine, and his energy was high
His go-tane was high octane, I was pretty sure he could fly

One day I asked him just what he was on
He said it was Juice, should get some before it is gone

Enthusiasm he said is a decision you make
It is a magical elixir; a mental Juice that you take

Juice, he said, doesn't really come in a glass
Your Juice is your own, the supply always lasts

It comes from inside of you, everyone has some
When you add Juice to your life, you will love what you become

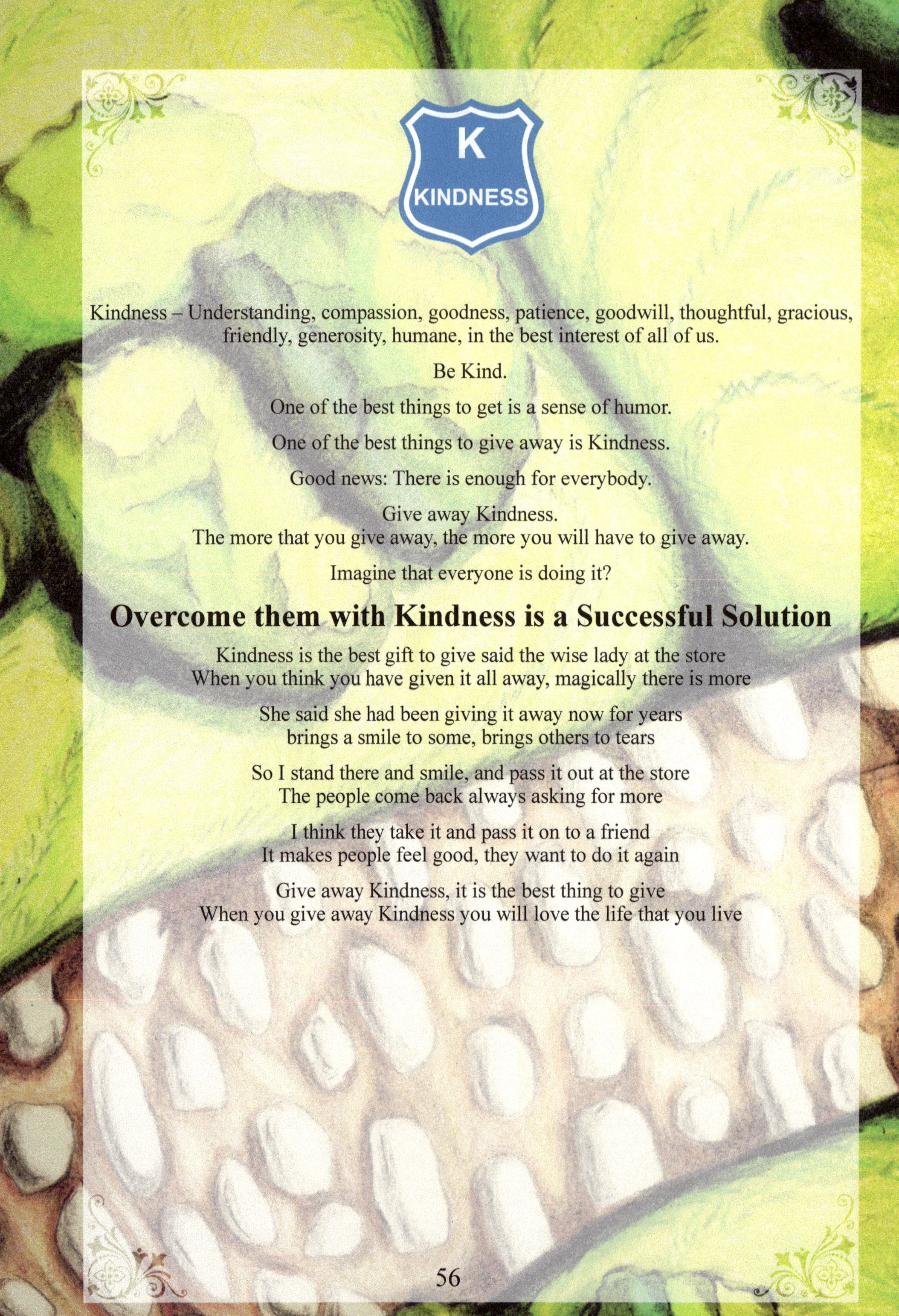

Kindness – Understanding, compassion, goodness, patience, goodwill, thoughtful, gracious, friendly, generosity, humane, in the best interest of all of us.

Be Kind.

One of the best things to get is a sense of humor.

One of the best things to give away is Kindness.

Good news: There is enough for everybody.

Give away Kindness.
The more that you give away, the more you will have to give away.

Imagine that everyone is doing it?

Overcome them with Kindness is a Successful Solution

Kindness is the best gift to give said the wise lady at the store
When you think you have given it all away, magically there is more

She said she had been giving it away now for years
brings a smile to some, brings others to tears

So I stand there and smile, and pass it out at the store
The people come back always asking for more

I think they take it and pass it on to a friend
It makes people feel good, they want to do it again

Give away Kindness, it is the best thing to give
When you give away Kindness you will love the life that you live

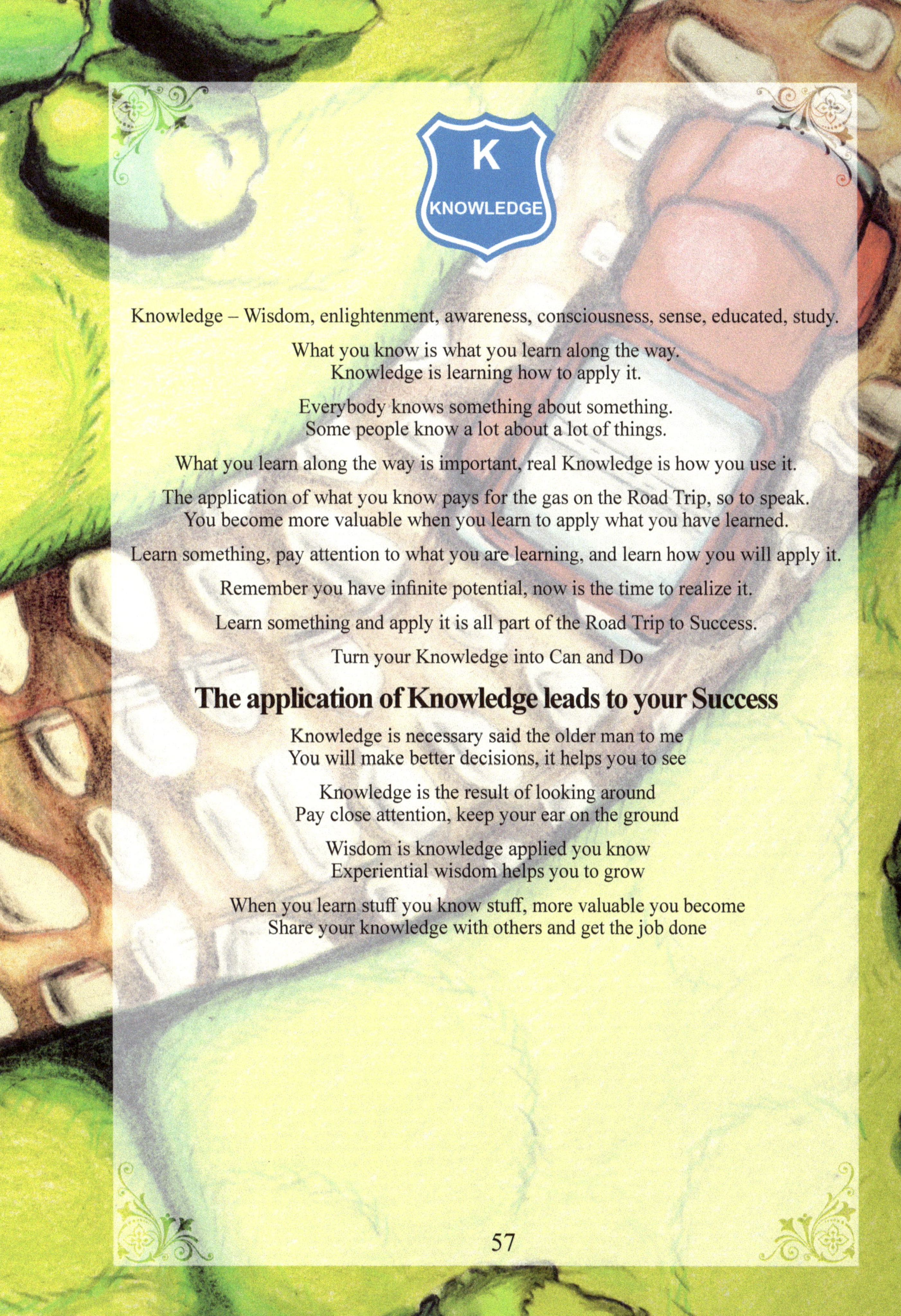

Knowledge – Wisdom, enlightenment, awareness, consciousness, sense, educated, study.

What you know is what you learn along the way.
Knowledge is learning how to apply it.

Everybody knows something about something.
Some people know a lot about a lot of things.

What you learn along the way is important, real Knowledge is how you use it.

The application of what you know pays for the gas on the Road Trip, so to speak.
You become more valuable when you learn to apply what you have learned.

Learn something, pay attention to what you are learning, and learn how you will apply it.

Remember you have infinite potential, now is the time to realize it.

Learn something and apply it is all part of the Road Trip to Success.

Turn your Knowledge into Can and Do

The application of Knowledge leads to your Success

Knowledge is necessary said the older man to me
You will make better decisions, it helps you to see

Knowledge is the result of looking around
Pay close attention, keep your ear on the ground

Wisdom is knowledge applied you know
Experiential wisdom helps you to grow

When you learn stuff you know stuff, more valuable you become
Share your knowledge with others and get the job done

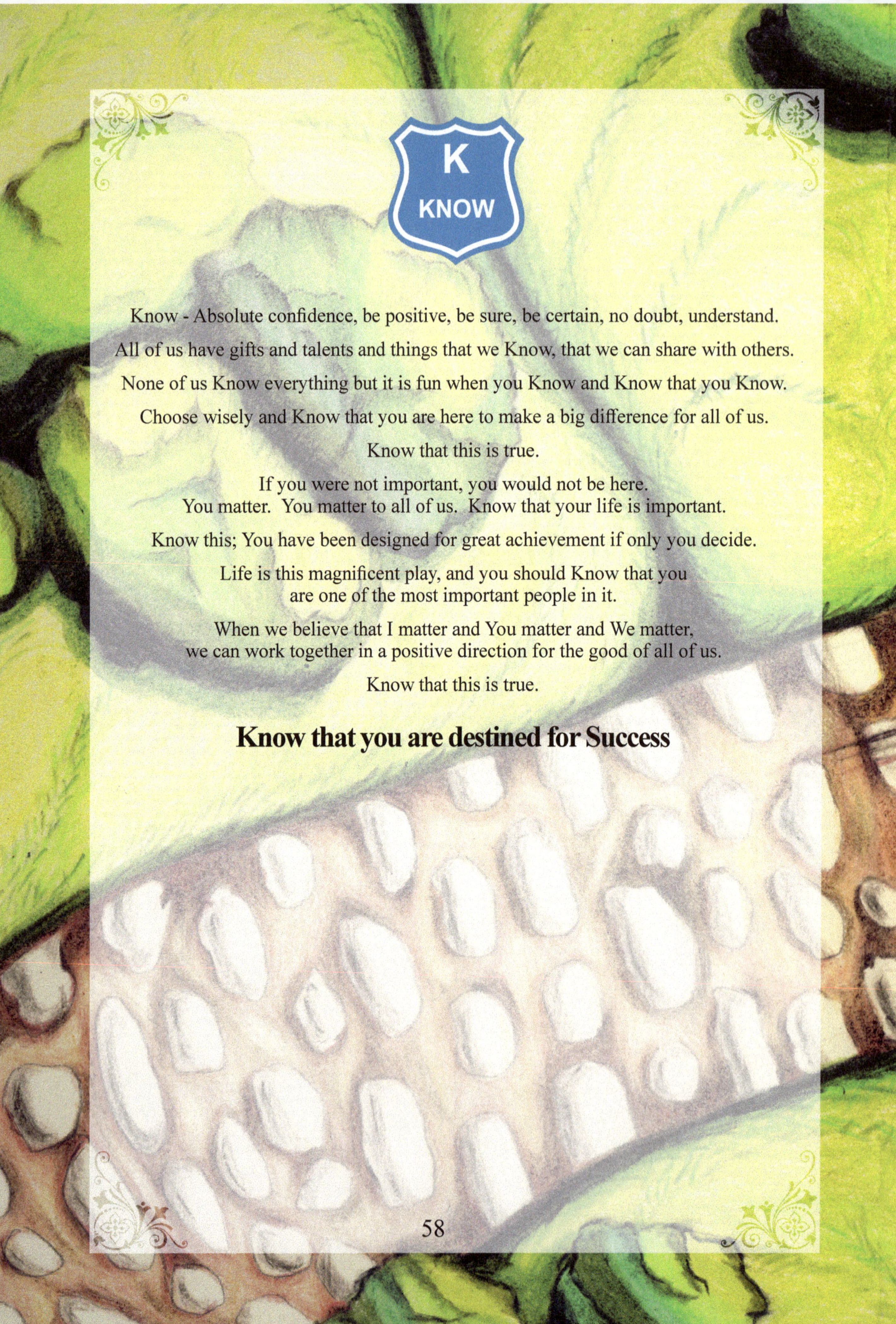

Know - Absolute confidence, be positive, be sure, be certain, no doubt, understand.

All of us have gifts and talents and things that we Know, that we can share with others.

None of us Know everything but it is fun when you Know and Know that you Know.

Choose wisely and Know that you are here to make a big difference for all of us.

Know that this is true.

If you were not important, you would not be here.
You matter. You matter to all of us. Know that your life is important.

Know this; You have been designed for great achievement if only you decide.

Life is this magnificent play, and you should Know that you
are one of the most important people in it.

When we believe that I matter and You matter and We matter,
we can work together in a positive direction for the good of all of us.

Know that this is true.

Know that you are destined for Success

I call it reflective training and you look at yourself in the mirror
You look at yourself, eye to eye, to make the reflection clearer

The first thing to say is I Love you; I am really glad to Know you
Today is going to be a great day, I am excited, can't wait to show you

I believe in my life with all my heart, and I like the person that I am
I read up above that I am here because I matter, and I Know that I can

So I say this to you, believe that it is true
Know you will make the world better because of what you will do

Love – The best feeling, esteem, admiration, friendship, brotherhood, goodwill.

Conditional Love is an oxymoron, unconditional Love is redundant.

Love is all and only Love.

Love is why we are here.

It is because of Love that we have life and the abundance that goes with it.

Love is what makes everything possible.

Love in our heart brings out the joy in our lives.

Love is the light that guides and protects us.

Love is the very essence of life.

Love is the fruit of life.

The tree of Love is dependent on the seeds of Love that we are planting.

More seeds, more trees, more fruit, more Love.

It is because of Love that we are here to begin with.

If you knew that Love is where you came from
you would live your life from Love.
If you live your life from Love, you will Love the life you live.

Realize the power of Love.
"It" is all about Love.

Success is full of Love

There is always Sunshine where I come from?

Living in the sun
Feeling it everyday
What do you think it is?
Why would I always feel this way?

Perhaps I am a pilot
and above the clouds I fly
Perhaps I am a King
and that's the reason why

What if I said…..
it was neither of the above
What if I told you the sunshine
is all about Love

You see sunshine is an attitude
It comes from the inside out
When your soul is full of sunshine
there is no room for clouds of doubt

With gratitude we realize
that we have got it made
The sunshine shines much brighter
Thinking about some trees, looking for some shade?

Keep the light on in your life
the source is everywhere
When we believe in Love
the sunshine is always there

"It" is all about Love

Loyal – Faithful, steadfast, true, constant, reliable, trustworthy, dependable, staunch, firm, scrupulous.

That sounds pretty good.

Loyal is an essential part of all Relationships.

Trustworthy, Reliable, True?
Put Loyal on the team

Be Loyal to yourself, be Loyal to others.

Loyal will never let you down.

Success is Loyal

Loyal is a necessary commitment you know
Loyal is strong, makes relationships grow

Loyal is an idea not to be misunderstood
Loyal is solid and feels really good

Be Loyal adds strength in all that you do
Loyal makes us strong, me and you

Life – Life is a gift. Life is positive energy. Life is alive. Life is growing.

Love and Life are synonymous.

Your Life is very important.

Your Life has power in it.

You will make an important impact with your Life.

Our Life is a gift to us, what we do with our Life is our gift back to Life.

Love Life is the best place to start.
Love your Life

Your Life is important, that is why you are here.

Your Life is a huge Success

Life is about perspective, what you think comes into play
Where does perspective come from? Use Good Words to help you say

Your Life is your responsibility to make the most of why you are here
Your perspective is about how you think, use Good Words to make it clear

Think about your Life, your perspective is about Success
Understand the gift of Life, Gratitude is best

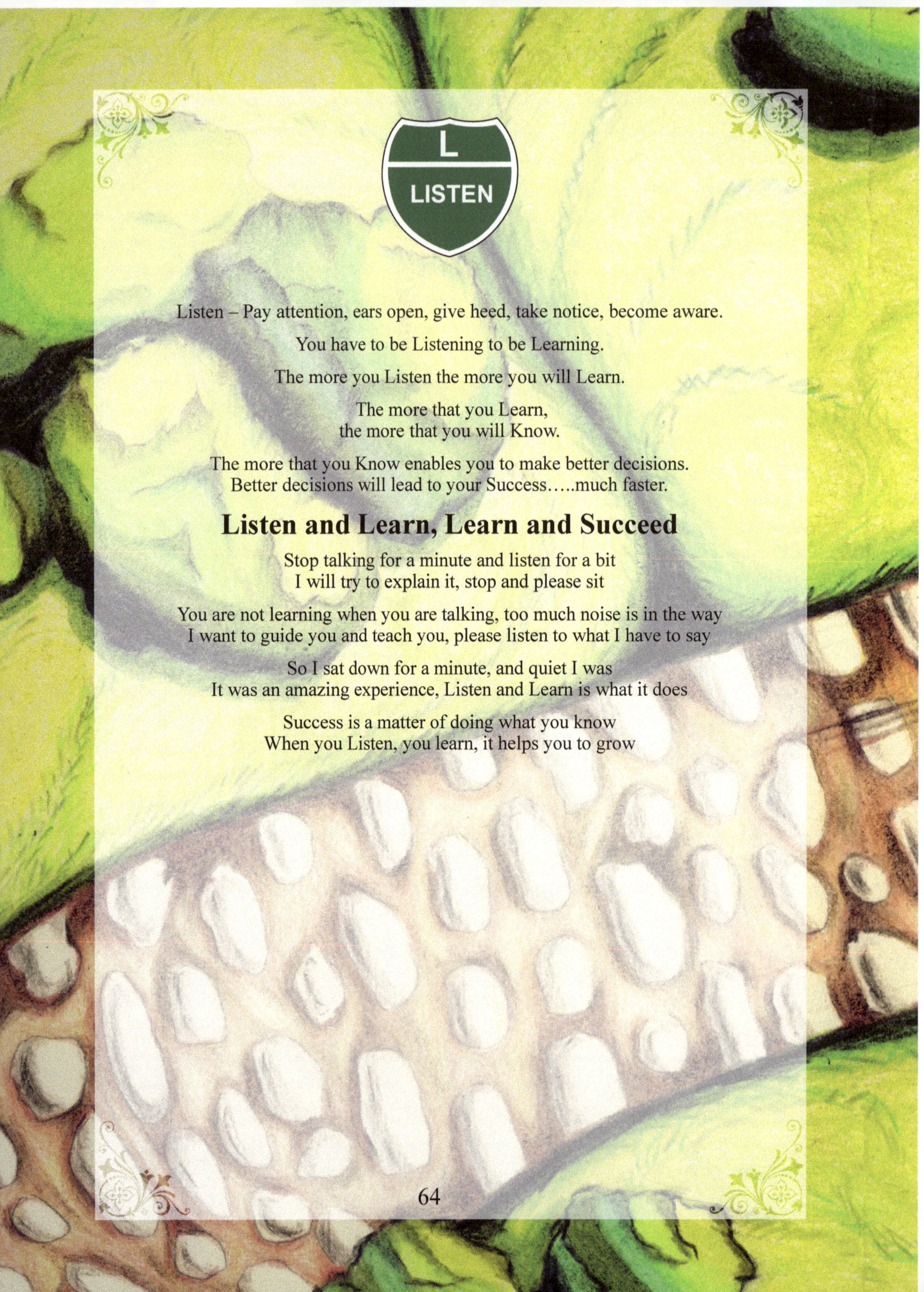

Listen – Pay attention, ears open, give heed, take notice, become aware.

You have to be Listening to be Learning.

The more you Listen the more you will Learn.

The more that you Learn,
the more that you will Know.

The more that you Know enables you to make better decisions.
Better decisions will lead to your Success…..much faster.

Listen and Learn, Learn and Succeed

Stop talking for a minute and listen for a bit
I will try to explain it, stop and please sit

You are not learning when you are talking, too much noise is in the way
I want to guide you and teach you, please listen to what I have to say

So I sat down for a minute, and quiet I was
It was an amazing experience, Listen and Learn is what it does

Success is a matter of doing what you know
When you Listen, you learn, it helps you to grow

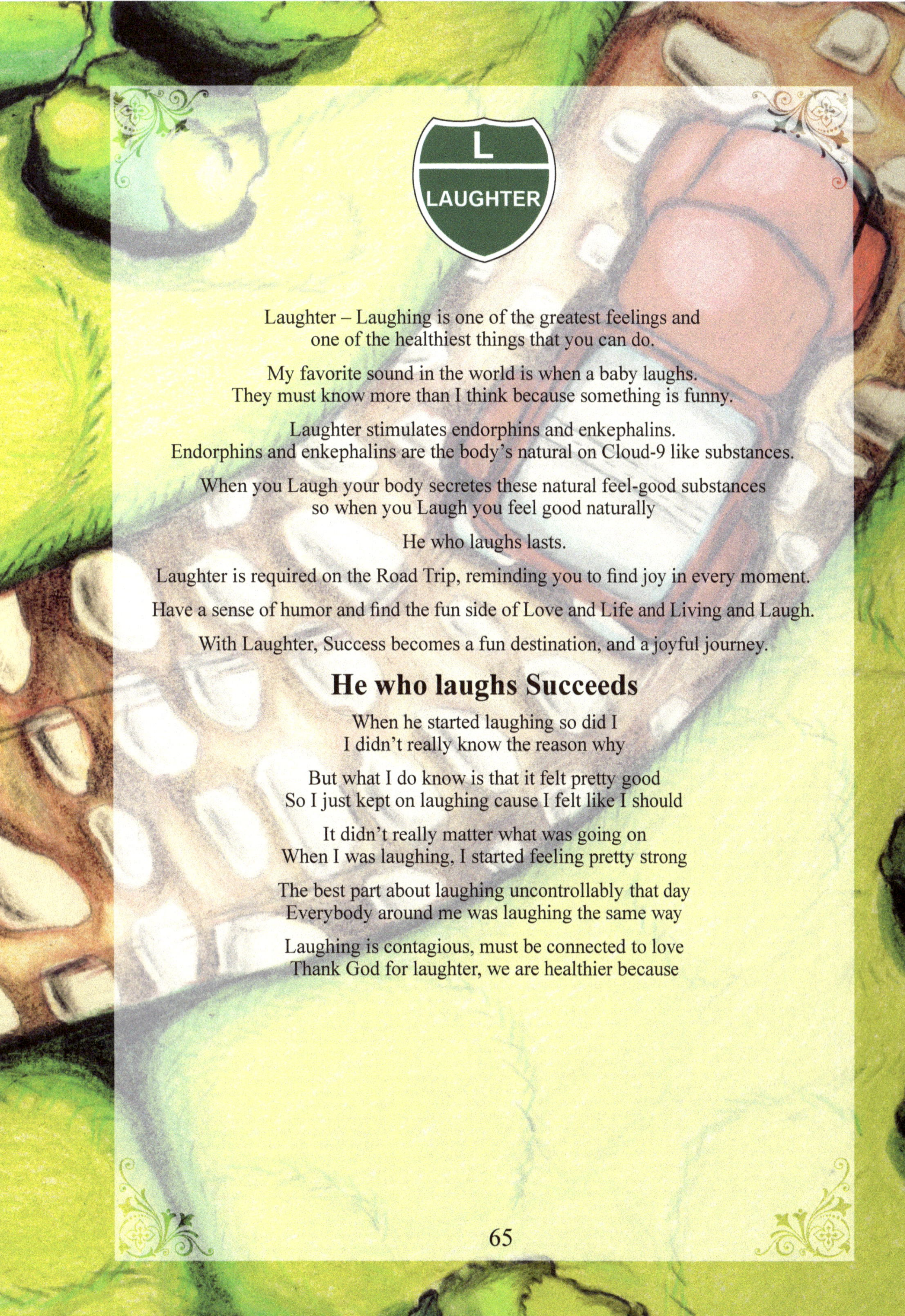

Laughter – Laughing is one of the greatest feelings and
one of the healthiest things that you can do.

My favorite sound in the world is when a baby laughs.
They must know more than I think because something is funny.

Laughter stimulates endorphins and enkephalins.
Endorphins and enkephalins are the body's natural on Cloud-9 like substances.

When you Laugh your body secretes these natural feel-good substances
so when you Laugh you feel good naturally

He who laughs lasts.

Laughter is required on the Road Trip, reminding you to find joy in every moment.

Have a sense of humor and find the fun side of Love and Life and Living and Laugh.

With Laughter, Success becomes a fun destination, and a joyful journey.

He who laughs Succeeds

When he started laughing so did I
I didn't really know the reason why

But what I do know is that it felt pretty good
So I just kept on laughing cause I felt like I should

It didn't really matter what was going on
When I was laughing, I started feeling pretty strong

The best part about laughing uncontrollably that day
Everybody around me was laughing the same way

Laughing is contagious, must be connected to love
Thank God for laughter, we are healthier because

Manifest – Magic, Imagication, clear, evident, apparent, visible, palpable, obvious, reveal, known, display, show me, I see it, unveil.

Visualize your Dreams with clarity and let your intentions guide your actions. What is it that you are Thinking? Write it down and put it out there.

What is the behavior required? Practice the behavior.

With unwavering Focus and Determination, you have the power to Manifest your Dreams into reality.

There is an unbelievable force, a source of MC2, that will come to assist you.

Unseen forces will come to support you. Where did the soldiers on horses come from?

Trust in the process, stay aligned with your goals, Watch as the Universal Energy helps makes your Dreams come home.

Success is yours to Manifest, one Manifestation at a Time.

Manifest your Success

I see it and I believe it and I know it can be true
Manifest Success is what I am going to do

Just write it down and read it is what RHJ said
Write it down and read it, at night, before you go to bed

Think about your life and put it on paper
The Universe takes over and gets involved in the caper

The next thing you know about what you wrote down
It Manifests itself, just look around

Mind – Your Mind is your house for your thoughts.

Your Thoughts are the Seeds from which your future Grows,
so your Thoughts are very important.

Your Mind can only hold one Thought at a Time and
you control which Thought you keep in the house.

The Thought that You hold in your Mind will make you feel
either good or bad depending on the thought that you are thinking.

If you live in the beautiful Energy of Love and Light,
then your thoughts are of the same.

Train your Mind to hold positive thoughts and thoughts that make you feel good or
motivate you or inspire you or relax you or help you love one another.

The cool thing about your Mind is that if your thoughts do not do the above,
you can rewind, rewrite and replay a Better Thought.

Better Thoughts come from the Good Words that you know.
Use them.

When you use Good Words to fill your Mind full of Better Thoughts,
You will be in a very Successful place.

Success is a state of Mind

I love the house that I get to live in because it is all up to me
I built it with my thoughts, and my Mind is a fun place to be

Your thoughts hold all your power, they give your strength to you
Your thoughts also give you contentment and they help you see things through

Your Mind sits high on a mountaintop, the view is quite amazing
When your Mind is full of positive your bonfire of thoughts will be blazing

Motivation – Motive, reason, impulse, impetus, driving force.

Are You Motivated?

Motivation is what causes your light to burn so brightly.

Motivation is the stimulus to have or be or do.

Motivation gets you off the couch and shuts the door behind you.

Motivation is the first of the month when the rent is due.

If Ambition is the fuel for the engine, Motivation is the Ignition.

Motivation is where Determination, Persistence and Success come from.

Motivation is the beginning of your Road Trip to Success.

Start your engine……….Success is Running!

Please explain Motivation, explain it I certainly Can
There was a pretty lady selling apples, she was waving her hand

I was Motivated to meet her because I was hungry for sure,
but it was really because she was pretty with such an allure

Motivation is full of surprises you know,
It's what starts your engine and makes you go

Motivation is the stimulus that helps get you there
Could have been the apples, perhaps it was her hair

The story will now come to an end
Motivation is what gets it started again

Mojo – Energy, charisma, power, positive motion, harmony,
soul juice, electricity, fire, magic.

Everyone has Mojo.

Your Mojo is unique to you.

Your Mojo is Up to you.

Your Mojo is what makes you special.

Mojo is charisma, Mojo is Energy, Mojo has rhythm, Mojo is the X-Factor of your soul.

Mojo is Panama Jack, Mojo is the guy in the Dos Equis commercial,
Mojo is the ironworker building a high rise.
Superman has Mojo.
What about The Rock?

I think you get the idea.

What does your Mojo look like?

Is your Mojo Working?

The answer should most definitely be, YES!

Success is all about Mojo

Mojo is your Energy, you are the only one
Mojo is part of what you will inevitably become

Your Mojo is yours, doesn't come out of a box
It is a brilliant display of what your soul's got

Mojo is the Energy that makes you Be You
Know your Mojo is awesome, truly unique is what you do

Now – The present time, immediately, current.

All there is, is the present moment that you are in right Now.

Right Now time.

This is the only time that you have to get it done.

Focus on Now.

Stay focused on this moment and live one moment at a time.

There are Infinite possibilities for the future when we stay focused in the Now.

There is huge potential in Now.

It is right Now. Enjoy it Now. Embrace it Now.

When we are focused in the Now of each moment
we are more actively engaged and focused on what we are doing.

The HUGE potential in each moment is
because of the realized potential in the last moment
which makes the next moment pretty exciting.

Live it Now.

Enjoy Now.

Be in the Now.

Have a Good Now!

Now is a good time for Success

It finally occurred to me that time was moving on
I realized that life moves quickly and soon it might be gone

I set my clocks all well ahead, so I had more Time in my thinking
I thought about time and how fast it can go, a bit like a ship when it is sinking

I kept thinking about Now and I made a decision,
to live only Now and avoid any revision

Live in the Now, the only place you can be
Now time is a good time to live Happily

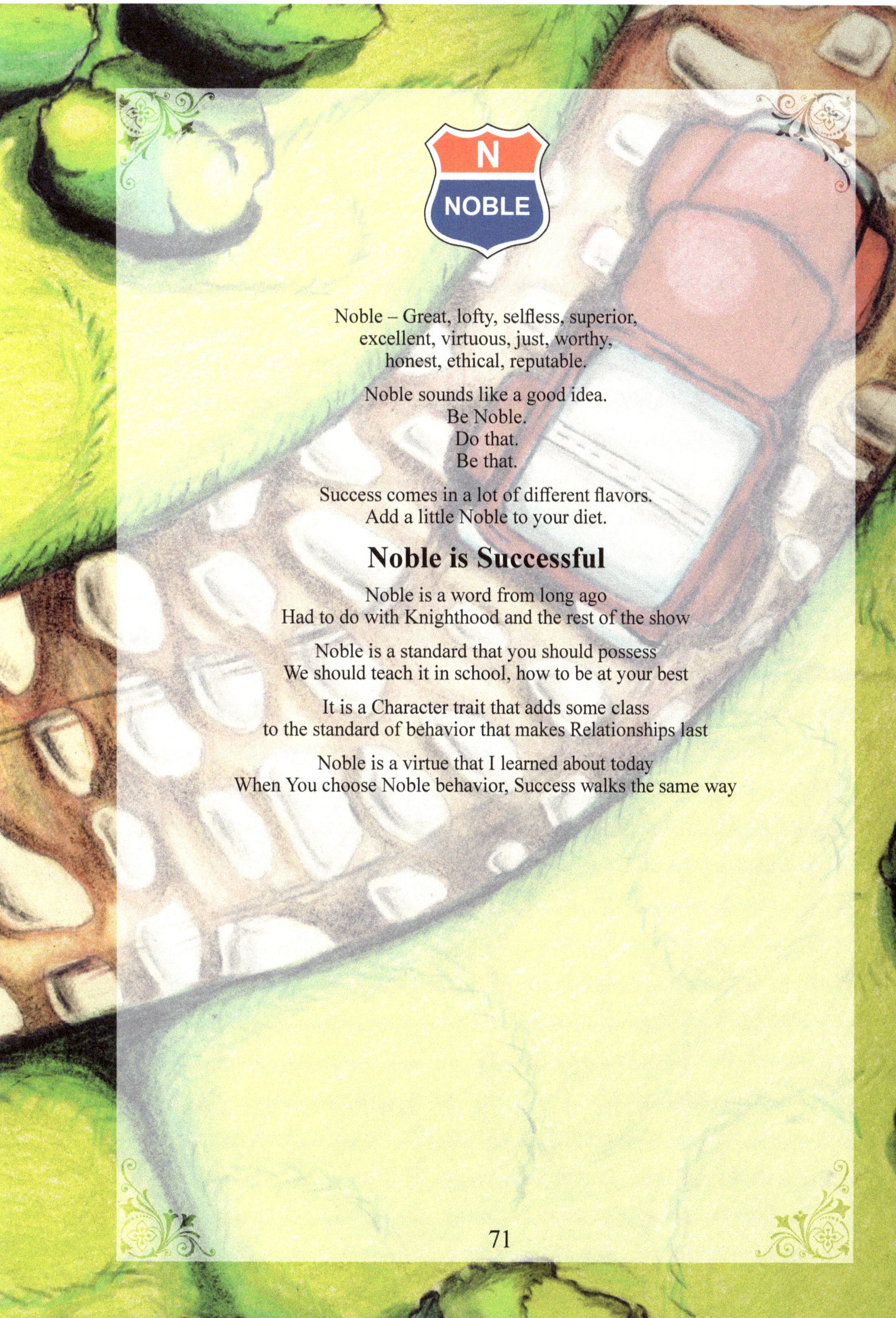

Noble – Great, lofty, selfless, superior,
excellent, virtuous, just, worthy,
honest, ethical, reputable.

Noble sounds like a good idea.
Be Noble.
Do that.
Be that.

Success comes in a lot of different flavors.
Add a little Noble to your diet.

Noble is Successful

Noble is a word from long ago
Had to do with Knighthood and the rest of the show

Noble is a standard that you should possess
We should teach it in school, how to be at your best

It is a Character trait that adds some class
to the standard of behavior that makes Relationships last

Noble is a virtue that I learned about today
When You choose Noble behavior, Success walks the same way

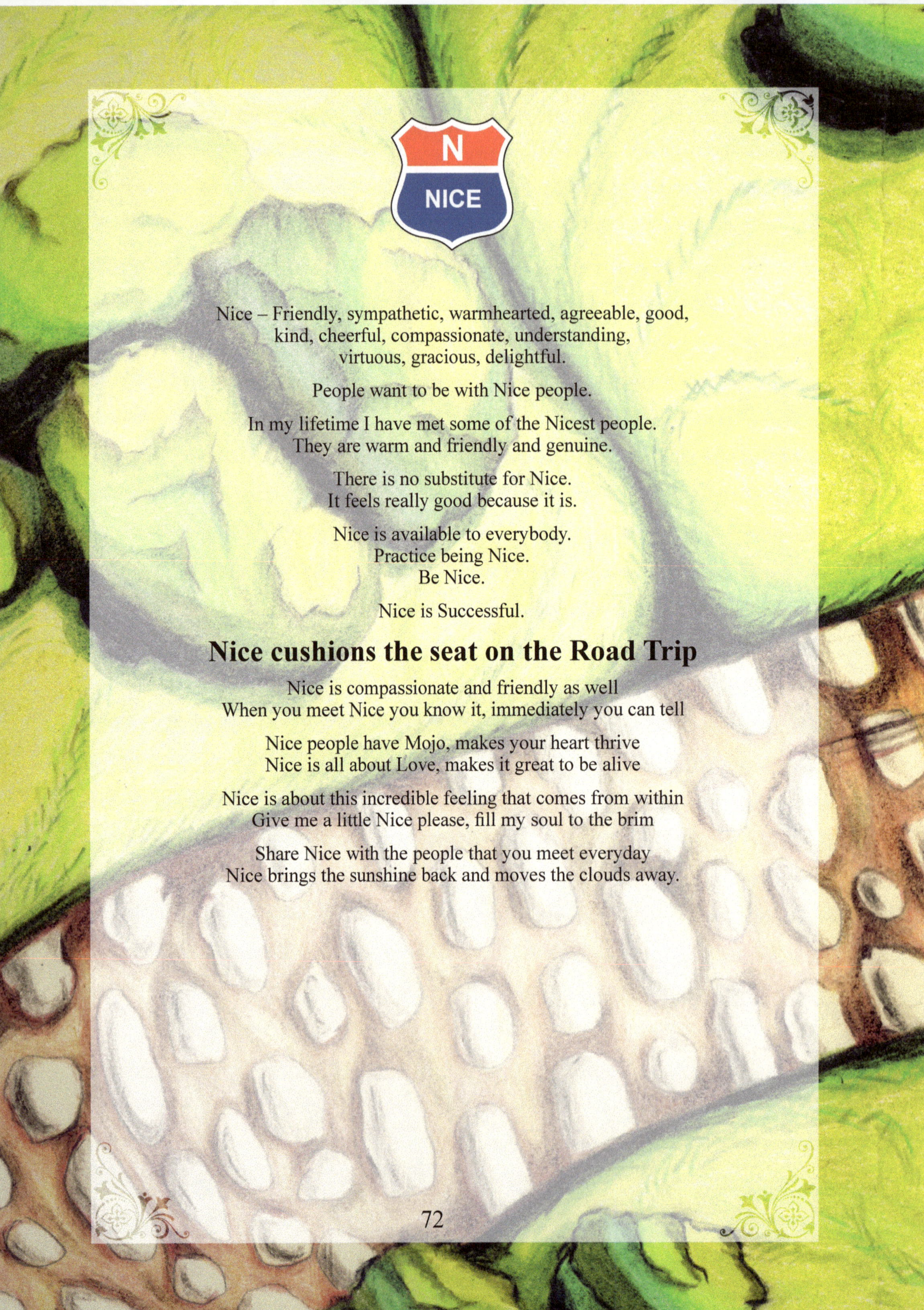

Nice – Friendly, sympathetic, warmhearted, agreeable, good,
kind, cheerful, compassionate, understanding,
virtuous, gracious, delightful.

People want to be with Nice people.

In my lifetime I have met some of the Nicest people.
They are warm and friendly and genuine.

There is no substitute for Nice.
It feels really good because it is.

Nice is available to everybody.
Practice being Nice.
Be Nice.

Nice is Successful.

Nice cushions the seat on the Road Trip

Nice is compassionate and friendly as well
When you meet Nice you know it, immediately you can tell

Nice people have Mojo, makes your heart thrive
Nice is all about Love, makes it great to be alive

Nice is about this incredible feeling that comes from within
Give me a little Nice please, fill my soul to the brim

Share Nice with the people that you meet everyday
Nice brings the sunshine back and moves the clouds away.

Open – Begin, commence, start, initiate, air flow

Open - Come on in!

Open minded.
Now we are getting somewhere.

Start all things with an Open Mind.

Start with Yes I am Open

Be Open to Possibilities outside of your box.

Your box? It is the house that you think in.

Get a bigger box!

Open your Mind and Open your heart and
you will Open the door of your Success.

Success is wide Open!

None of us know everything, quite a bit to know
Our Mind must stay Open for us to grow

There is so much to see and to learn and to do
Keep an Open Mind and new ideas will come to you

Keep your Mind Open and you will like what shows up
An Open Mind is Successful, even adds a little luck

Optimism – Confidence, hopeful, enthusiastic, encouraged, promising, bright, positive.

Believe in Possible.

Be Optimistic.

Confidence and Can.

There is always a blessing in every situation or circumstance,
Optimism is the map to help us find it.

Bring Optimism into your life and you will Open the treasure chest of Success.

Pretty Optimistic about a Successful Road Trip

Optimism is Positive about what's going on
What are you Thinking, are you weak or are You Strong?

If you have fears and doubts in your life
Get a dose of Optimism, get rid of that knife

Believe in yourself and believe in your plan
Optimism gives you the Energy to Believe that You Can

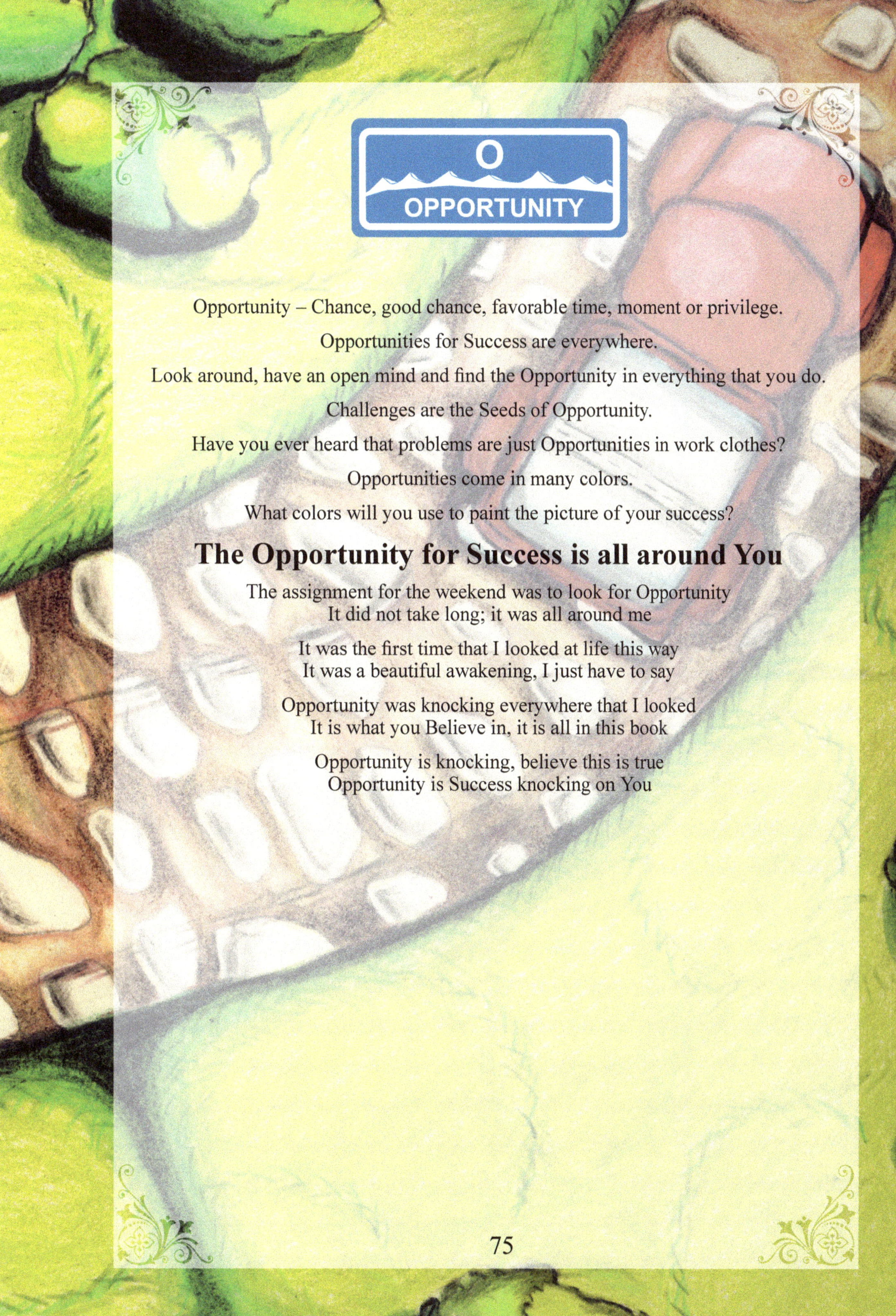

Opportunity – Chance, good chance, favorable time, moment or privilege.

Opportunities for Success are everywhere.

Look around, have an open mind and find the Opportunity in everything that you do.

Challenges are the Seeds of Opportunity.

Have you ever heard that problems are just Opportunities in work clothes?

Opportunities come in many colors.

What colors will you use to paint the picture of your success?

The Opportunity for Success is all around You

The assignment for the weekend was to look for Opportunity
It did not take long; it was all around me

It was the first time that I looked at life this way
It was a beautiful awakening, I just have to say

Opportunity was knocking everywhere that I looked
It is what you Believe in, it is all in this book

Opportunity is knocking, believe this is true
Opportunity is Success knocking on You

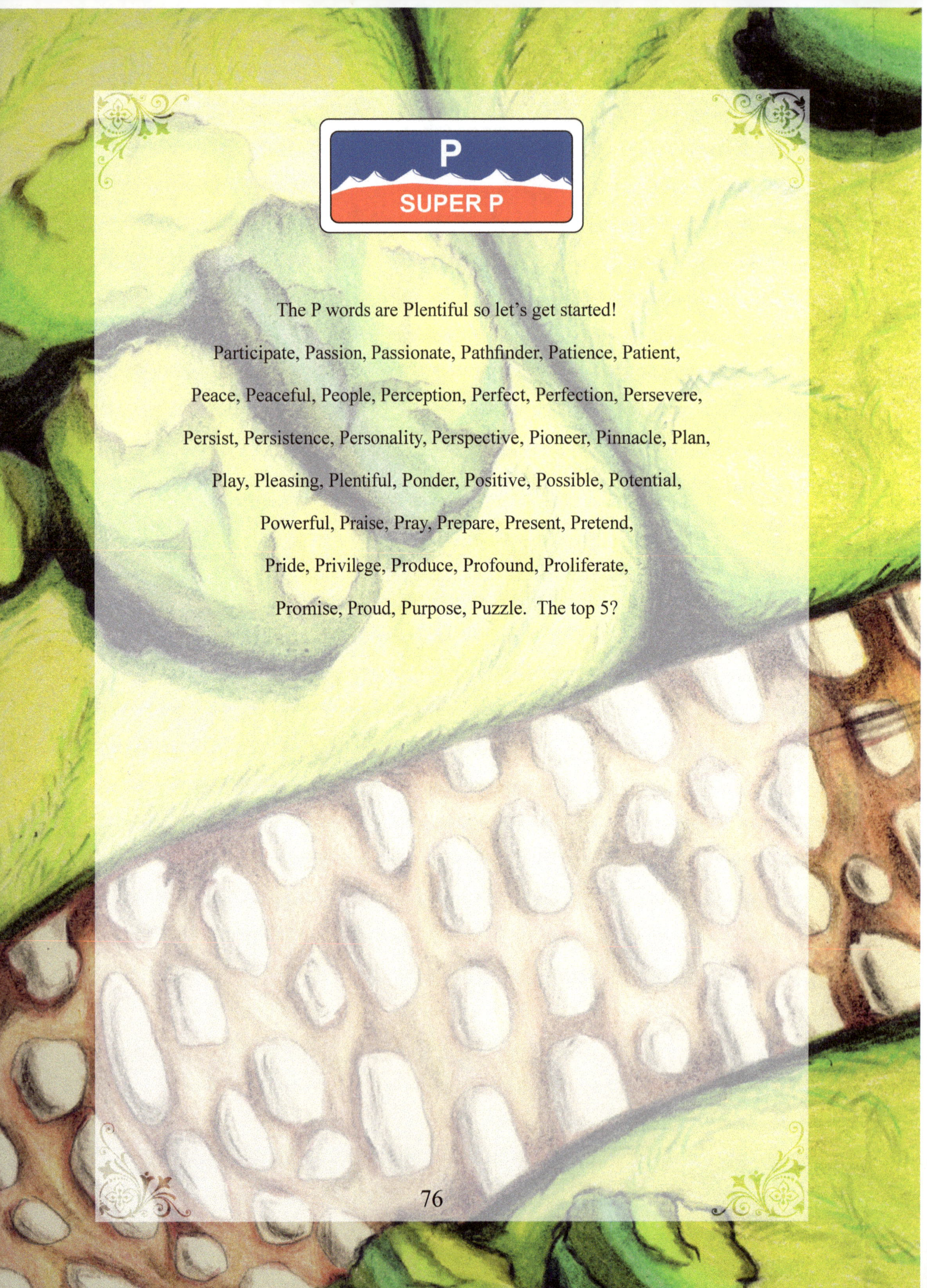

The P words are Plentiful so let's get started!

Participate, Passion, Passionate, Pathfinder, Patience, Patient,

Peace, Peaceful, People, Perception, Perfect, Perfection, Persevere,

Persist, Persistence, Personality, Perspective, Pioneer, Pinnacle, Plan,

Play, Pleasing, Plentiful, Ponder, Positive, Possible, Potential,

Powerful, Praise, Pray, Prepare, Present, Pretend,

Pride, Privilege, Produce, Profound, Proliferate,

Promise, Proud, Purpose, Puzzle. The top 5?

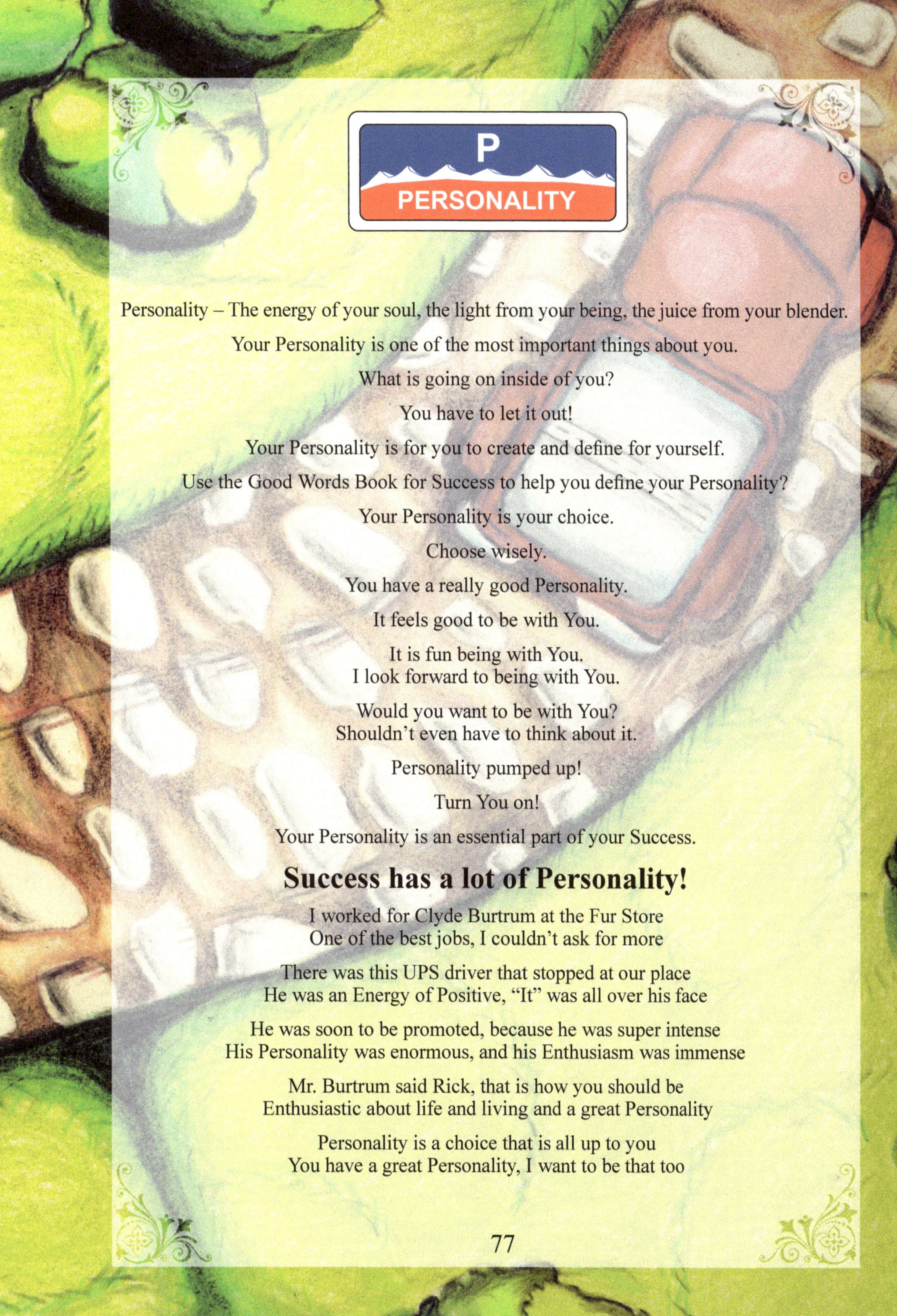

Personality – The energy of your soul, the light from your being, the juice from your blender.

Your Personality is one of the most important things about you.

What is going on inside of you?

You have to let it out!

Your Personality is for you to create and define for yourself.

Use the Good Words Book for Success to help you define your Personality?

Your Personality is your choice.

Choose wisely.

You have a really good Personality.

It feels good to be with You.

It is fun being with You.
I look forward to being with You.

Would you want to be with You?
Shouldn't even have to think about it.

Personality pumped up!

Turn You on!

Your Personality is an essential part of your Success.

Success has a lot of Personality!

I worked for Clyde Burtrum at the Fur Store
One of the best jobs, I couldn't ask for more

There was this UPS driver that stopped at our place
He was an Energy of Positive, "It" was all over his face

He was soon to be promoted, because he was super intense
His Personality was enormous, and his Enthusiasm was immense

Mr. Burtrum said Rick, that is how you should be
Enthusiastic about life and living and a great Personality

Personality is a choice that is all up to you
You have a great Personality, I want to be that too

Purpose – Goal, aim, ambition, aspiration, object, objective, mission, intent, intention, target, resolution, plan, motive, design, scheme, project, desire, wish, resolve, expectation, determination, hope, motivation, will, persist, persevere.

Why are you here?

What do you want to do with your life?

What will you do with your life?

How will you benefit others?

The Purpose of this book is to help you figure that out.

Anything is possible if only you Believe but you have to Believe in something.

The something is your Purpose.

Success is a good Purpose

I awoke very early and decided to get up out of bed
There was a swarm of ideas buzzing around in my head

I had spoken with a teacher, just the day before
It was all about Purpose and what I thought I was here for

Never really thought about it, is what I said
However, I thought about it again, as I went to bed

I am Up Now because my life has more meaning to me
A direction, a Purpose, what am I going to be?

Purpose is the reason that you and I are here
Believe in you and your Purpose, no doubt, no fear

Purpose gives you the reason to wake up every day
Your life makes a difference, thanks for thinking this way

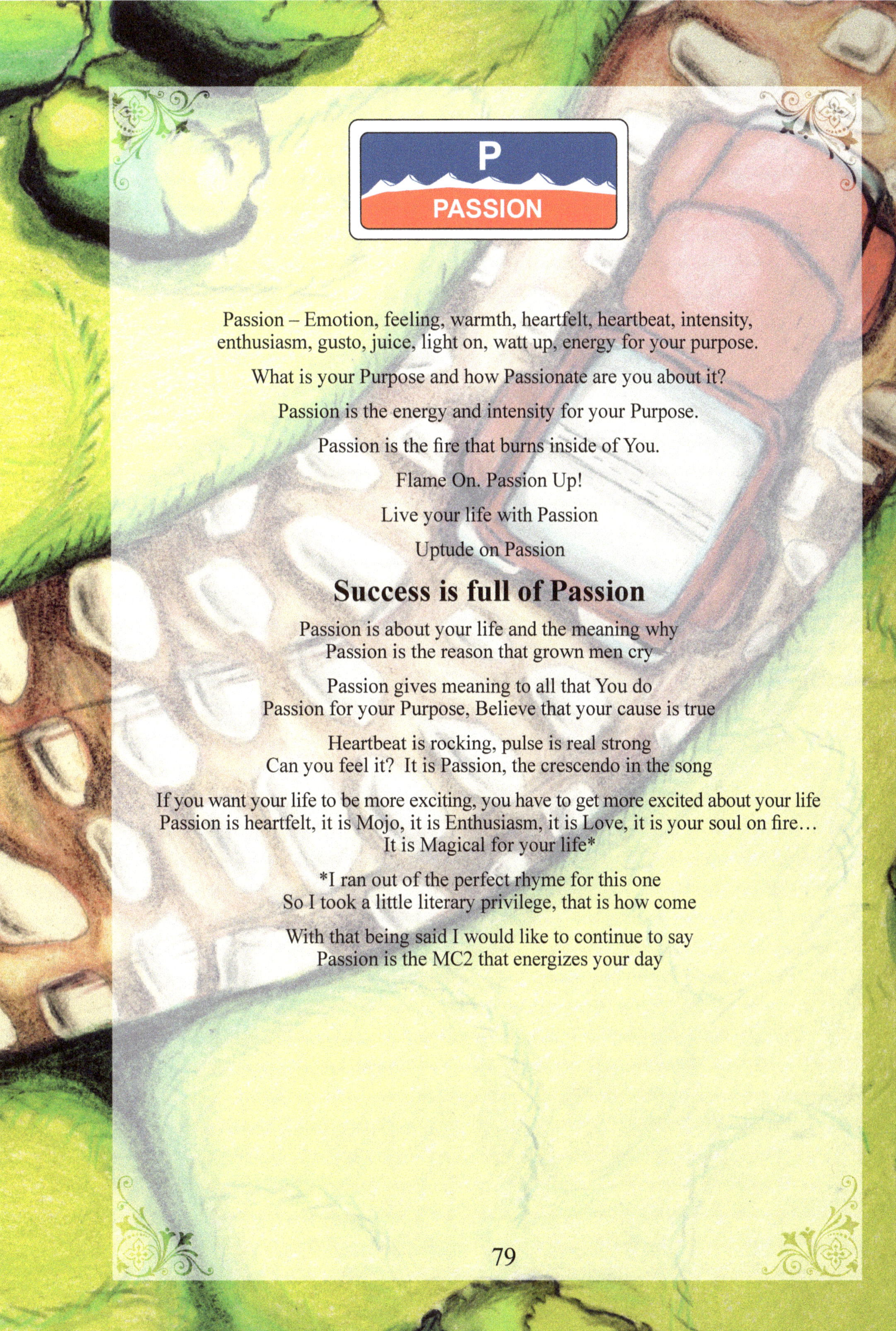

Passion – Emotion, feeling, warmth, heartfelt, heartbeat, intensity, enthusiasm, gusto, juice, light on, watt up, energy for your purpose.

What is your Purpose and how Passionate are you about it?

Passion is the energy and intensity for your Purpose.

Passion is the fire that burns inside of You.

Flame On. Passion Up!

Live your life with Passion

Uptude on Passion

Success is full of Passion

Passion is about your life and the meaning why
Passion is the reason that grown men cry

Passion gives meaning to all that You do
Passion for your Purpose, Believe that your cause is true

Heartbeat is rocking, pulse is real strong
Can you feel it? It is Passion, the crescendo in the song

If you want your life to be more exciting, you have to get more excited about your life
Passion is heartfelt, it is Mojo, it is Enthusiasm, it is Love, it is your soul on fire…
It is Magical for your life*

*I ran out of the perfect rhyme for this one
So I took a little literary privilege, that is how come

With that being said I would like to continue to say
Passion is the MC2 that energizes your day

Positive – Optimistic, bright side, useful, helpful, beneficial,
good, affirmative, absolute, definite, real. Light On. Say Yes.
Of course we can. Living the dream. Love.

Be Positive.

Think Positive and Pass it on,

Pass the Positive®

You have a choice to add light or take it away by your thinking.

By Being Positive and Thinking Positive,
You will create more light in your life and the lives of others.

More Positive, more light.

More light, easier to see.

Positive shines the light on your Success.

I have had the good fortune of being exposed to a lot of Positive wisdom
early on in my life and the Positive side of life is where I live.

It is not that I have not had some significant learning curves
in multiple spokes of my wheel, but my choice was always to look for
and find the value in any situation or circumstance.

Not always that easy, but Possible.

Positive becomes the Virtue
"Believe in Possible and Overcoming" is the theme song.

A true story:

I was in a Chamber meeting and we are discussing Possibilities for the future.

I am excited.

I am thinking pretty Positive and one of the members said that
they appreciated my input but he said he was a realist.

He went on to say he thought I might be a little too optimistic.
He further suggested that maybe I was even living in a space suit.

Then I started thinking.

I love simple.

I call this the Battery Theory.

There are only 2 poles.

Positive	negative
Light On	light off
Up	down
Partly Sunny	partly cloudy
½ Full	½ empty
Law of Attraction	no clue
Yes	no
Possible	don't think so
Probable	doubt it
Optimist	pessimist
Realist? Real Positive	realist? real negative
Enthusiasm	why?
Excited	not so much

Aside from that I am not really sure how to explain it,
other than it feels much better living in a space suit!

Success is all lit up with Positive!

It was 2009 when I was feeling a little low
Money was tight and business was slow

The financial world was in chaos and the sky was apparently falling
I wasn't sure what to do, no one was answering when I was calling

So I said to myself, "You have to think differently"
I grabbed a big bucket of Positive and set my soul free

Pass the Positive I thought, Think Positive and Pass it On
It doesn't mean that nothing is wrong

It just adds light to the situation at hand
A better dimension of thinking, like a song with a band

I will forever just say it, think Positively
The light is much brighter, much easier to see

Pass the Positive®

Think Positive and Pass it On is the motto
Pass the Positive is the slogan.

I came up with this a few years ago and have been wearing silicone bracelets ever since.

Pass the Positive is about Love, Hope and Optimism rolled up
in to a big ol' ball of Passion about life and our existence.

Pass the Positive is about the opportunity to make a positive difference
for our planet and the people that live here.

Pass the Positive is about light and energy and the true joy
of being alive. We want to make it this way for everybody.

Pass the Positive is about peace and harmony and
the possibility that we can all live together and like it.

The best part about PtP is that we are all in this together.
You don't have to go it alone.

All of us are in the same race, the Human Race.

We need everyone in.

Think Positive and Pass it on…...
Pass the Positive

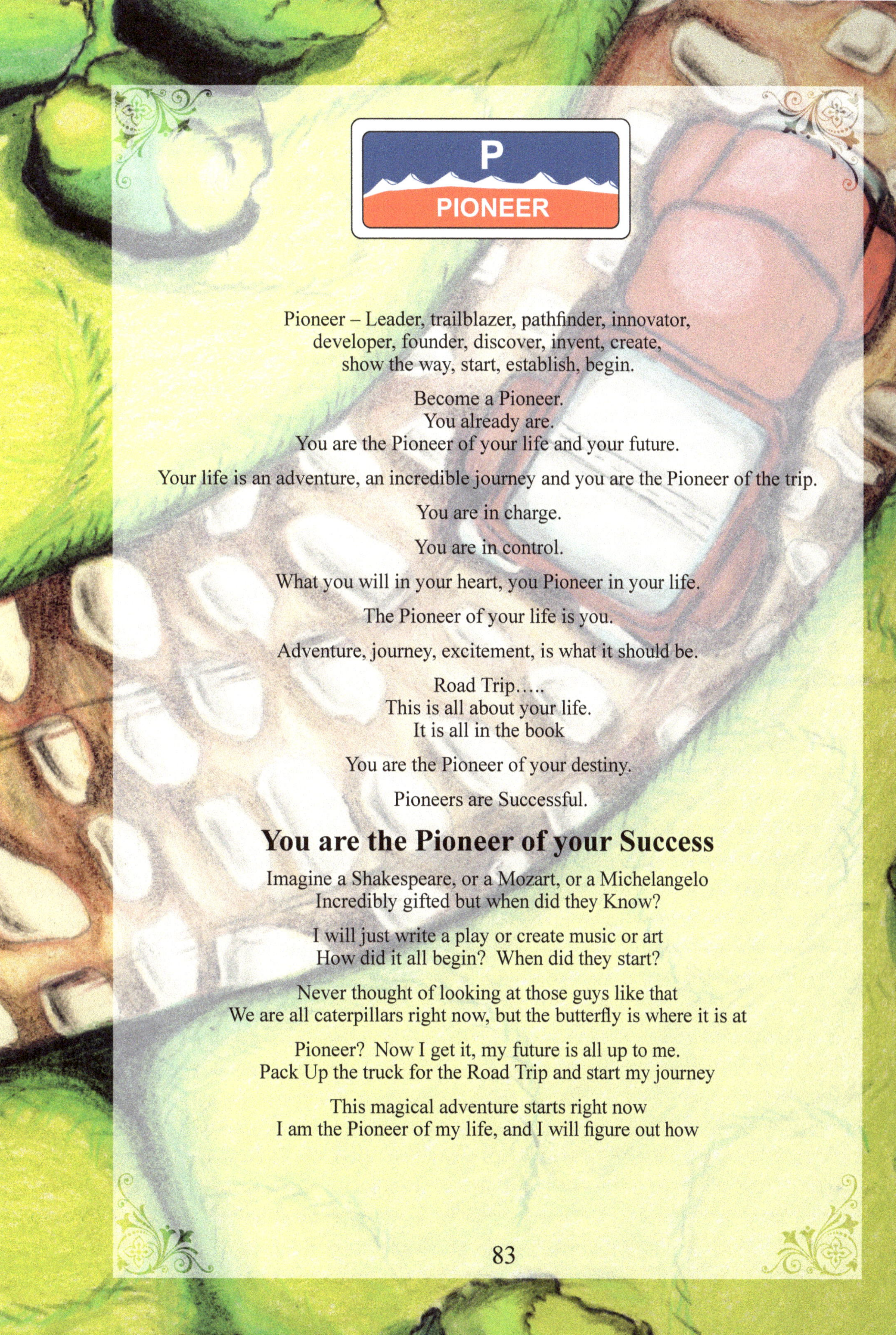

Pioneer – Leader, trailblazer, pathfinder, innovator,
developer, founder, discover, invent, create,
show the way, start, establish, begin.

Become a Pioneer.
You already are.
You are the Pioneer of your life and your future.

Your life is an adventure, an incredible journey and you are the Pioneer of the trip.

You are in charge.

You are in control.

What you will in your heart, you Pioneer in your life.

The Pioneer of your life is you.

Adventure, journey, excitement, is what it should be.

Road Trip…..
This is all about your life.
It is all in the book

You are the Pioneer of your destiny.

Pioneers are Successful.

You are the Pioneer of your Success

Imagine a Shakespeare, or a Mozart, or a Michelangelo
Incredibly gifted but when did they Know?

I will just write a play or create music or art
How did it all begin? When did they start?

Never thought of looking at those guys like that
We are all caterpillars right now, but the butterfly is where it is at

Pioneer? Now I get it, my future is all up to me.
Pack Up the truck for the Road Trip and start my journey

This magical adventure starts right now
I am the Pioneer of my life, and I will figure out how

Patience – Calm, self-control, peaceful, relaxed, understanding,
compassionate, considerate, steady, meaningful, restful, accomplished.

Stay Focused on your Goals and be Patient.
Good timing is the key to all Success.
Patience is usually why it is good timing.

The Universal Energy has a Universal Timeline.
The Universe says Yes but the Universe is a wee bit wiser and controls the timeline.

Learning to Be Patient is essential on the Road Trip.
Have Faith.
God's timing is always on time.

Patience is the virtue that allows you to trust Father Time.
Things typically work out the way they are supposed to.

With Patience as a pillar, you can overcome challenges and setbacks,
obstacles and potholes, trips and falls, and Get Back Up!

Make a plan, work your plan and be Patient.
Patience allows things to fall into place in the necessary order required for Success.

Success is full of Patience

The dude was full of Patience, he was standing in a pretty long line
There was calm in his demeanor, like he had an unlimited amount of time

I am a people watcher, and I am a pretty curious guy
I had to find out how he was the way he was and the reason why

This is what he told me, when he was standing there
I learned a very long time ago, the line is the line, and I am not going anywhere

I take an Imagication Vacation, I can go anywhere that I choose
Patience is the Virtue that you never want to lose

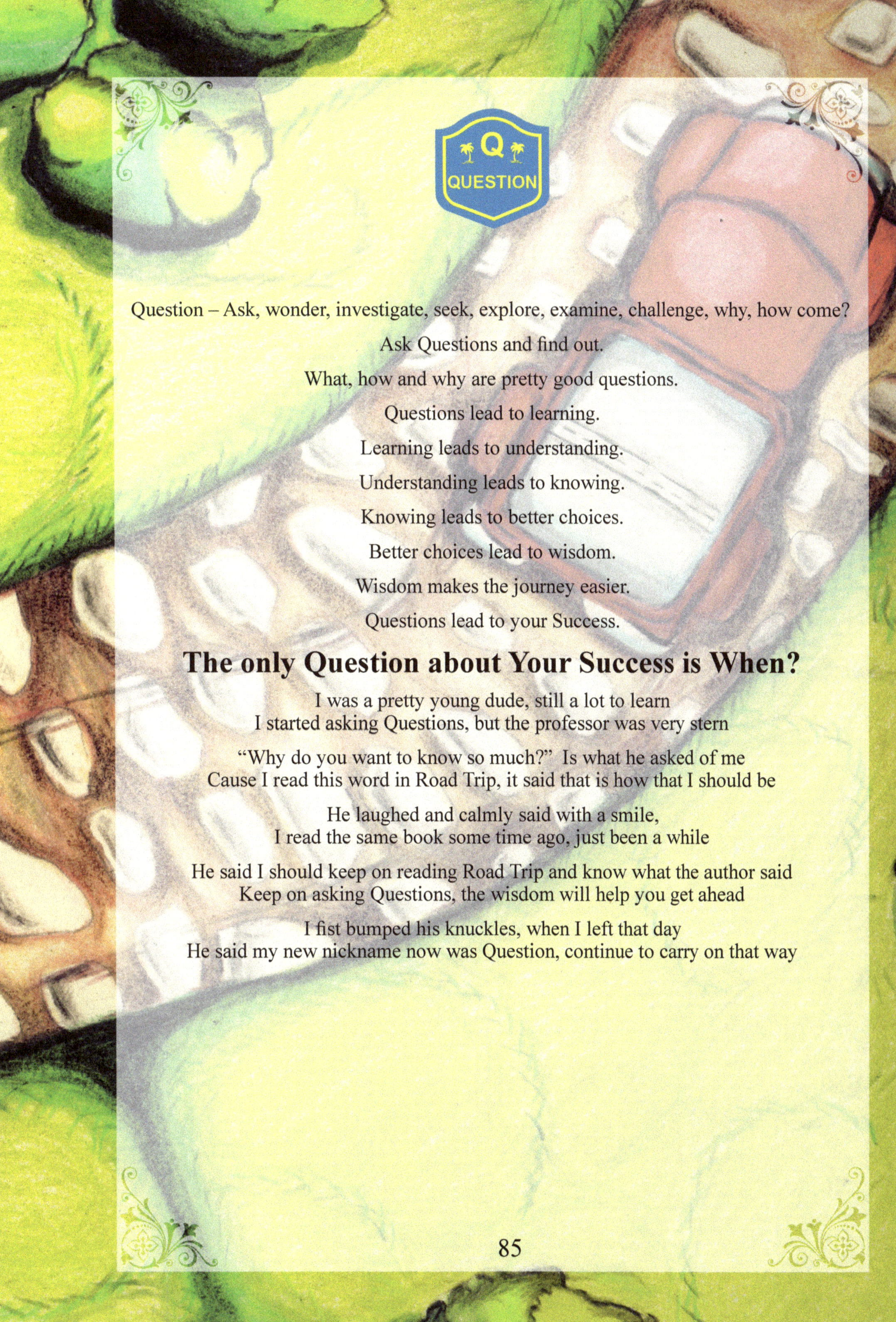

Question – Ask, wonder, investigate, seek, explore, examine, challenge, why, how come?

Ask Questions and find out.

What, how and why are pretty good questions.

Questions lead to learning.

Learning leads to understanding.

Understanding leads to knowing.

Knowing leads to better choices.

Better choices lead to wisdom.

Wisdom makes the journey easier.

Questions lead to your Success.

The only Question about Your Success is When?

I was a pretty young dude, still a lot to learn
I started asking Questions, but the professor was very stern

"Why do you want to know so much?" Is what he asked of me
Cause I read this word in Road Trip, it said that is how that I should be

He laughed and calmly said with a smile,
I read the same book some time ago, just been a while

He said I should keep on reading Road Trip and know what the author said
Keep on asking Questions, the wisdom will help you get ahead

I fist bumped his knuckles, when I left that day
He said my new nickname now was Question, continue to carry on that way

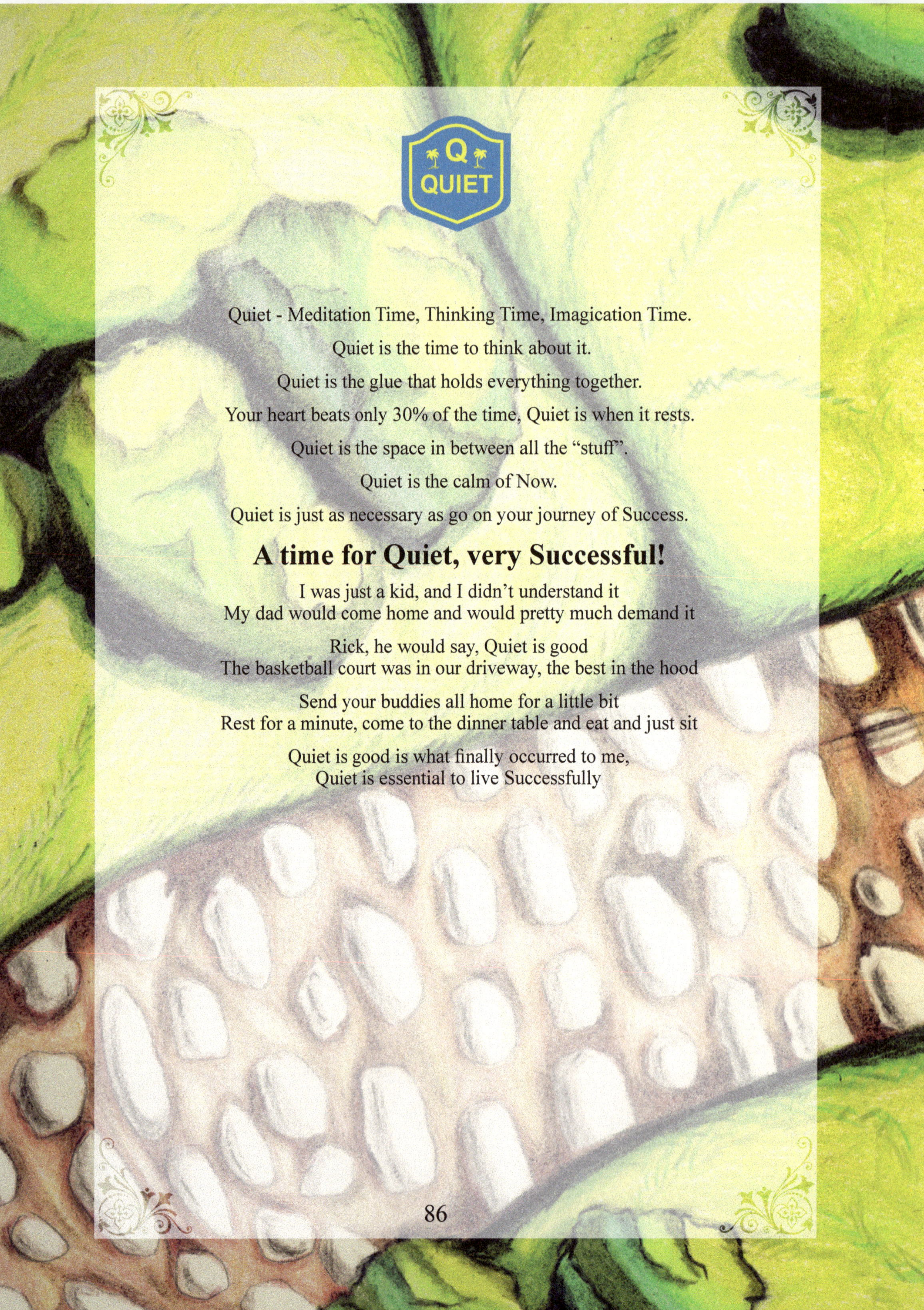

Quiet - Meditation Time, Thinking Time, Imagication Time.

Quiet is the time to think about it.

Quiet is the glue that holds everything together.

Your heart beats only 30% of the time, Quiet is when it rests.

Quiet is the space in between all the "stuff".

Quiet is the calm of Now.

Quiet is just as necessary as go on your journey of Success.

A time for Quiet, very Successful!

I was just a kid, and I didn't understand it
My dad would come home and would pretty much demand it

Rick, he would say, Quiet is good
The basketball court was in our driveway, the best in the hood

Send your buddies all home for a little bit
Rest for a minute, come to the dinner table and eat and just sit

Quiet is good is what finally occurred to me,
Quiet is essential to live Successfully

Quality – Characteristic, attribute, trait, nature, feature,
integrity, value, worth, eminence, distinction, dignity.

Inherent Quality in all of us.
Made from Quality materials.

Quality goods and services.
Thread count.

What is the Quality of your life experience?
What do you want it to be?
Highest, best, top drawer, #1.

Quality is about Contentment.
Quality Life experiences
Quality time with people that You Love

Good Words are Quality Words.
Use Good Words to describe and plan your life and you will
In Joy the Quality of your Success.

Success is Quality time

Quality is meaningful, not just about the label
Quality of life means that you are willing and able

Quality is individual and defined by us all
Quality is awesome, whether it is big or small

Wake up every day and In Joy Quality time
It starts when your eyes open, choose Quality thoughts for your mind

I am going to have a Quality Day
My Quality thinking is what makes me feel this way

Respect – Regard, esteem, appreciation, affection, reverence,
praise, admiration, approval, recognition, consideration.

Respect for people, places and things.
Respect other people's time.

Respect allows you to become genuinely interested in other people and learn who they are.
Respect helps you to appreciate what other people have to say and the things they have done.

Respect is the beginning of Successful Relationships.

Find out what people like to do and discover what they are good at.
Respect gives you the pause to appreciate and listen.

You need to know how you might be able to work together.
Respect Opens that door for the good of you and the people around you.

Respect means that you care about what you are doing and what you are saying.

Respect your elders, people that are older than you.
There is no substitute for their experiential wisdom.

They have Successfully traveled the road that you are now on.

It has been said that the best teacher is experience.
Pay attention, watch what is going on and learn from it.

It is usually easier to learn from the experience of others but for some reason,
each generation must learn the stove is hot by touching it for themselves.

Respect minimizes the number of times in your life
that you will have to "touch the stove" for yourself.

Respect is one of the most important spokes on the wheel of Success.

Respect Success

Respect creates a better ride on the Road Trip
Respect is the beginning of Successful Relationships

Respect other people that are older than you
You do not know their life story or what they have been through

Respect younger people and spend time with them
They will be our leaders in the future, never know when

Respect is noble, a virtue that you should possess
Respect is an important part of Success

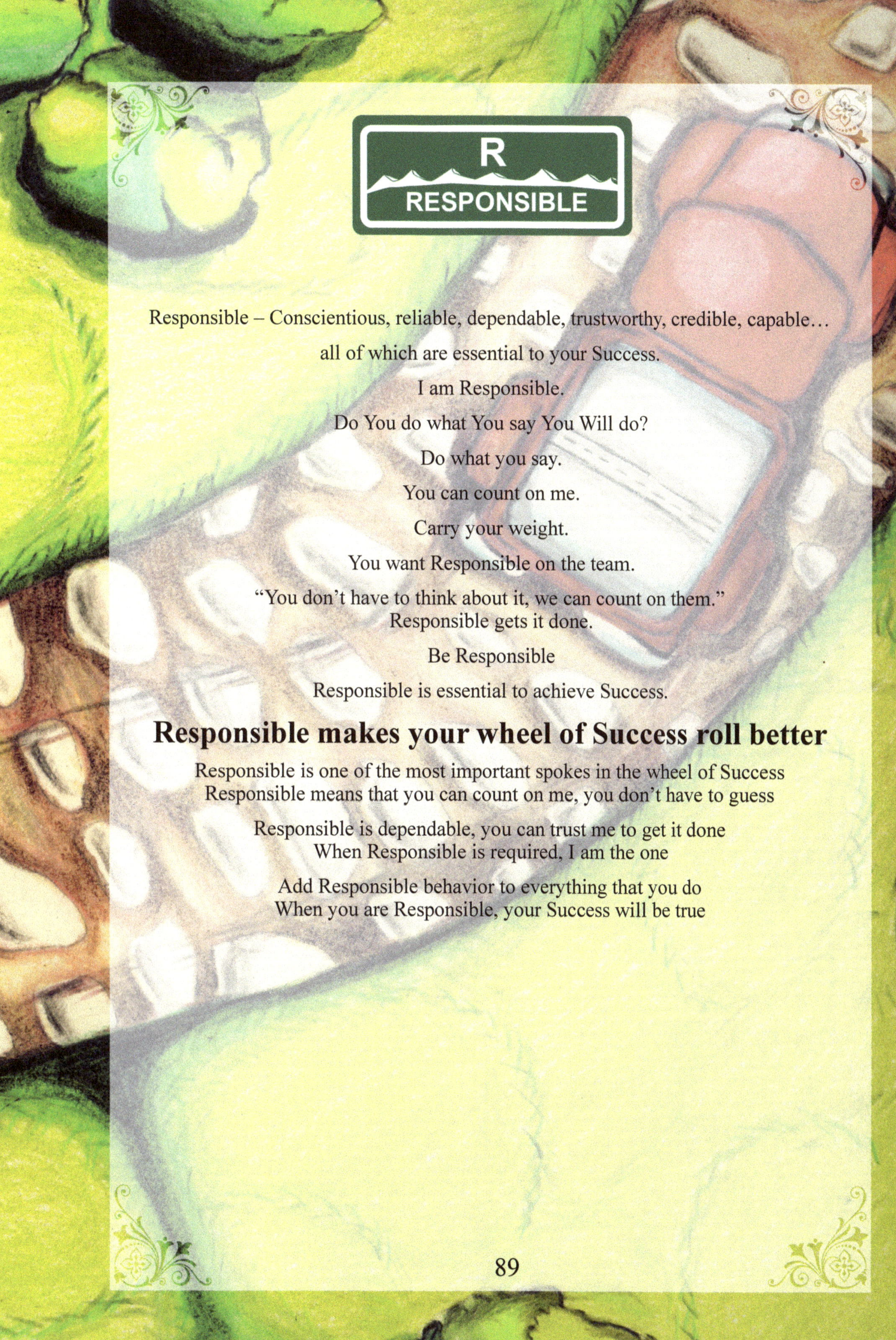

Responsible – Conscientious, reliable, dependable, trustworthy, credible, capable…

all of which are essential to your Success.

I am Responsible.

Do You do what You say You Will do?

Do what you say.

You can count on me.

Carry your weight.

You want Responsible on the team.

"You don't have to think about it, we can count on them."
Responsible gets it done.

Be Responsible

Responsible is essential to achieve Success.

Responsible makes your wheel of Success roll better

Responsible is one of the most important spokes in the wheel of Success
Responsible means that you can count on me, you don't have to guess

Responsible is dependable, you can trust me to get it done
When Responsible is required, I am the one

Add Responsible behavior to everything that you do
When you are Responsible, your Success will be true

Righteous – Moral, honorable, honest, just, fair, good, virtuous, reverent, trustworthy.

Do the right thing.

Be Righteous with each other.

Look out for one another.

Take Care of people.

The Golden Rule is Righteous.
"Do unto others as You would have them do unto You".

Love one another is what Righteous is all about.

Good Words are Righteous.

Righteous is Successful.

Success is full of Righteous

Righteous is this incredible feeling
It is Peaceful, it is Quiet, Love with no ceiling

Think about it for a minute, here what I say
When you give away Righteous, Righteous comes back your way

I imagine creating a Positive Thinking Culture of Us
Righteous is the hub of the wheel on the bus

Love is the glue that holds all of us together
Righteous is the behavior that makes our lives better

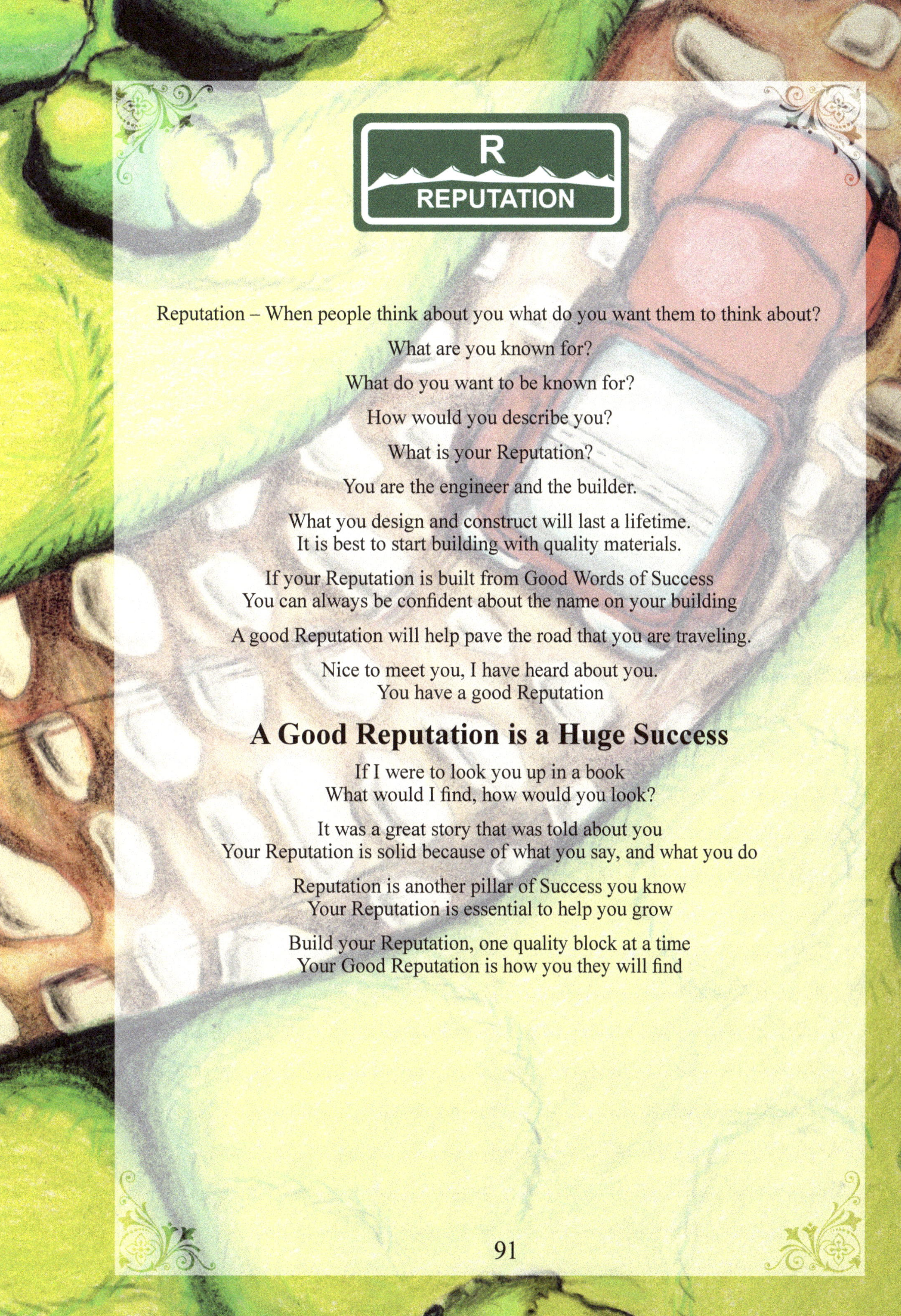

Reputation – When people think about you what do you want them to think about?

What are you known for?

What do you want to be known for?

How would you describe you?

What is your Reputation?

You are the engineer and the builder.

What you design and construct will last a lifetime.
It is best to start building with quality materials.

If your Reputation is built from Good Words of Success
You can always be confident about the name on your building

A good Reputation will help pave the road that you are traveling.

Nice to meet you, I have heard about you.
You have a good Reputation

A Good Reputation is a Huge Success

If I were to look you up in a book
What would I find, how would you look?

It was a great story that was told about you
Your Reputation is solid because of what you say, and what you do

Reputation is another pillar of Success you know
Your Reputation is essential to help you grow

Build your Reputation, one quality block at a time
Your Good Reputation is how you they will find

Resilience – Resistant, irrepressible, hardy, recover rapidly, against all odds,
tenacious, adaptable, determined, get up, get up again.

Resilience is the ability to bounce back from setbacks and continue to charge forward.

Resilience helps you face obstacles and overcome challenges
with determination and perseverance.

Success is about Overcoming, Overcoming is about Resilience.

Build your Success with Resilience

There was a story about a man in the paper
It was a story about Resilience, he wanted to be a deal maker

Everything he tried met with temporary defeat,
but he never gave up, his family needed shelter and something to eat

He continued to get up everyday
Because he kept trying, deals started coming his way

Years went by and he became a very Successful man
Resilience was the reason, he never gave up on I Can

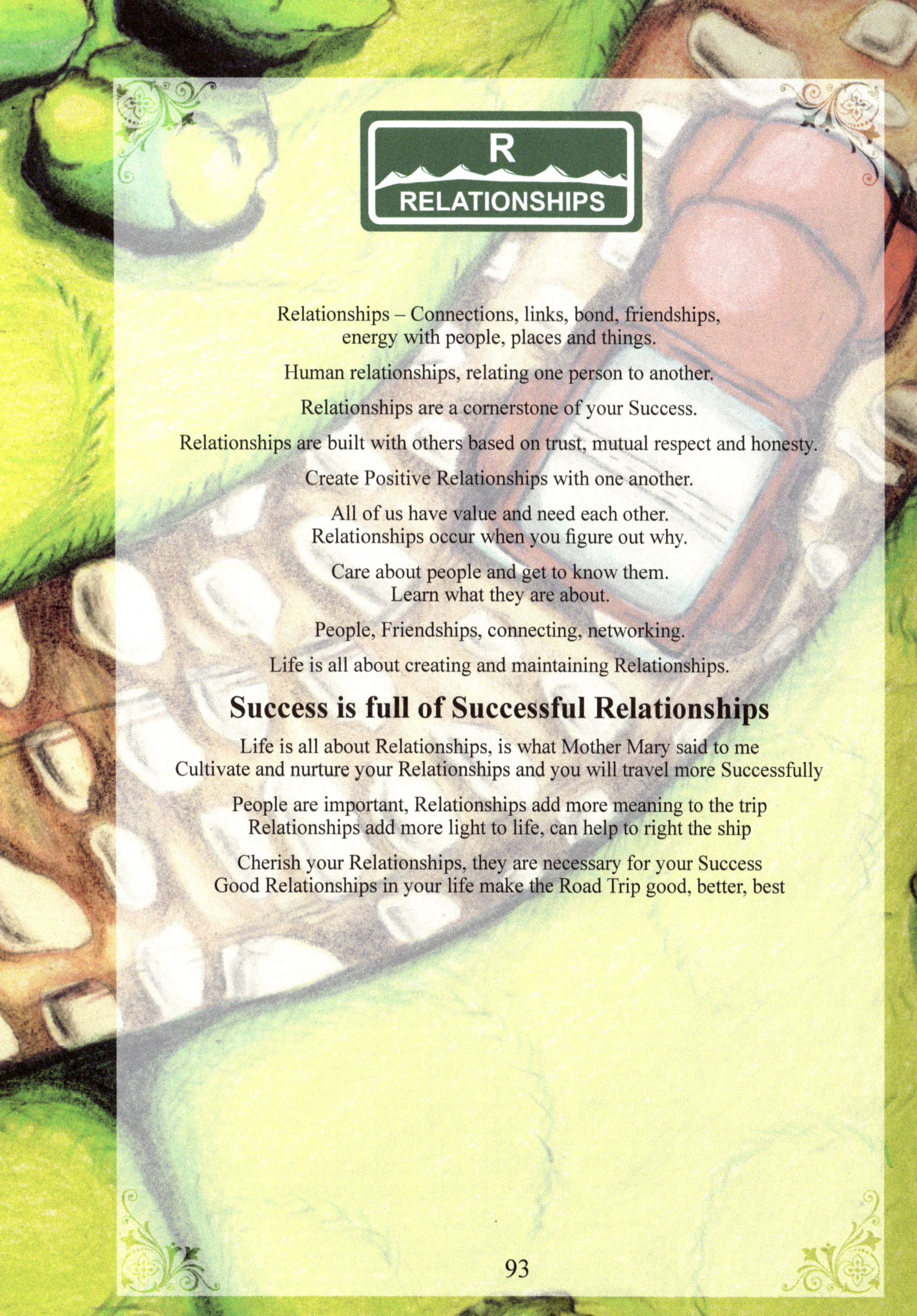

Relationships – Connections, links, bond, friendships,
energy with people, places and things.

Human relationships, relating one person to another.

Relationships are a cornerstone of your Success.

Relationships are built with others based on trust, mutual respect and honesty.

Create Positive Relationships with one another.

All of us have value and need each other.
Relationships occur when you figure out why.

Care about people and get to know them.
Learn what they are about.

People, Friendships, connecting, networking.

Life is all about creating and maintaining Relationships.

Success is full of Successful Relationships

Life is all about Relationships, is what Mother Mary said to me
Cultivate and nurture your Relationships and you will travel more Successfully

People are important, Relationships add more meaning to the trip
Relationships add more light to life, can help to right the ship

Cherish your Relationships, they are necessary for your Success
Good Relationships in your life make the Road Trip good, better, best

Spirit – Soul, vital essence, mind, disposition, mood, feelings, energy,
vigor, zest, liveliness, animation, vitality, enthusiasm, drive, zeal, will,
fire, warmth, courage, daring, fortitude, substance, purpose.

Those are a lot of great possibilities of what Spirit might look like.

Everyone has Spirit.

What does your Spirit look like?
How does it feel to you?
How does your Spirit impact other people?

Turn it on and dial it up

Your Spirit is your Juice, it is your Mojo, it is Zest for your Purpose.

It is the energy that you bring to the table of your life.

Spirit is alive and full of enthusiasm and willpower.

Indomitable Spirit?
It is just about impossible to beat an energy that will not give up.
Imagine facing that challenge?
Be that.
Determination, Grit, Tenacity.

Success, Overcoming, Indomitable, Conquer, Can

Now that's the Spirit!

Your Spirit lights Up your Success

She was a pretty small girl, but her Spirit was large
I knew when I met her that she was in charge

She was Determined and Passionate, the obstacles didn't matter
She would make the world better, let her be the batter

She said if we lived by the law of Love
The world would be better certainly because

When I asked her how she thought it should go
She said it is all about Love and Kindness, you Know

Her Spirit was buzzing and was dialed up high
She would definitely Succeed, with whatever she tried

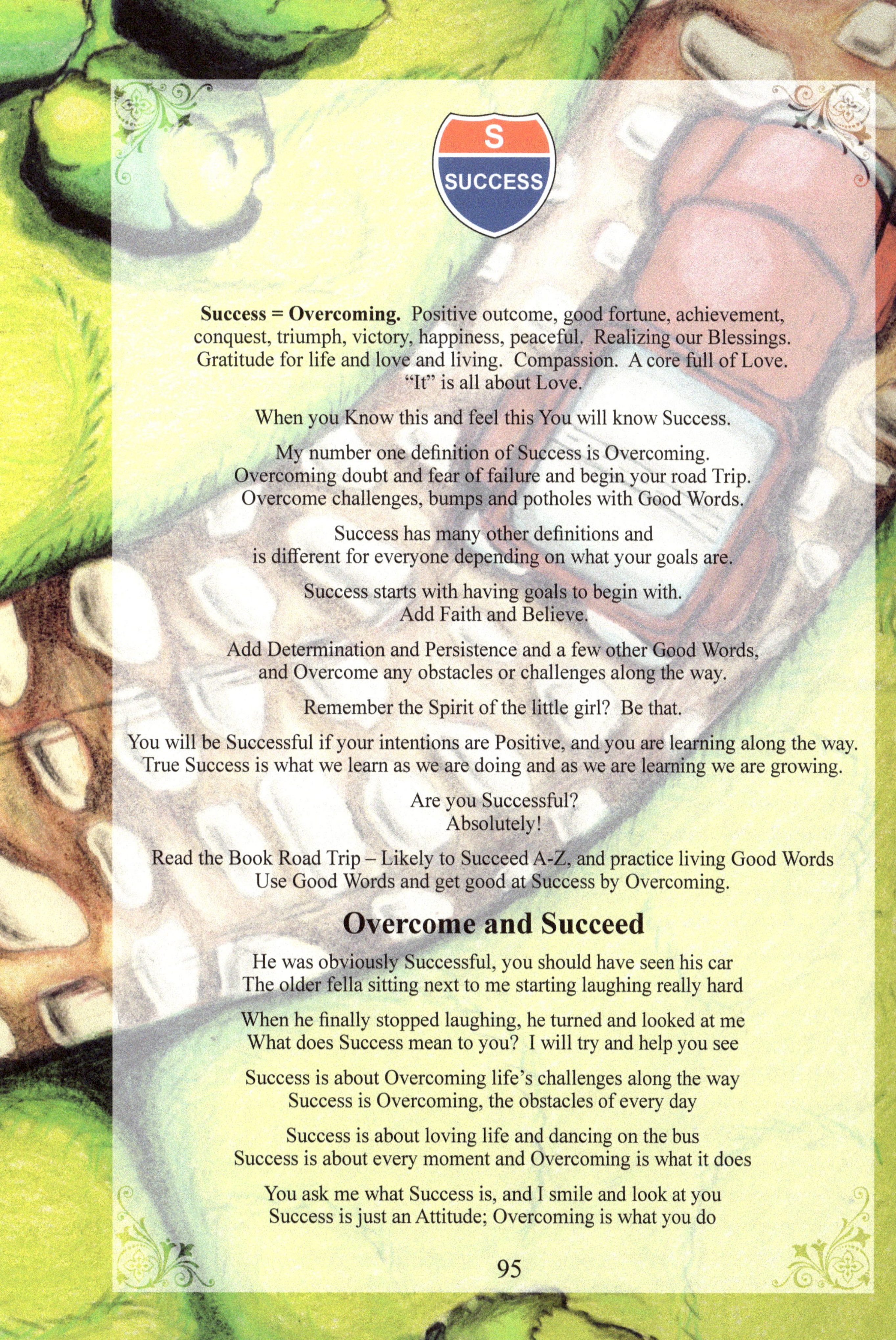

Success = Overcoming. Positive outcome, good fortune, achievement, conquest, triumph, victory, happiness, peaceful. Realizing our Blessings. Gratitude for life and love and living. Compassion. A core full of Love. "It" is all about Love.

When you Know this and feel this You will know Success.

My number one definition of Success is Overcoming. Overcoming doubt and fear of failure and begin your road Trip. Overcome challenges, bumps and potholes with Good Words.

Success has many other definitions and is different for everyone depending on what your goals are.

Success starts with having goals to begin with. Add Faith and Believe.

Add Determination and Persistence and a few other Good Words, and Overcome any obstacles or challenges along the way.

Remember the Spirit of the little girl? Be that.

You will be Successful if your intentions are Positive, and you are learning along the way. True Success is what we learn as we are doing and as we are learning we are growing.

Are you Successful?
Absolutely!

Read the Book Road Trip – Likely to Succeed A-Z, and practice living Good Words Use Good Words and get good at Success by Overcoming.

Overcome and Succeed

He was obviously Successful, you should have seen his car
The older fella sitting next to me starting laughing really hard

When he finally stopped laughing, he turned and looked at me
What does Success mean to you? I will try and help you see

Success is about Overcoming life's challenges along the way
Success is Overcoming, the obstacles of every day

Success is about loving life and dancing on the bus
Success is about every moment and Overcoming is what it does

You ask me what Success is, and I smile and look at you
Success is just an Attitude; Overcoming is what you do

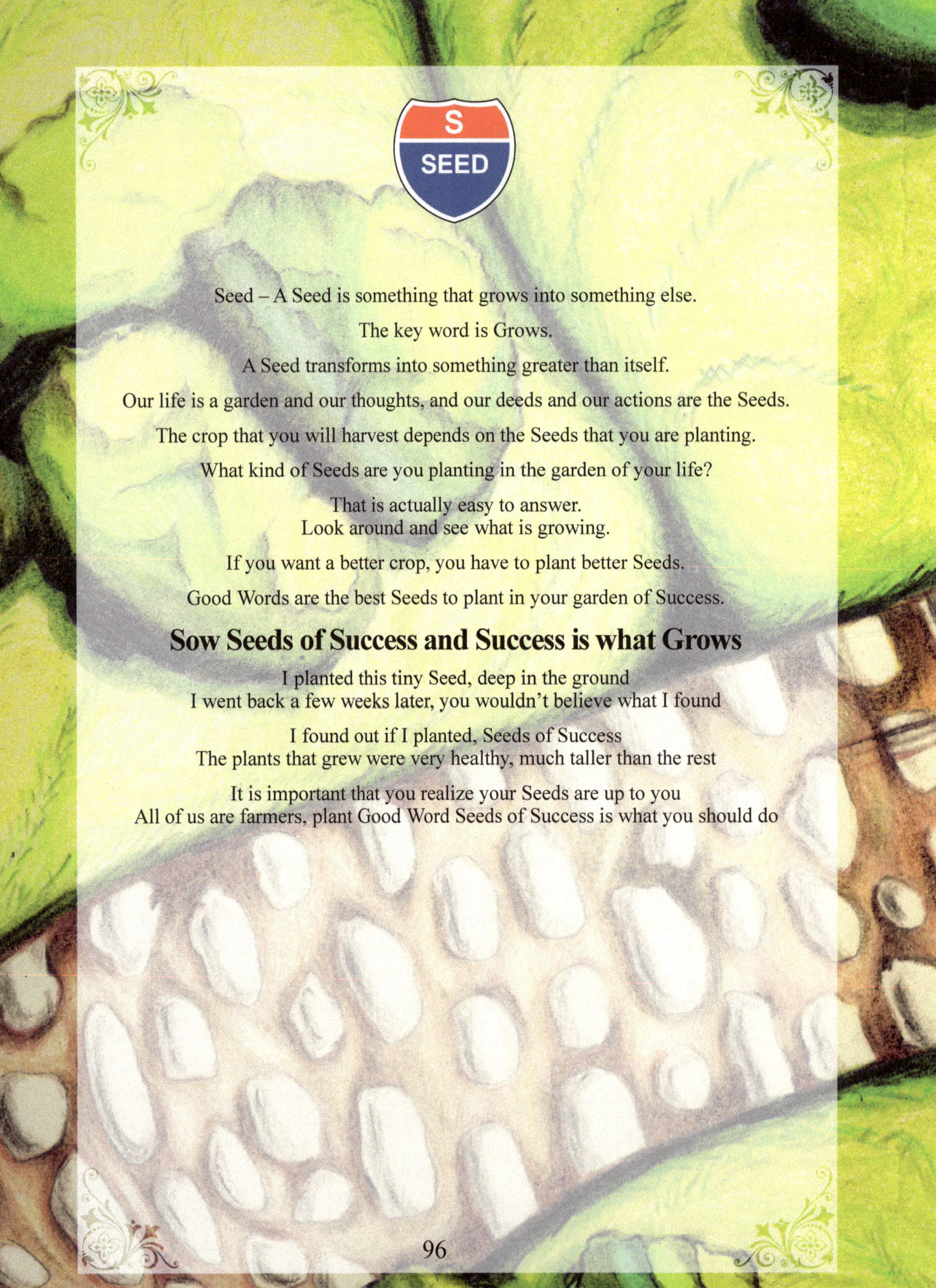

Seed – A Seed is something that grows into something else.

The key word is Grows.

A Seed transforms into something greater than itself.

Our life is a garden and our thoughts, and our deeds and our actions are the Seeds.

The crop that you will harvest depends on the Seeds that you are planting.

What kind of Seeds are you planting in the garden of your life?

That is actually easy to answer.
Look around and see what is growing.

If you want a better crop, you have to plant better Seeds.

Good Words are the best Seeds to plant in your garden of Success.

Sow Seeds of Success and Success is what Grows

I planted this tiny Seed, deep in the ground
I went back a few weeks later, you wouldn't believe what I found

I found out if I planted, Seeds of Success
The plants that grew were very healthy, much taller than the rest

It is important that you realize your Seeds are up to you
All of us are farmers, plant Good Word Seeds of Success is what you should do

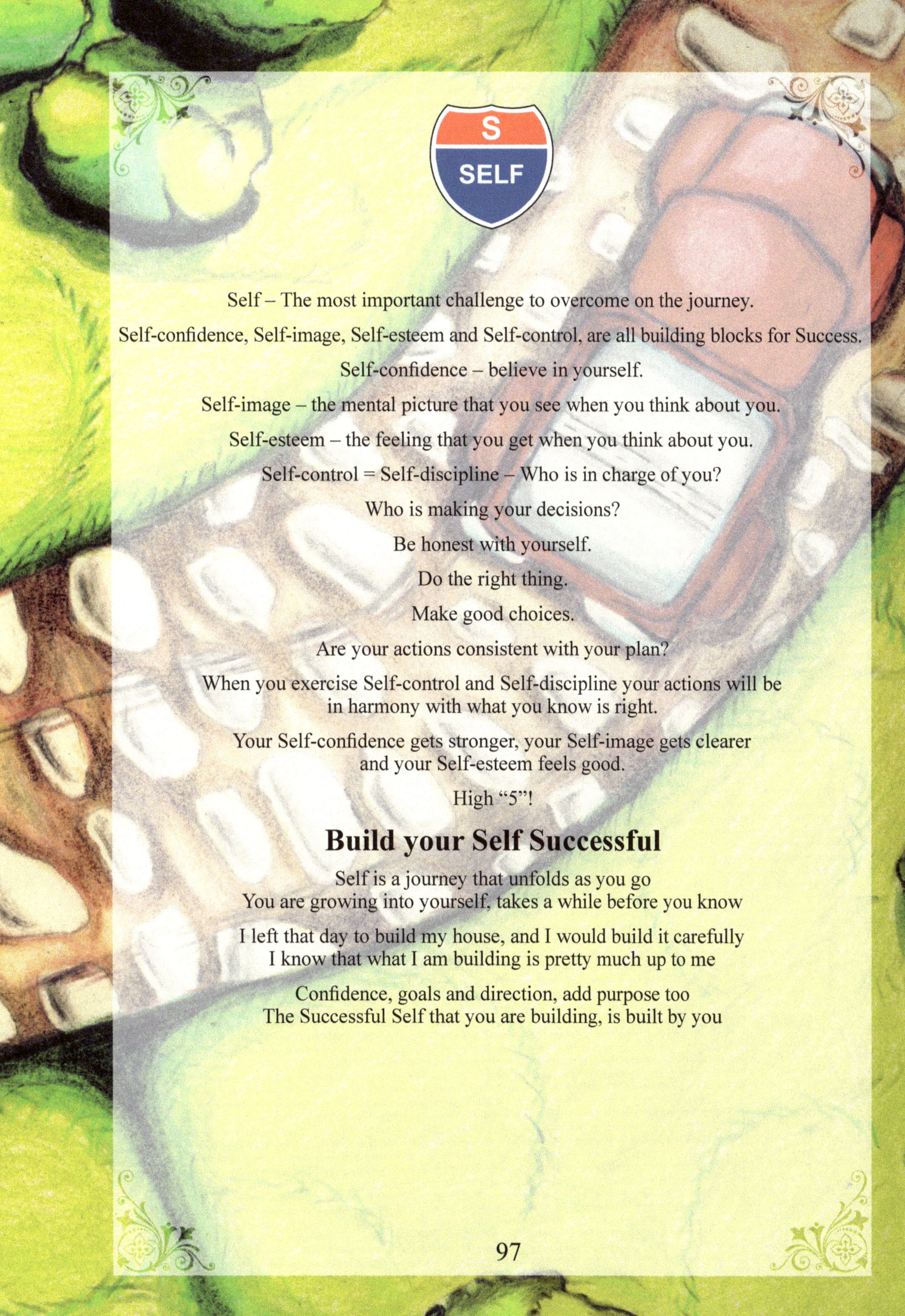

Self – The most important challenge to overcome on the journey.

Self-confidence, Self-image, Self-esteem and Self-control, are all building blocks for Success.

Self-confidence – believe in yourself.

Self-image – the mental picture that you see when you think about you.

Self-esteem – the feeling that you get when you think about you.

Self-control = Self-discipline – Who is in charge of you?

Who is making your decisions?

Be honest with yourself.

Do the right thing.

Make good choices.

Are your actions consistent with your plan?

When you exercise Self-control and Self-discipline your actions will be in harmony with what you know is right.

Your Self-confidence gets stronger, your Self-image gets clearer and your Self-esteem feels good.

High "5"!

Build your Self Successful

Self is a journey that unfolds as you go
You are growing into yourself, takes a while before you know

I left that day to build my house, and I would build it carefully
I know that what I am building is pretty much up to me

Confidence, goals and direction, add purpose too
The Successful Self that you are building, is built by you

Think – Believe, conceive, imagine, dwell, reason, reflect, intend, purpose, create, dream.

That could keep a person pretty busy doing all that!

How important is it?

Critical, essential, mandatory, necessary, required, get on it, get down with that, must do it!

To be Successful, you must Think about it.

Think about you and your life.

Thinking produces thoughts and your thoughts are the seeds that grow into your future.

Success is dependent on thinking and planting seeds.

Planning and creating a direction, that you would like to go.

Where do your thoughts come from?

What you see
What you hear
What you read
What you have been taught

Which all ultimately formulates what you Think and what you Believe in.
Good Words help you to write your thoughts more productively.
The key word is write.

Think on paper and write down what you are thinking about.
And read it. Amend it. Add to it.
Think about it.

Take time to Think about Success……. Every day.

Think about your Success, it is just one Thought away!

They say that we should Think on paper, write down what you would like to see
It starts with a Positive Attitude and believing in the future and what Can Be

Spend a few minutes of your day Thinking, meditation time is good
Think about what is possible and believe in could

The premise is that Life is naturally good and should be a pretty good time
It is just a matter of Thinking about it, and what is possible will fall in line

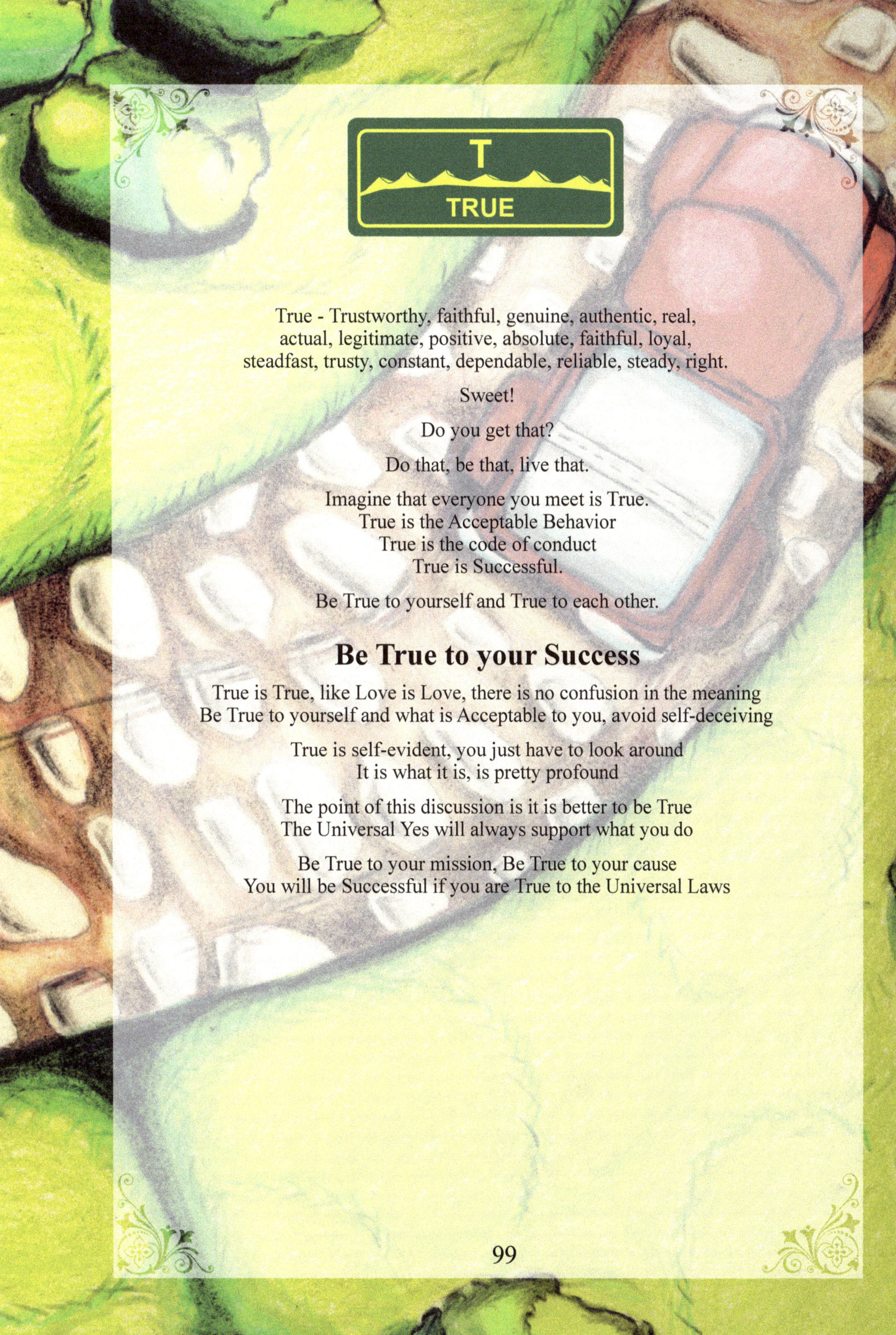

True - Trustworthy, faithful, genuine, authentic, real,
actual, legitimate, positive, absolute, faithful, loyal,
steadfast, trusty, constant, dependable, reliable, steady, right.

Sweet!

Do you get that?

Do that, be that, live that.

Imagine that everyone you meet is True.
True is the Acceptable Behavior
True is the code of conduct
True is Successful.

Be True to yourself and True to each other.

Be True to your Success

True is True, like Love is Love, there is no confusion in the meaning
Be True to yourself and what is Acceptable to you, avoid self-deceiving

True is self-evident, you just have to look around
It is what it is, is pretty profound

The point of this discussion is it is better to be True
The Universal Yes will always support what you do

Be True to your mission, Be True to your cause
You will be Successful if you are True to the Universal Laws

Time – What Time is it? What Time do you want it to be?

When we are younger, we want Time to be later.
When we are older we want Time to be earlier.

When we are young Time seems to take forever and when we are older Time goes by so fast.

All that there really is of Time is Now Time.

The Time is Now.

Now is the blissful side of Time.

The fun thing about life and living is that there is the possibility of future Nows.

The other side of Now Time.

When you are making plans for your life, realize the value of timing and patience.

One-three-five-year periods are much shorter than you think.

Good Timing is always a key to your Success.

Is go Time Now Time or is the best Time next Time?

Now is a good Time for Your Success!

I was with my good friend Terry, and he noticed the time that was on my clock
He laughed and he smiled at me and said the time was up to Doc

He knew that I set all my clocks, 30 minutes fast
I have done that for a long, long time, hoping somehow time would last

Now is a precious moment, the only time we truly have
Best to get wrapped up in it, so the moments don't go by so fast

Life is just an Attitude, a Now attitude is the way to go
Living one Now at a time gives your life a little slow

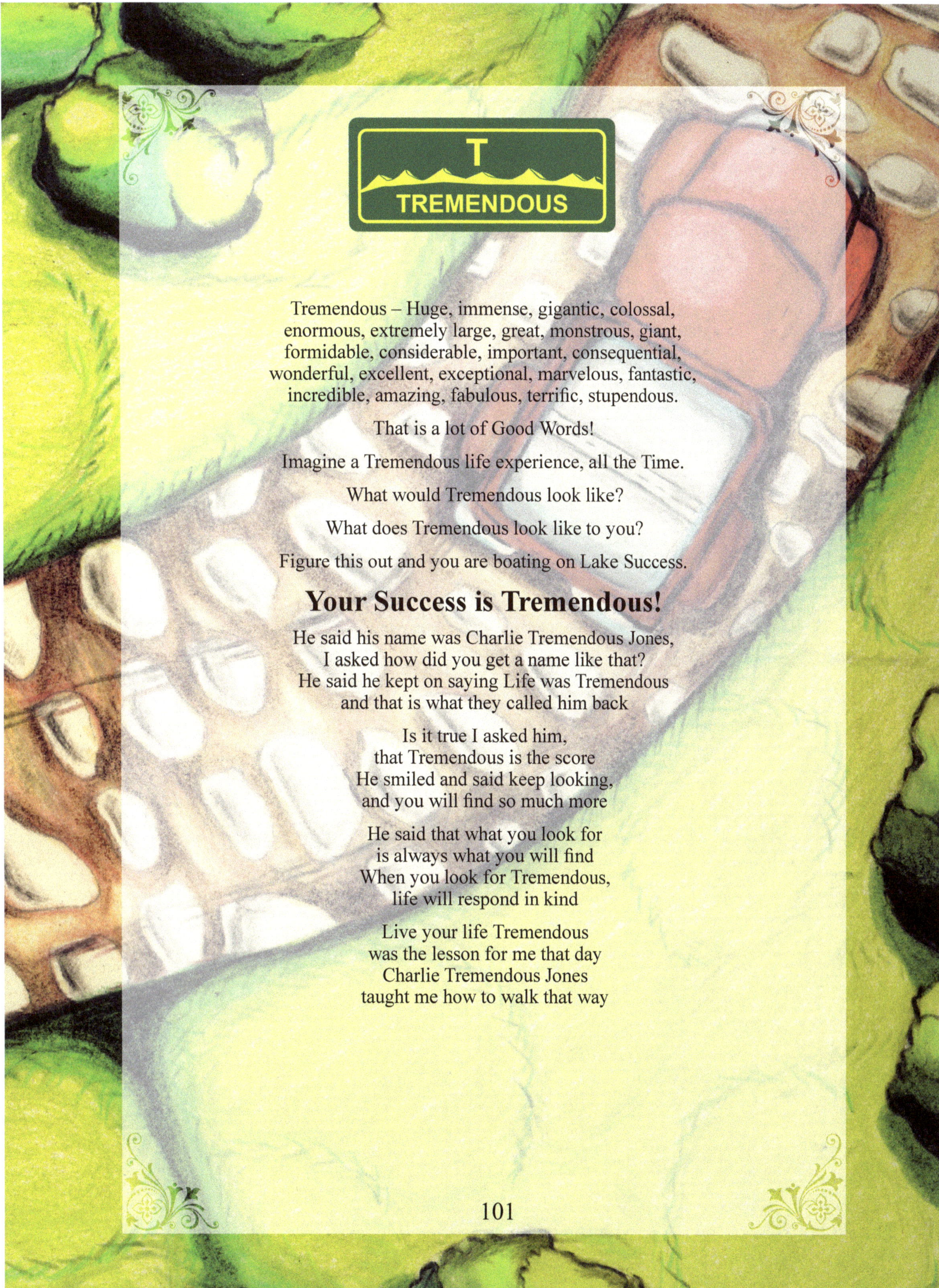

Tremendous – Huge, immense, gigantic, colossal,
enormous, extremely large, great, monstrous, giant,
formidable, considerable, important, consequential,
wonderful, excellent, exceptional, marvelous, fantastic,
incredible, amazing, fabulous, terrific, stupendous.

That is a lot of Good Words!

Imagine a Tremendous life experience, all the Time.

What would Tremendous look like?

What does Tremendous look like to you?

Figure this out and you are boating on Lake Success.

Your Success is Tremendous!

He said his name was Charlie Tremendous Jones,
I asked how did you get a name like that?
He said he kept on saying Life was Tremendous
and that is what they called him back

Is it true I asked him,
that Tremendous is the score
He smiled and said keep looking,
and you will find so much more

He said that what you look for
is always what you will find
When you look for Tremendous,
life will respond in kind

Live your life Tremendous
was the lesson for me that day
Charlie Tremendous Jones
taught me how to walk that way

Unafraid – Fearless, confident, strong; full of Faith.
Unafraid is a keystone on the Road Trip to your Success.

When your bag of words has a few Good Words like:
Think, Thoughts, Seeds, Focus, Energy, Ambition, Passion, Motivation,
Resilient, Persistence, Enthusiasm and Determination and…..
You Believe in yourself and
you are Confident because you are full of Faith,
you can be strong and fearless and Unafraid.

When we stay Focused on the Positive, fear doesn't fit.

Unafraid gets easy.

Unafraid? Absolutely!

Your Thoughts are the Seeds from which your future Grows.
Unafraid is because you understand this.

Success is Unafraid

Just go get it done is what I heard him say
What about…..he stopped me cold and said don't think that way

What are you afraid of? He asked with a passionate voice
I said I was a bit afraid, he asked why would I make that choice?

It is about what you believe in, if you can get it done
The only way to accomplish anything is to believe it can become

Believe in you and doing, Unafraid is about Fortitude
Unafraid is easy, it is just an Attitude

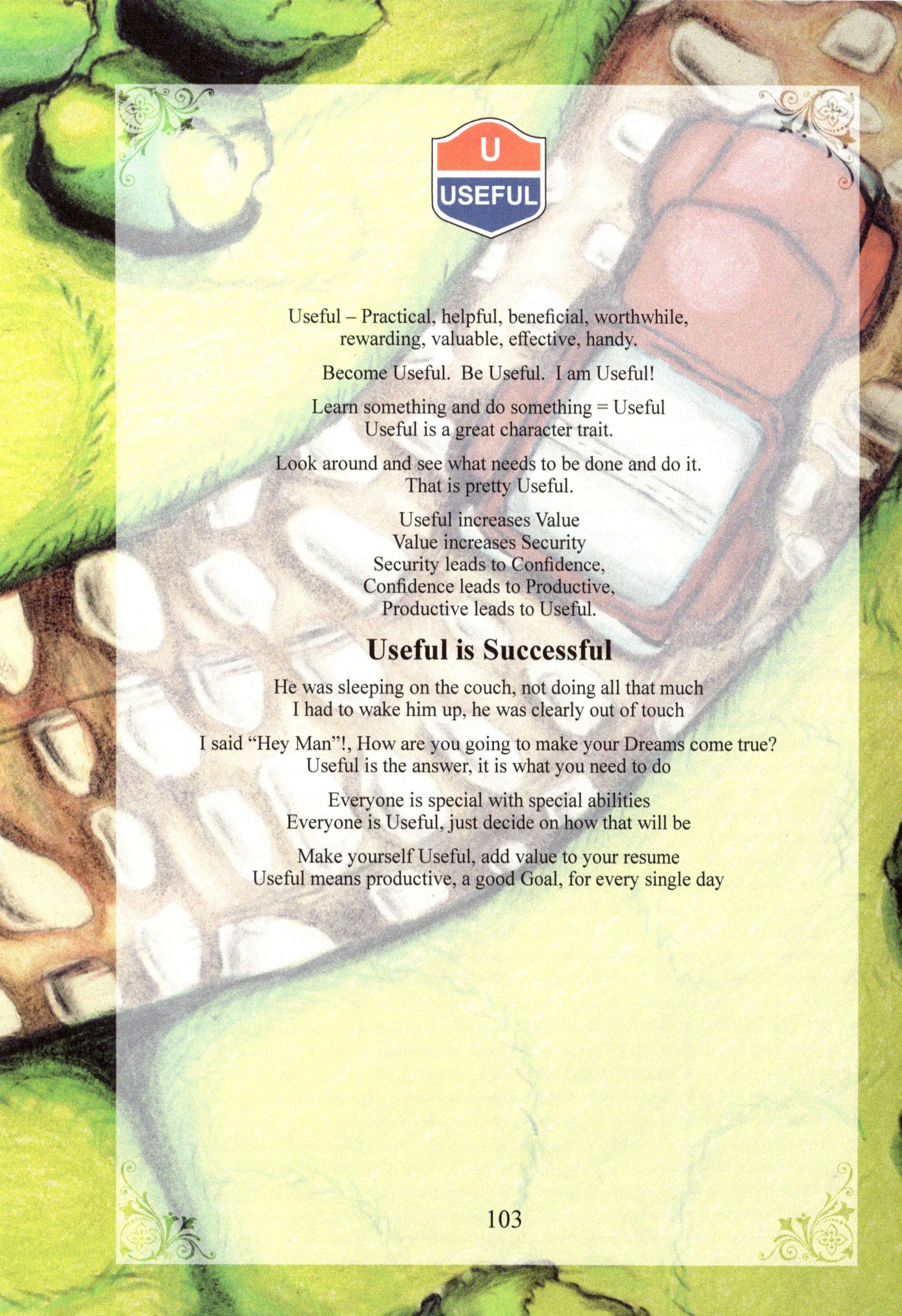

Useful – Practical, helpful, beneficial, worthwhile,
rewarding, valuable, effective, handy.

Become Useful. Be Useful. I am Useful!

Learn something and do something = Useful
Useful is a great character trait.

Look around and see what needs to be done and do it.
That is pretty Useful.

Useful increases Value
Value increases Security
Security leads to Confidence,
Confidence leads to Productive,
Productive leads to Useful.

Useful is Successful

He was sleeping on the couch, not doing all that much
I had to wake him up, he was clearly out of touch

I said "Hey Man"!, How are you going to make your Dreams come true?
Useful is the answer, it is what you need to do

Everyone is special with special abilities
Everyone is Useful, just decide on how that will be

Make yourself Useful, add value to your resume
Useful means productive, a good Goal, for every single day

Up – Up. There is only one way to go, go Up.

Go vertical. Straight Up.

When you look up you go up.

When someone falls down help them Up.

When someone's Spirit is down use Good Words and lift it Up

The Attitude of the day is helping other people go Up

Success is a process of trying and learning and getting Up and looking Up again.

Success requires a Positive – Up Attitude.

New word: Uptude – Positive Up Attitude – Uptude.

Turn your Uptude Up!

Fire your Uptude Up!

Get Up, Go Up, Live Up

Success is about Uptude on Up

He had an incredible Attitude, he was always looking Up
Hey man, how did you get this way? He said it was a little Uptude luck

He said that it all started when he was just a boy
It was like one day he just woke up and his soul was full of Joy

I asked him what he thought it was, that he would be this way
He wasn't sure, he did not know, he really could not say

I guess that my real question is how do I get some Up?
He said it is just a mental drink I drink, that I drink from the Uptude Cup

The cup wasn't exactly empty but it looked pretty dry to me
I held it up and drank it up and thought I would just wait and see

It was an imaginary elixir is what I learned that day
Looking Up and going Up is the Uptude way to play

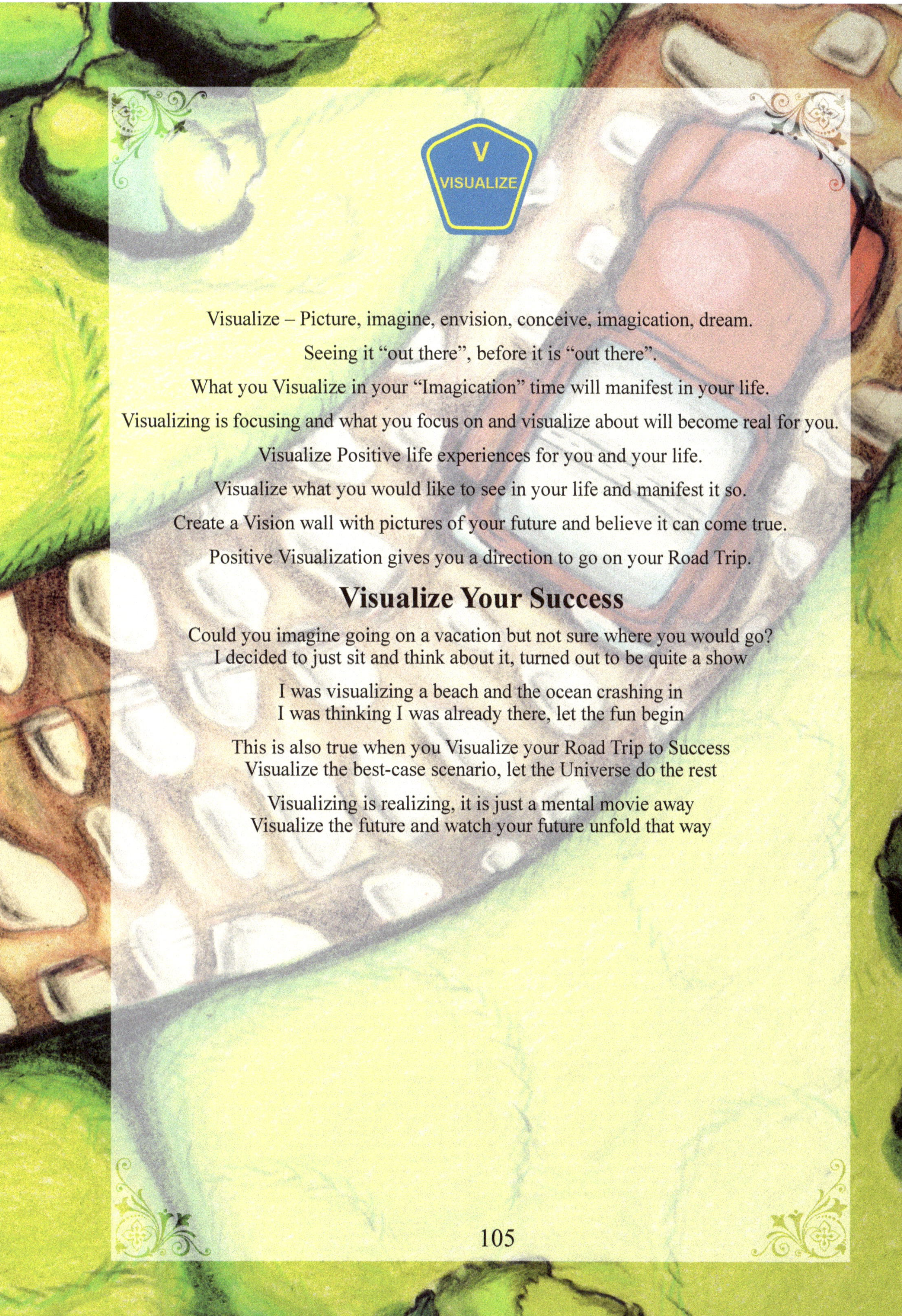

Visualize – Picture, imagine, envision, conceive, imagication, dream.

Seeing it "out there", before it is "out there".

What you Visualize in your "Imagication" time will manifest in your life.

Visualizing is focusing and what you focus on and visualize about will become real for you.

Visualize Positive life experiences for you and your life.

Visualize what you would like to see in your life and manifest it so.

Create a Vision wall with pictures of your future and believe it can come true.

Positive Visualization gives you a direction to go on your Road Trip.

Visualize Your Success

Could you imagine going on a vacation but not sure where you would go?
I decided to just sit and think about it, turned out to be quite a show

I was visualizing a beach and the ocean crashing in
I was thinking I was already there, let the fun begin

This is also true when you Visualize your Road Trip to Success
Visualize the best-case scenario, let the Universe do the rest

Visualizing is realizing, it is just a mental movie away
Visualize the future and watch your future unfold that way

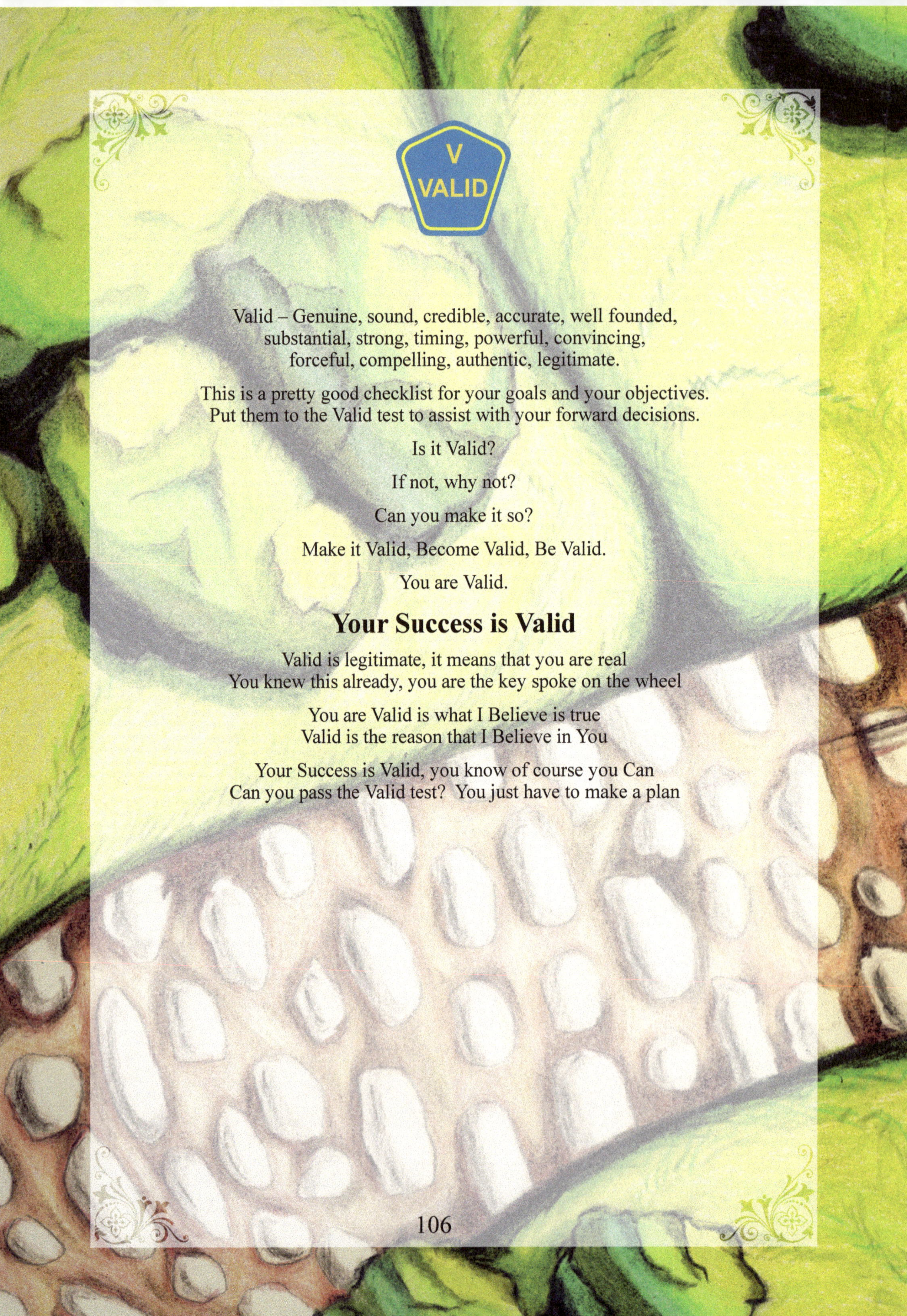

Valid – Genuine, sound, credible, accurate, well founded,
substantial, strong, timing, powerful, convincing,
forceful, compelling, authentic, legitimate.

This is a pretty good checklist for your goals and your objectives.
Put them to the Valid test to assist with your forward decisions.

Is it Valid?

If not, why not?

Can you make it so?

Make it Valid, Become Valid, Be Valid.

You are Valid.

Your Success is Valid

Valid is legitimate, it means that you are real
You knew this already, you are the key spoke on the wheel

You are Valid is what I Believe is true
Valid is the reason that I Believe in You

Your Success is Valid, you know of course you Can
Can you pass the Valid test? You just have to make a plan

Virtue - Moral goodness, righteousness, honor, honesty, integrity, strength.

Virtue is doing the right thing.

Virtue is merit.

Virtue is Noble.

Virtue is Positive Intention.

Virtue is Positive Action.

Road Trip and Good Words A-Z is full of Virtues
Learn the words and practice the behavior and add Virtue to your Success.

Your Success is full of Virtue

Virtue and Noble and Chivalry too
Love one another, Compassion for me and for you

Virtue is something they should sell at the store
Imagine a world where everybody buys a little more

Could you imagine that our culture looked like this?
This would be a dream come true, a world that's full of bliss

Virtues make your life more peaceful, contentment of the soul
Live your life with Virtue, it changes how your life will roll

Will – Will Power – Determination, passion, resilient, positive, strength of purpose, force of courage, self-discipline, ownership of self, self-control, tenacious, possible, probable. Get it Done.

There is huge potential with human Will Power.

The possibilities are infinite for those that realize the power of their own Will.

Will it so and the energy to make it so, Will come together.

Will strength ends all doubt.

The strength of your Will is the cement for the building blocks of your Success.

Your Success? Will it so!

Will Power is a powerful source,
Will it so is an amazing force

Will Power and the Will to do is about Determination
Anything is possible is the important part of the equation

Focus on it and believe it and you can Will it so
With Will Power on your team, there is only one way you will go

Will yourself Successful and Success is what will be
It was just a little seed you know that Willed itself a tree

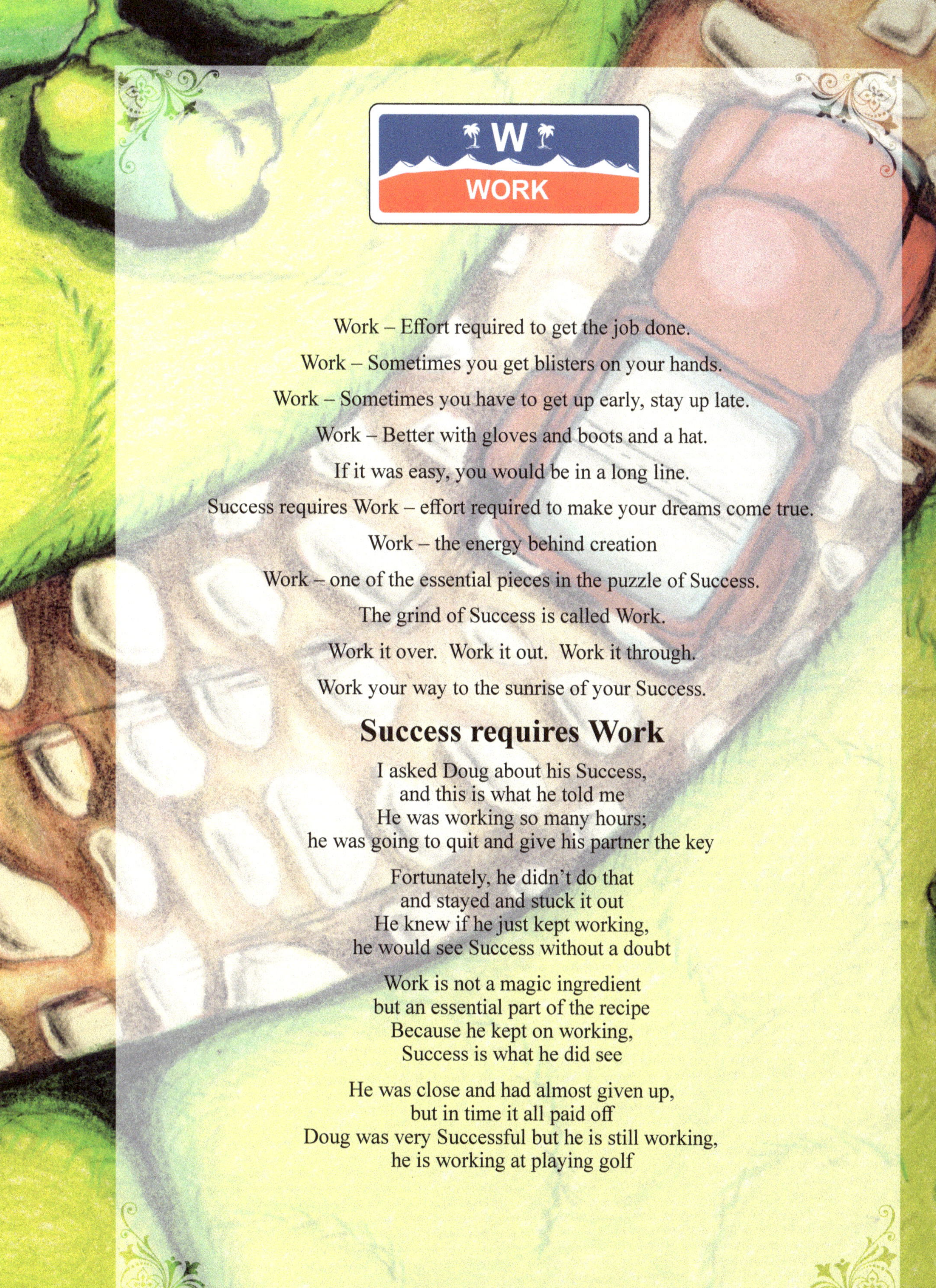

Work – Effort required to get the job done.

Work – Sometimes you get blisters on your hands.

Work – Sometimes you have to get up early, stay up late.

Work – Better with gloves and boots and a hat.

If it was easy, you would be in a long line.

Success requires Work – effort required to make your dreams come true.

Work – the energy behind creation

Work – one of the essential pieces in the puzzle of Success.

The grind of Success is called Work.

Work it over. Work it out. Work it through.

Work your way to the sunrise of your Success.

Success requires Work

I asked Doug about his Success,
and this is what he told me
He was working so many hours;
he was going to quit and give his partner the key

Fortunately, he didn't do that
and stayed and stuck it out
He knew if he just kept working,
he would see Success without a doubt

Work is not a magic ingredient
but an essential part of the recipe
Because he kept on working,
Success is what he did see

He was close and had almost given up,
but in time it all paid off
Doug was very Successful but he is still working,
he is working at playing golf

Words – The tools used to describe or define your life, past, present and future.

The tools used to stimulate or describe your thoughts.

The Words that you know and use, determine your behavior.

Choose your Words wisely as they create the "vehicle" that you get to ride in.

How important are the Words that you use in your life?

Good Words are very important.

Good Words make the journey less bumpy.

Good Words give you a better ride.

Good Words are Positive Words.

Positive words allow you to see the Positive Possibilities
in the situations and circumstances along the way.

Good Words will bring the sunshine back, when it gets a little cloudy in your life.
Good Words are the building blocks of Your Success

Build Your Success with Good Words

Words are fun to have around
but it depends on what words you use
Likely to Succeed, A-Z, is about your life experience
because of the words that you choose

Your thoughts are the seeds from which your future grows
and are defined by our choices
Choose Good Words, choose Positive Words,
the Words you choose have little voices

When your energy is fed with Good Words,
Good Words energy shows up in your life
Good Words used on a daily basis,
makes the Road Trip pretty Nice

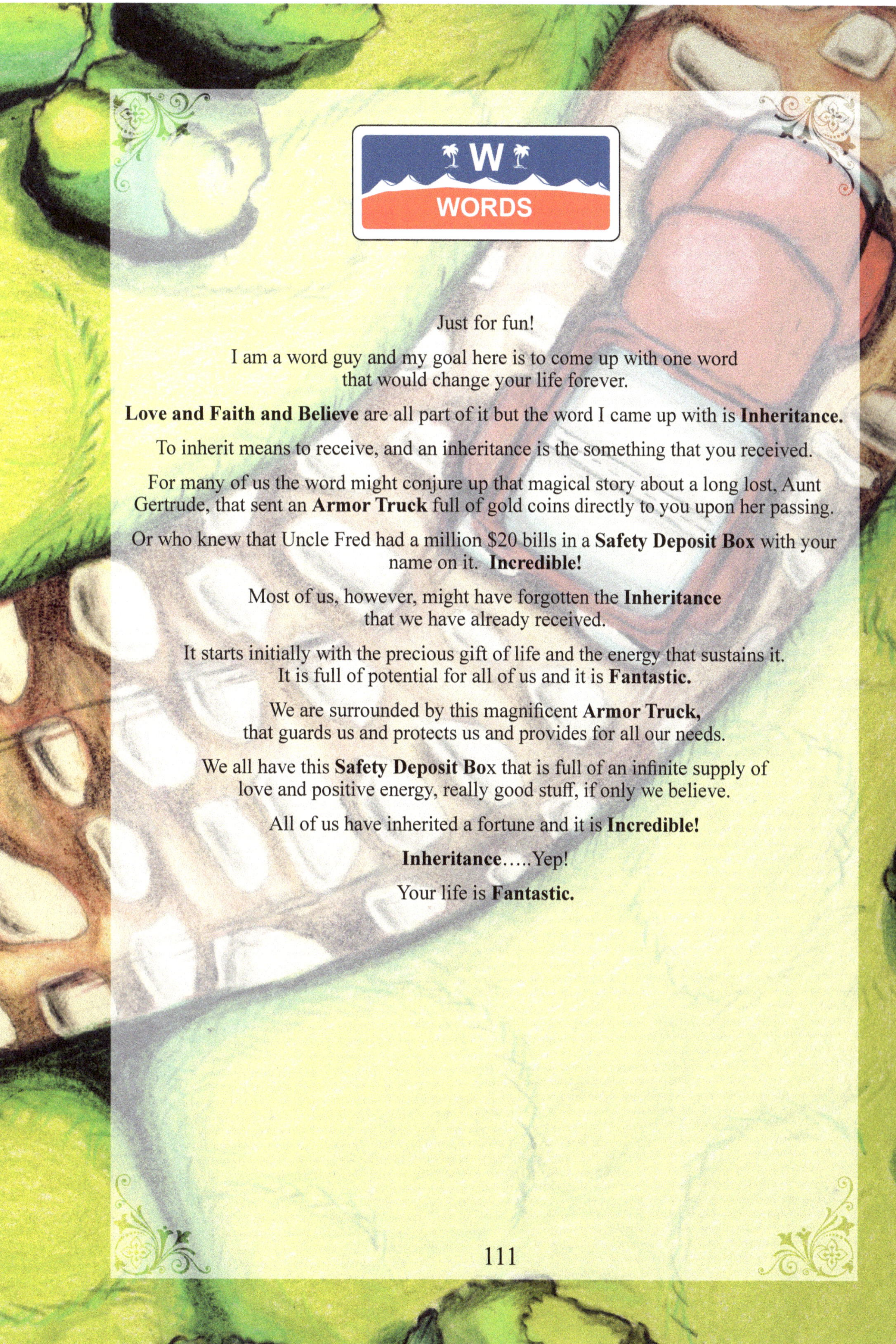

Just for fun!

I am a word guy and my goal here is to come up with one word
that would change your life forever.

Love and Faith and Believe are all part of it but the word I came up with is **Inheritance.**

To inherit means to receive, and an inheritance is the something that you received.

For many of us the word might conjure up that magical story about a long lost, Aunt
Gertrude, that sent an **Armor Truck** full of gold coins directly to you upon her passing.

Or who knew that Uncle Fred had a million $20 bills in a **Safety Deposit Box** with your
name on it. **Incredible!**

Most of us, however, might have forgotten the **Inheritance**
that we have already received.

It starts initially with the precious gift of life and the energy that sustains it.
It is full of potential for all of us and it is **Fantastic.**

We are surrounded by this magnificent **Armor Truck,**
that guards us and protects us and provides for all our needs.

We all have this **Safety Deposit Box** that is full of an infinite supply of
love and positive energy, really good stuff, if only we believe.

All of us have inherited a fortune and it is **Incredible!**

Inheritance…..Yep!

Your life is **Fantastic.**

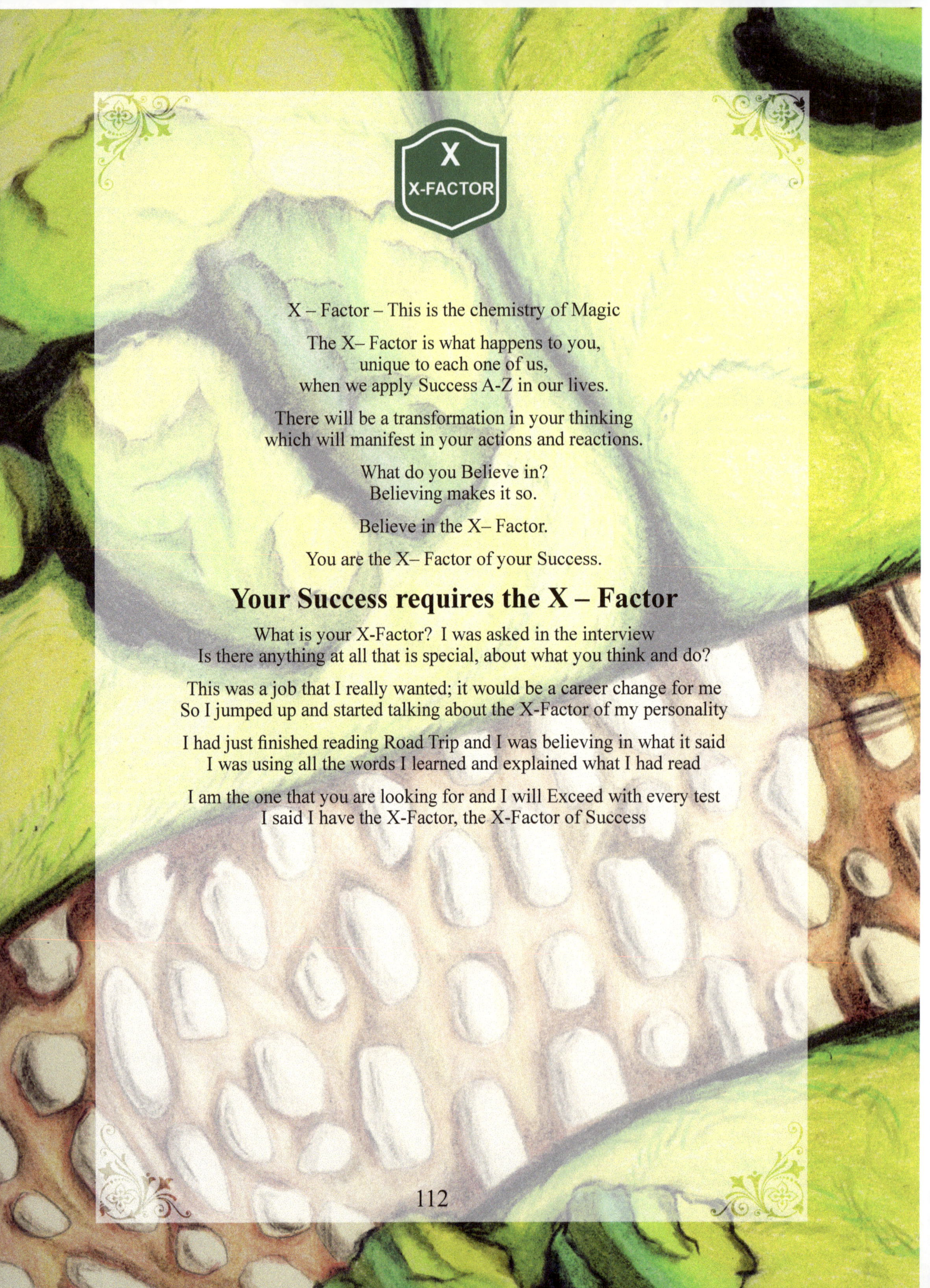

X – Factor – This is the chemistry of Magic

The X– Factor is what happens to you,
unique to each one of us,
when we apply Success A-Z in our lives.

There will be a transformation in your thinking
which will manifest in your actions and reactions.

What do you Believe in?
Believing makes it so.

Believe in the X– Factor.

You are the X– Factor of your Success.

Your Success requires the X – Factor

What is your X-Factor? I was asked in the interview
Is there anything at all that is special, about what you think and do?

This was a job that I really wanted; it would be a career change for me
So I jumped up and started talking about the X-Factor of my personality

I had just finished reading Road Trip and I was believing in what it said
I was using all the words I learned and explained what I had read

I am the one that you are looking for and I will Exceed with every test
I said I have the X-Factor, the X-Factor of Success

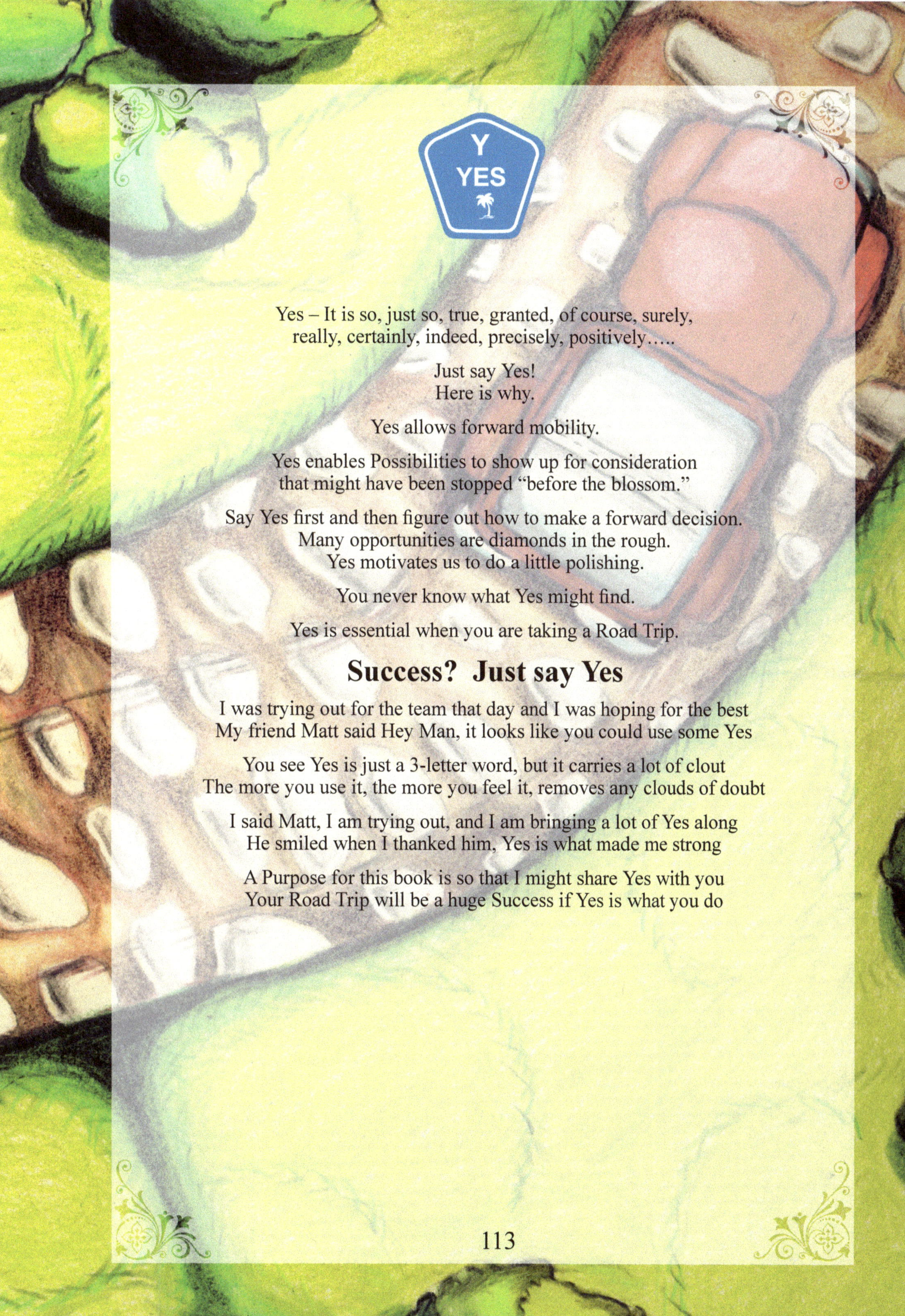

Yes – It is so, just so, true, granted, of course, surely,
really, certainly, indeed, precisely, positively…..

Just say Yes!
Here is why.

Yes allows forward mobility.

Yes enables Possibilities to show up for consideration
that might have been stopped "before the blossom."

Say Yes first and then figure out how to make a forward decision.
Many opportunities are diamonds in the rough.
Yes motivates us to do a little polishing.

You never know what Yes might find.

Yes is essential when you are taking a Road Trip.

Success? Just say Yes

I was trying out for the team that day and I was hoping for the best
My friend Matt said Hey Man, it looks like you could use some Yes

You see Yes is just a 3-letter word, but it carries a lot of clout
The more you use it, the more you feel it, removes any clouds of doubt

I said Matt, I am trying out, and I am bringing a lot of Yes along
He smiled when I thanked him, Yes is what made me strong

A Purpose for this book is so that I might share Yes with you
Your Road Trip will be a huge Success if Yes is what you do

You are You, the person that you are.

Who are You?

Your name is the frosting, the You is the cake.

You are unique, rare, one of a kind, currently #1 out of 8 billion on the planet.

When it comes to a picture puzzle and there is a piece missing,
the first thing that you notice is the missing piece.

There is a large block wall that is tall and wide, with many blocks in it,
but there is one block missing.

"Nice wall, did you know there was a block missing?"

When it comes to a safety pin,
which part of the balloon is more or less important
than any other part of the balloon?

What about You?
You are the missing piece in the puzzle,
You are the missing block in the wall.
You are the important part of the balloon.

We all are.

You are the only one of You.

That makes You valuable.

Realize it.

Know it.

You matter to all of us.

Your life is important.

Thanks for Being You!

Your Success is all about You

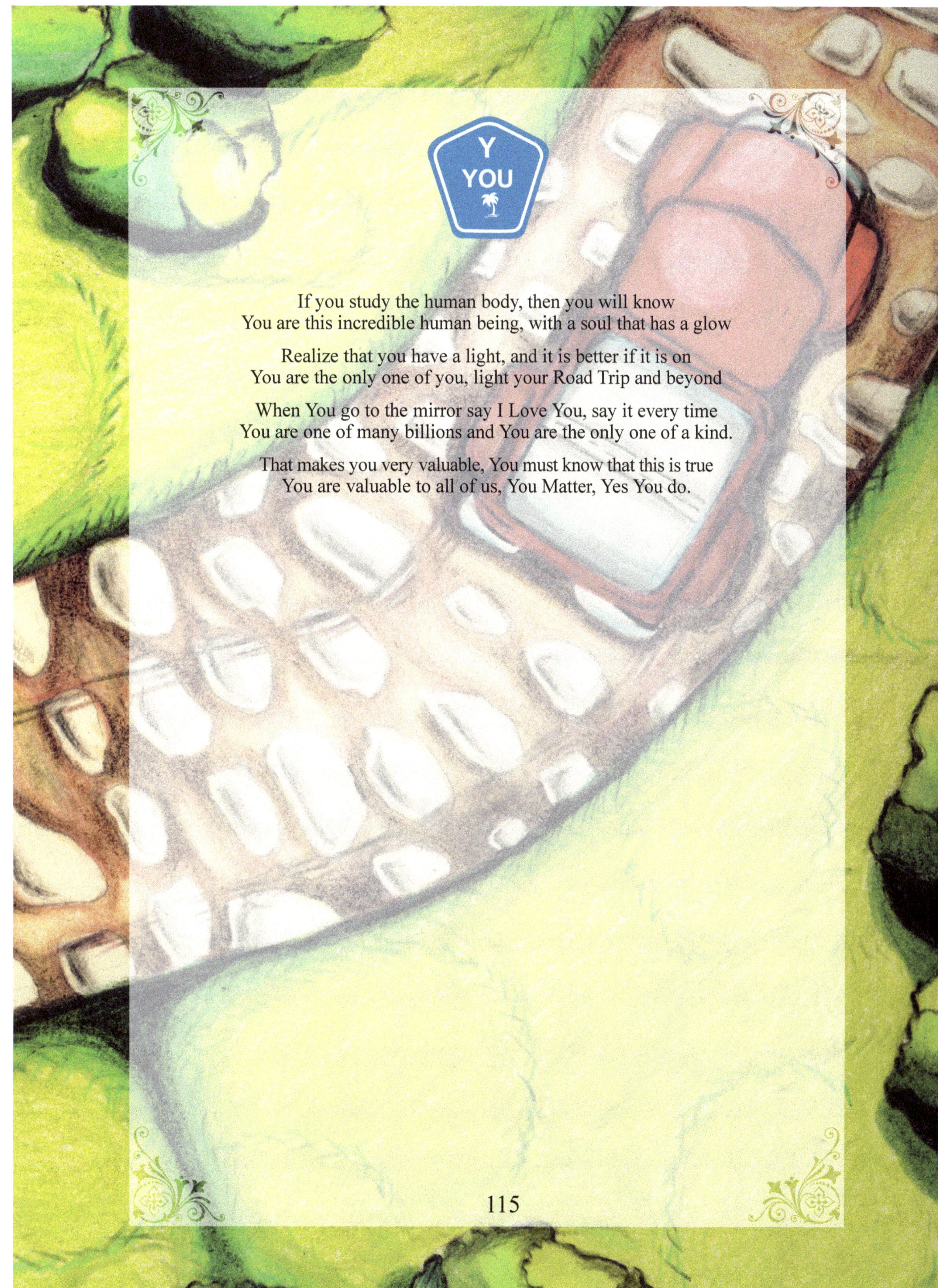

If you study the human body, then you will know
You are this incredible human being, with a soul that has a glow

Realize that you have a light, and it is better if it is on
You are the only one of you, light your Road Trip and beyond

When You go to the mirror say I Love You, say it every time
You are one of many billions and You are the only one of a kind.

That makes you very valuable, You must know that this is true
You are valuable to all of us, You Matter, Yes You do.

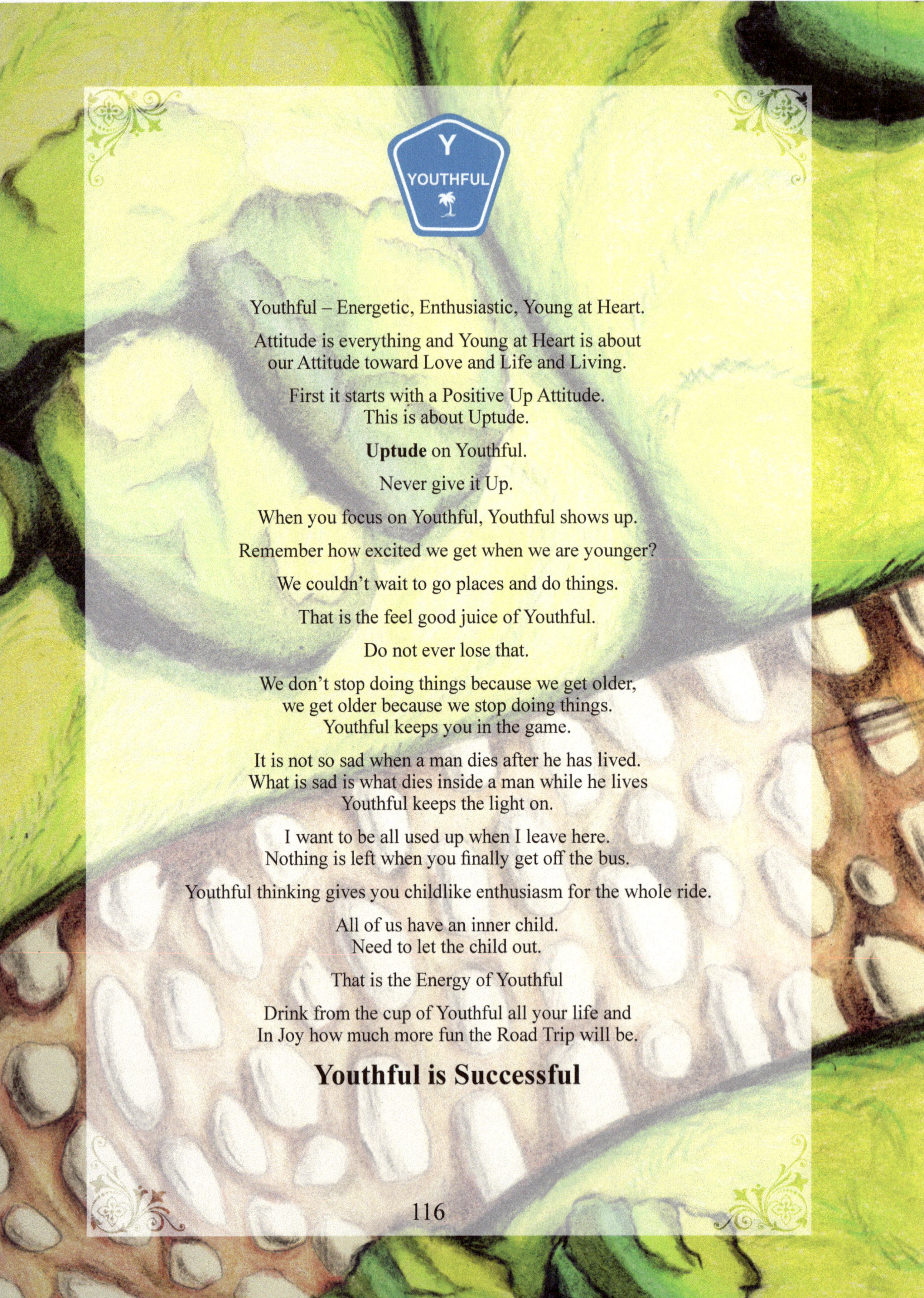

Youthful – Energetic, Enthusiastic, Young at Heart.

Attitude is everything and Young at Heart is about
our Attitude toward Love and Life and Living.

First it starts with a Positive Up Attitude.
This is about Uptude.

Uptude on Youthful.

Never give it Up.

When you focus on Youthful, Youthful shows up.

Remember how excited we get when we are younger?

We couldn't wait to go places and do things.

That is the feel good juice of Youthful.

Do not ever lose that.

We don't stop doing things because we get older,
we get older because we stop doing things.
Youthful keeps you in the game.

It is not so sad when a man dies after he has lived.
What is sad is what dies inside a man while he lives
Youthful keeps the light on.

I want to be all used up when I leave here.
Nothing is left when you finally get off the bus.

Youthful thinking gives you childlike enthusiasm for the whole ride.

All of us have an inner child.
Need to let the child out.

That is the Energy of Youthful

Drink from the cup of Youthful all your life and
In Joy how much more fun the Road Trip will be.

Youthful is Successful

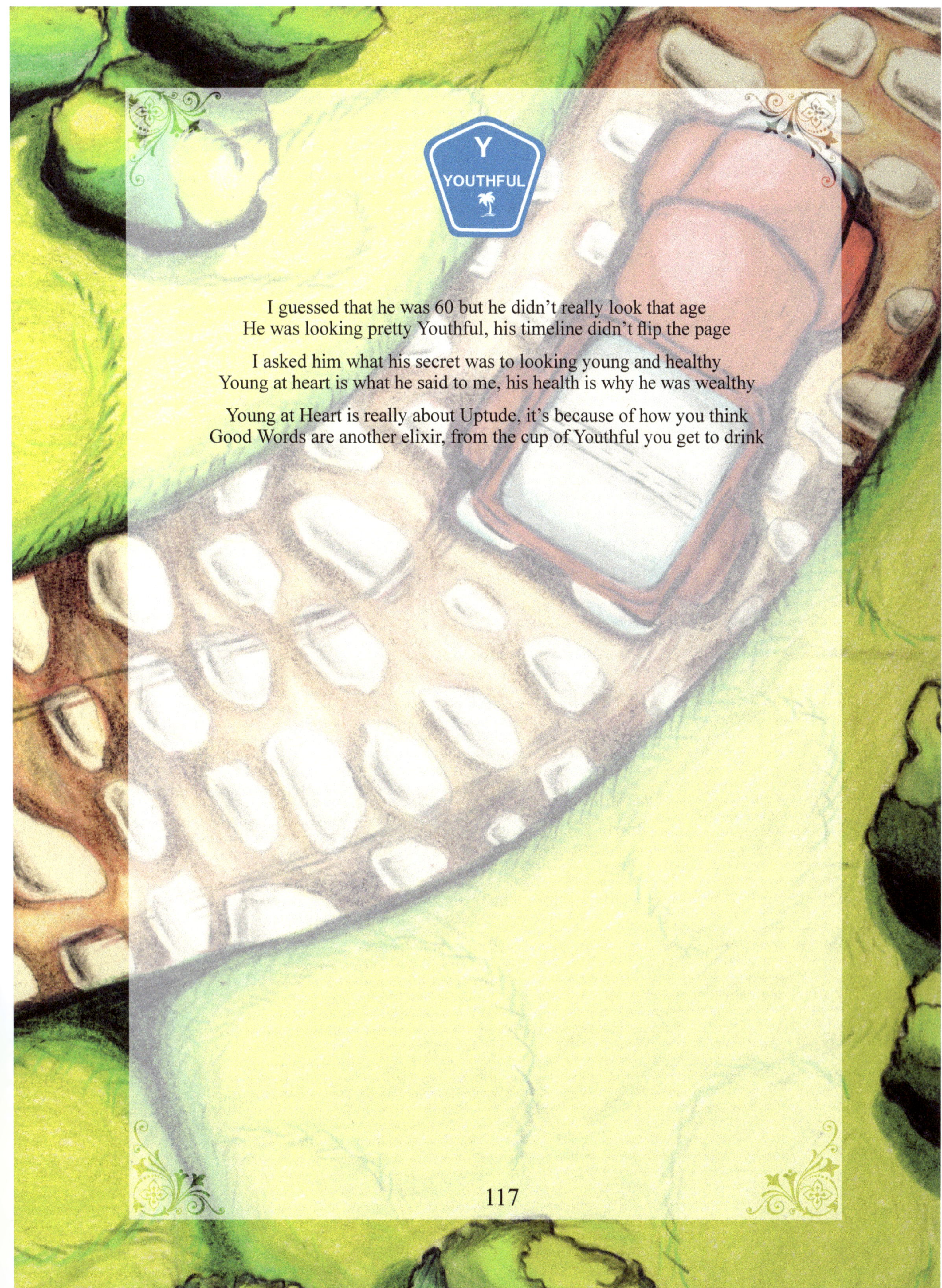

I guessed that he was 60 but he didn't really look that age
He was looking pretty Youthful, his timeline didn't flip the page

I asked him what his secret was to looking young and healthy
Young at heart is what he said to me, his health is why he was wealthy

Young at Heart is really about Uptude, it's because of how you think
Good Words are another elixir, from the cup of Youthful you get to drink

Zero – The best place to start.

The beginning.

Start here.

Ground Up.

Zero is peaceful.

Zero is the beginning of pumped up but it is the quiet of now.

Zero is base camp.

Success occurs in cycles of leaving Zero and returning to Zero.

Begin…..and Begin again.

Get started from ground Zero.

Zero on
Zero in
Zero up
Zero over
Repeat

Zero in on your Success

He was one of the greatest teachers in my life, Mr. Orr.
He was a previous Marine; we had no idea what was in store

We were only 6th graders and had so much to learn,
Sometimes we drove him crazy and to the blackboard he would turn

With the chalk he would try to draw, a perfect Zero on the board
He said he would be certifiably crazy, completely lost his gourd

Suddenly the class was quiet
We all went back to Zero, watching him try it

He never drew a perfect Zero, but he had accomplished his goal
By the time he finished drawing, the class was back in control

Zero is the place to return to, and occasionally you need to stay
Mr. Orr was a pretty good teacher, Zero, is what he taught us that day

Zest – Gusto, passion, exhilaration, excitement, enthusiasm
heart beating, blood pumping, breathing heavy,
thrill, delight, joy, satisfaction, zeal

Zest Pumped Up

Can You feel it?

Zest is a bounce in your step.
Zest is about excitement for the day.
Zest is Enthusiasm about your life.

Your life experience is about choices that you make with your thinking.
Zest is one of those choices.

Earlier we spoke about gratitude and what a great first thought in the morning.
Zest is right there with it.

The other day I was busy doing and I started thinking about playing life.
I thought about having to or getting to when it comes to what we do.

I laughed when I thought about the different words
that showed up in my thinking about the chore at hand.
To do or not to do could have gone a couple different ways.
I believe in what I am writing so it was a simple choice.

Kind of what Zest is all about.

Zest is what gets you from Z word #1 to Z word #3.

Zest Up!

Success is Zest for your Life

Zest is such a great word they named a soap after it
Zest is the carbonation for the elixir that gives your soul a lift

Zest is enthusiasm and excitement for your day
It is because of your thinking that you would feel this way

We are running out of letters on the Road Trip you know
Success is where you are, your Road Trip is a go

Remember the concept, and that "It" is all about Love
Love is what adds Zest to your life, it is almost unbelievable what it does

Zenith – Apex, vertex, best, pinnacle, the peak,
highest point, summit, climax, in the clouds.

Success.

The goal for me, was for you to get here in this book.
You made it.

Congratulations! You have reached the Zenith.

Zenith is a life peak and a worthy end of the journey.
The Zenith was the goal.

The real Zenith shows up when you apply it.

You Can do it!
Way to Go!

Success is the Zenith

Are You at the Zenith? The pinnacle of Success?
Always trying to do your best

It has been a long Road Trip, you have traveled quite far
The journey is about your becoming, just who you are

There are Zeros and there are Zeniths on the journey you are on
They both are important, they both come and then there gone

One Zenith after another perhaps, but never just one.
One Zenith after another is how you become

Growing is virtue, learning the best way to go
Good Words in your life give you the direction for you to grow

Life has many journeys, never give up
Drink the magical elixir, from the Good Words Cup

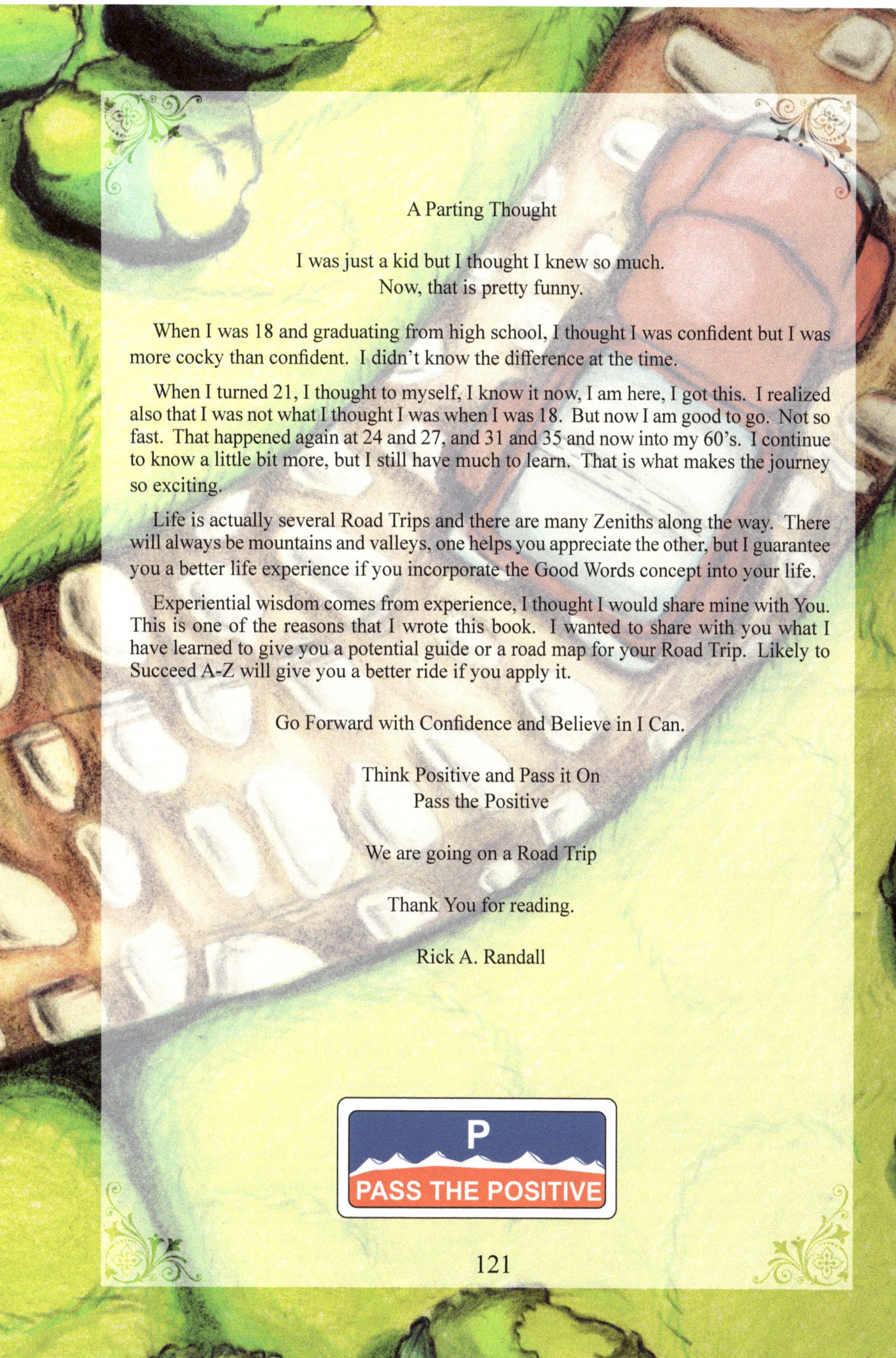

A Parting Thought

I was just a kid but I thought I knew so much.
Now, that is pretty funny.

When I was 18 and graduating from high school, I thought I was confident but I was more cocky than confident. I didn't know the difference at the time.

When I turned 21, I thought to myself, I know it now, I am here, I got this. I realized also that I was not what I thought I was when I was 18. But now I am good to go. Not so fast. That happened again at 24 and 27, and 31 and 35 and now into my 60's. I continue to know a little bit more, but I still have much to learn. That is what makes the journey so exciting.

Life is actually several Road Trips and there are many Zeniths along the way. There will always be mountains and valleys, one helps you appreciate the other, but I guarantee you a better life experience if you incorporate the Good Words concept into your life.

Experiential wisdom comes from experience, I thought I would share mine with You. This is one of the reasons that I wrote this book. I wanted to share with you what I have learned to give you a potential guide or a road map for your Road Trip. Likely to Succeed A-Z will give you a better ride if you apply it.

Go Forward with Confidence and Believe in I Can.

Think Positive and Pass it On
Pass the Positive

We are going on a Road Trip

Thank You for reading.

Rick A. Randall

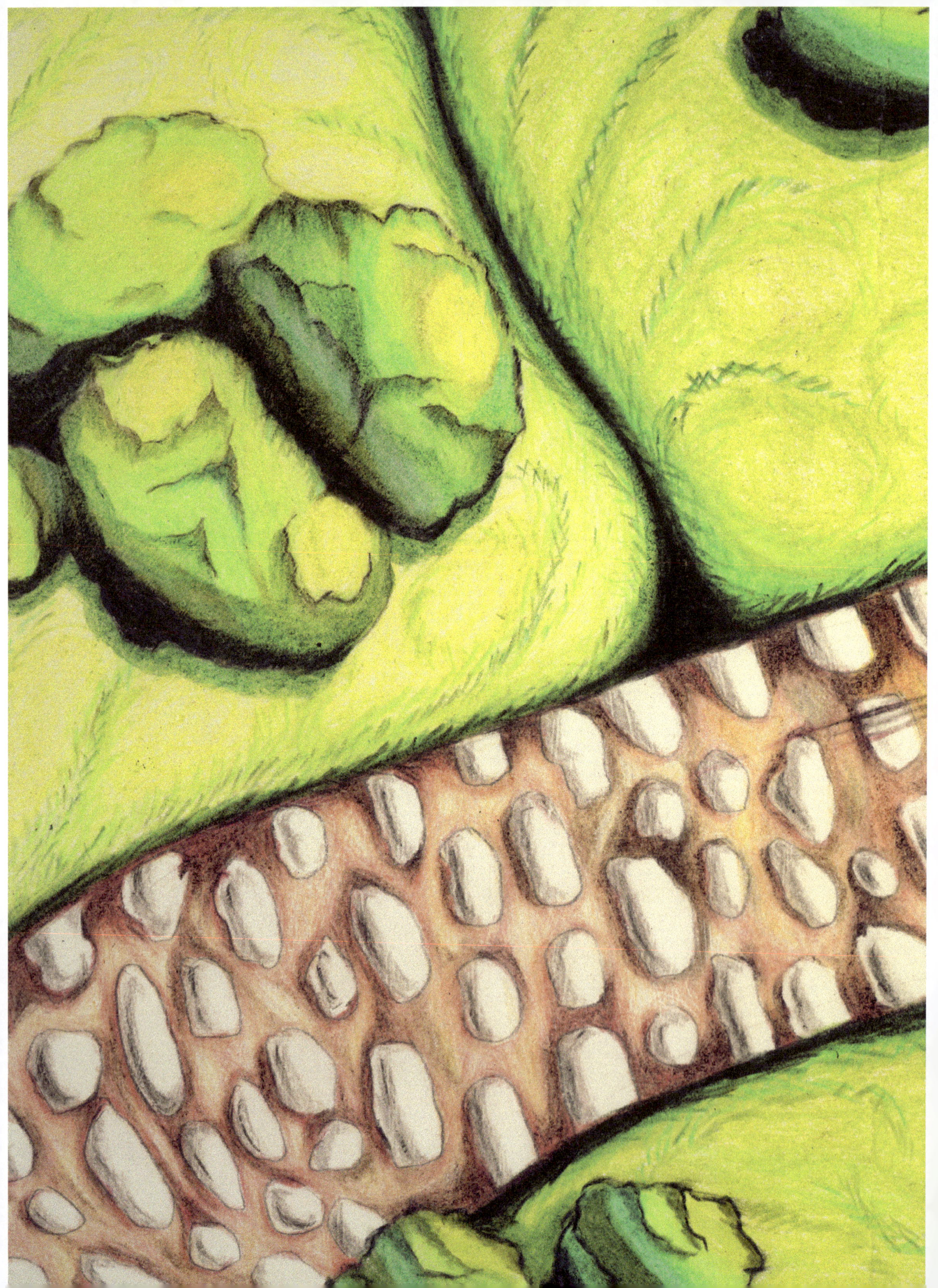

www.ingramcontent.com/pod-product-compliance
Lightning Source LLC
Chambersburg PA
CBHW042049010826
48978CB00023B/1329